Vagabonds

ELIAS WITHEROW

**THOUGHT
CATALOG**
Books

THOUGHTCATALOG.COM
NEW YORK·LOS ANGELES

THOUGHT
CATALOG
Books

Published by Thought Catalog Books, an imprint of the digital magazine Thought Catalog, which is owned and operated by The Thought & Expression Company LLC, an independent media organization based in Brooklyn, New York and Los Angeles, California. For bulk purchasing inquiries, please visit shopcatalog.com/about.

This book was produced by Thought Catalog. Cover by RebeccaCovers.
Visit us on the web at thoughtcatalog.com and shopcatalog.com.

Made in the USA.

ISBN 978-1-949759-39-6

AUTHOR'S NOTE

When I started writing this book, I really just wanted to have fun with it. This is my ninth book since 2015 and I had a strong desire to do something a little different. I'm a big fan of sci-fi and I incorporate the genre a lot into my horror fiction. This time, I decided to lean a little heavier into it, while maintaining my roots.

The book you hold in your hands is the result. I think you're going to enjoy it. It has *plenty* of violence for you blood-starved animals while maintaining the quick pacing you've come to expect. And if you find yourself longing for something darker after you've finished *Vagabonds*...don't fret. My next one is going to be brutal. And I mean downright awful.

But for now, please enjoy Vagabonds. Writing it felt like spring break and I'm extremely pleased with how it turned out.

Love you all.

—ELIAS

CHAPTER 1

The sun was a scorching slice of burnt orange stuck in a sizzling blue sky. The air was stiff and suffocating, the cloudless canvas offering nothing but relentless heat and blinding light. The desert plains stood motionless beneath the windless expanse, the dunes curling and rising like a dehydrated ocean. Bright red sandstone jutted from the earth like shattered, bloodied teeth, scattering the endless vastness with dips, peaks, and valleys, like the bottom of a drained sea doused in dirt, sand, and dust.

Ada shielded her eyes from the scorching brilliance and scanned the horizon, casting her eyes toward the distant white mountains that rose like broken bones across the far distance. Muttering to herself, she glanced down at the piece of parchment in her hands.

"We should head back," her sister Marah observed. "The Negative is close."

Ada scribbled their coordinates on her piece of parchment with a coal pencil and then folded it neatly into her loose-fitting shirt, into a hidden pocket. She shot the sky another look, noting the position of the great opaque circular lens that floated toward the sun, inching its strange, cosmic mass ever closer to its searing orange counterpart.

"We have an hour at least," Ada calculated quietly, brushing sand from her short black hair. "Keep your pants on."

"I just don't want to get stuck out here during it," Marah said softly. "We've been away longer than we should anyway. Papa's going to get worried."

"*Lord* Reston will be just fine," Ada snorted. "He's probably too busy arguing with the rest of the politicians about what color they should paint the Orbital Dome next year."

Marah gave a small smile. "You should have heard him and Mom arguing about that last night after curfew. I could hear them from my room."

"I guess when you're the boss, stupid crap becomes important," Ada said. "Like what color to paint a big piece of metal." She shook her head and turned toward their duster. "*So* stupid. If I ever get like that, please do something about it."

"You'll be great when the time comes," Marah said, stealing another glance at the shimmering, cloudy disc in the heavens. "Maybe you'll even figure out a way to eliminate the Negative."

"Eliminate it?" Ada asked, cocking an eyebrow, her green eyes sparkling in the desert sun. "Why? There's nothing sinister about it. I don't know why it makes you so jittery."

Marah rolled her own emerald eyes and marched over to their duster, popped the metal door open, and kicked one of the rubber tires. "Will you just get in and drive? You know this time of the day gives me the creeps so get your fat ass into the damn duster. We've surveyed enough of the salt mountains to keep Papa happy for now."

Ada ducked her head and climbed into one of the two cloth seats, turning the key to start the duster with a rumble. "Yeah, he'll be thrilled to discover the south range seems to go even further than we expected. He plans to start mining it sometime next year, from what he told me."

Marah climbed into the seat next to Ada and slammed the door shut, sealing them inside the snug vehicle. "I talked to Kevlar the other day and he said he can have crews out there in three months if Papa wants. It seems like the mining in the north range is going smoothly and he wants to get his crew chiefs started down this way as soon as possible."

Ada flipped a switch next to the steering wheel and the windshield darkened some, the tint softening the glare of the dunes and sandy plains before them.

"I'm sure Pap will be thrilled," Ada said, giving the duster some diesel, lurching them forward, the front tires kicking up sand while the treads in the back began to churn. "Nothing he enjoys more than sending reports off-world about how wealthy this planet is becoming. I figure we could build three more cities here on Pratus with the amount of salt we'll mine in the south."

Marah reclined a little in her seat. "Imagine how many more Orbital Domes Papa will be able to paint."

"He only needs one capital, Mar, don't go giving him any ideas. He's getting a little big in the head these days."

"Yeah, and his gut."

Ada grunted. "Heaven help our poor mother."

The duster rolled contentedly across the rolling dunes and around the jutting croppings of sandstone, all the while guided by Ada's steady hand at the wheel. They passed scraggles of dried-out trees, twisted and baked in the sun like gasping veins from Pratus's crust. In the distance, Ada could see little tufts of dust as the other survey crews made the journey back toward Typhon, the capital city of Pratus. It seemed as if no one else was eager to wait out the Negative either.

After a half-hour of traversal, Ada turned them east, taking the duster over a series of stilted ridges to crest a peak. As they reached the summit and began to descend, Typhon came into view. Each time Ada approached the sprawling city, she couldn't help but feel a sense of pride at what they had helped build, each generation adding to the massive settlement.

The city stood atop a cluster of colossal spires of red sandstone, hundreds of feet high. The tops of each were flat, spanning dozens of miles to allow for construction, housing, and what Ada knew as her home. There were nine towers of sandstone in total that made up Typhon, with the one in the center being the largest and the one that hosted the Orbital Dome where she lived, along with her mother, father, sister, and hundreds of others. The dome itself was a grand thing, a half-sphere of brilliant silver that hosted an array of satellite towers, weather radars, and blinking, short-range com relays. The dome was clearly visible among the smaller spires which mostly held vendors, housing, and machine operations. On the outer rim of Typhon's cluster, circling the city, were the titanic

Glo Cannons, the one thing about the settlement her father loathed but deemed necessary in case unwelcome guests decided to raid their home from space. It wasn't the cannons themselves that Ada's father hated, but the glo that powered them, with its strange, unexplainable energy that, upon discovery four hundred years ago, had pushed technological progress into overdrive. It was the reason space travel was possible and it carved the way for new, incredible, and intuitive tech.

Beyond that, according to the records, it had been discovered that Glo could be injected into human beings, thought that perhaps the strange liquid would advance evolution itself. The long-term effect had been devastating for those who had experimented, shortening their life span by a staggering number of years, but not without some incredible, terrible benefits.

I would never even think to inject myself with that poison, Ada thought as she drove the duster closer toward Typhon, watching as the great Glo Cannons idly rotated, their massive barrels pointed toward the sky. *Never in a million years. And heaven help me if those juicers ever found their way here to Pratus.*

Despite her concern, she knew it was a distant worry. Almost all of the people who lived and worked here were born on Pratus. Offworlders were extremely rare. She was of the third generation of settlers and it had been their generation, along with her father's, that had put the planet of Pratus on the map, in terms of universal value. Her father's expansion and growth of the mining colony, along with his brilliant mind for business and survival, had far exceeded the expectations of the offworlders who had initially funded the excursion. In the next decade, if things continued, her father would put in an application for their planet to be accepted into the Minor Ring. If accepted, the off-world traffic would explode and their economy would flourish, the recognition bringing with it a host of benefits, including wealthy mining corporations that would be eager to continue funding her father's operations. U-Creds would start pouring in at a ridiculous rate, allowing the mined salt to be converted into currency, giving Pratus two separate forms of wealth. Perhaps even enough to build a terraformer and finally fulfill her father's dream of turning Typhon into a lush paradise.

A sudden flare across the windshield brought her quickly out of her thoughts. Despite the tint, she squinted and felt her heart leap into her throat as she realized what she was seeing. She slammed the brakes and heard Marah gasp from the passenger seat. Dust swirled past the windows and Ada leaned forward in her seat, her pulse quickening.

The Glo Cannons had been activated.

Not only that, but something was hurtling toward Typhon from the far horizon, something huge, and the massive guns all swirled in unison toward it, tracking its progression.

"Ada?" Marah whispered, her voice shaking. "Ada, what is that?"

Ada's eyes widened as the air began to hum with the sound of the cannons powering up, the colossal structures beginning to glow with blue energy.

"What is he doing?" Ada hissed, her own fear present in her thin voice.

Marah craned her neck to look out the side window at the black mass on the horizon, a massive thing that grew closer with every passing second.

"Is that some kind of ship?" she breathed nervously. "Is Papa going to shoot it down? Ada? Ada!"

"I don't know!" Ada snapped, feeling her chest flutter. What the hell was going on? It had been thirty years since pirates had dared attempt to steal from Typhon's salt reserves, which had been a good five years before she had even been born.

The roar of power coming from the distant Glo Cannons was unmistakable now, the blinding neon light emanating from the barrel's cores casting a blue wash across the sky.

"Are we under attack?" Marah sputtered, squirming in her seat. "Is this a raid?!"

Ada was about to tell her sister to shut up, but before she could, the Glo Cannons let out a blast, a singular detonation that rattled her teeth. Marah let out a cry of terror as the nine constructs fired in unison, an eruption of blue, a pulsing wave of power that rocketed toward the far-off ship.

At the last second, the dark mass in the sky shuddered to the left in an attempt to avoid the incoming barrage, but it was in vain. The back part of the craft was clipped, sending a shower of wreckage smoking across the sky. From this distance, it took a full two seconds before Ada heard the impact, a booming explosion of shattering metal, titanium, and super-charged power conduits. Blue splashed out of the black smoke and the great ship, its details obscured from this distance, slowly spun off course and then dipped and fell toward the western part of the planet, far and away from Typhon. It left a trail of smoke and fuming black in its wake, arcing across the sky to finally, horribly, disappear beyond the rising red-stone of Typhon.

Ada didn't breathe for a couple of seconds, the shock of what had just happened still buzzing in her head. She stared out at the trail of inky smoke that painted the sky, a filthy line of grime across the open blue as if the atmosphere itself had been cut open.

"Ada," Marah whispered. "Ada, we need to get back right now and find Papa. Ada!"

Ada shook herself and looked at her sister. Her face was white and her eyes were large and shimmering.

"Right," Ada said, blinking. "Right. Let's go." She gave the duster a pump of diesel and they accelerated once more.

"What the hell," Ada muttered, her throat tight. "I mean just *what in the hell...?*"

Marah wrung her hands together as the duster raced toward the ga-rages at the base of Typhon.

"Did they shoot at us?" Marah asked, her voice much too high. "Do you think there's going to be more of them? I mean if we're under attack then I think we need to—"

"Shut up, Marah," Ada said stiffly, finally finding her center again. "Just keep it buttoned until we find Pap. There's no use speculating until we know what the hell is going on." She glanced at the sky, past the dim-ming Glo Cannons, toward the sun and the eerie, hazy disk to its right as it slipped closer toward the light. The world was already beginning to gray.

What horrible timing, she thought almost frantically.

They reached the garages and Ada parked in bunker 12, waving past the personnel who rushed their duster. She could hear them shouting at her and Marah, panic plastered to their confused faces.

She parked the duster and climbed out into the flat gray garage, signaling for Marah to sign them out with the Auto Captain while she hitched the lock bar to their duster. As she worked, other crews returned from their own missions, exiting their vehicles with similar looks of bewildered fear. The mechanics and diesel crews flooded Ada and Marah with worried questions, along with the other scouts, but no one seemed to know what was going on. The bunker was a hive of noise and dust, each voice rising higher than the last.

Ada grabbed Marah and pulled her away from the Auto Captain who seemed more concerned with what was happening than checking in their duster. He raised a hand to them as they left, questions bubbling from his lips, but Ada ignored him.

They reached the lifts and Ada shoved Marah into one before following. Once the grate had been secured, they began to rise, soaring up along the metal track, ascending hundreds of feet toward Typhon high above.

When they reached the Orbital Dome, Ada saw that everyone inside was pressed against the massive, curving windows that striped the structure. The noise in the garage seemed quiet compared to the roar in here. The eateries and offices sat abandoned, the metal pathways that crisscrossed over Ada's head were heavy with the sound of rushing feet, and the blare of the emergency alert system droned heavily in her ears, the mechanical voice blasting over the loudspeakers.

"*Please remain calm and return to your stations. Captain Reston has the situation under control. You will be informed of our status when deemed appropriate. Please return to your stations. Orbital Clerks will assist in cases of non-compliance.*"

The loudspeakers continued to blare the message on loop and Ada watched as everyone slowly, reluctantly began to wander back to their duties, the sting of panic bleeding out of the air like poison. Orbital Clerks hurried past Ada and Marah, dressed in their combat attire, their copper-plated armor and face shields daring anyone to disobey.

"Come on Marah," Ada said, pushing past the throngs of people. "Let's see if Pap really has this thing under control or not."

Together they threaded their way through the strings of connected metal pathways, up the stairs toward the higher levels, rushing through each raised plate to the next set of staircases. Each of the raised plates was crowded with shops, armories, off-world communication offices, news stations, scrappers, duster dealers, and every other operation of life. Each of the massive metal plates was encircled by large transparent walls without a ceiling, creating an airy, open feeling to the entirety of the Orbital Dome no matter which level, pathway, or plate you were standing on.

When Ada and Marah reached the top plate, they approached the only structure with a ceiling, a completely enclosed section of the Dome that was reserved for the most wealthy and important people in Typhon. It was nestled against the far curve of the outer dome, giving it a private, almost hidden feel as one approached the massive double doors that were guarded by a host of Orbital Clerks.

When Ada approached the doors, one of the captains raised a hand to her, his face hidden beneath the copper faceplate of his battle armor.

"I wouldn't, Ada." He said gravely. "Maybe come back in a couple hours when your father has had time to calm things down."

"Where is he?" Ada asked with more hostility than she intended.

The Orbital Clerk took a step back, surprised by her tone. "He's in Operations Control, but I wouldn't-"

"Are we under attack?" Marah blurted out.

The Clerk shook his head, "I'm not authorized to—"

"We're his daughters!" Marah practically shouted.

The Clerk nodded, almost embarrassed. "I'm aware of who you both are but-"

"Let us in," Ada said, her teeth clenched. "Don't waste your breath trying to talk us out of it. I want to know what the hell is going on and why our father just activated the Glo Cannons after nearly thirty years of silence."

"Look, we all want-" the Clerk started, but Ada bit off the end of his sentence.

"Open the *fucking* doors."

The Clerk sighed and then waved to his crew. The doors opened and Ada and Marah practically flew inside. Together they whisked down the stark white hallways, past the residential quarters, past their private rooms, beyond the rec halls and lounge cabins, and headed straight for Operations Control.

The blinking white door whisked open to reveal a wash of natural light, the command center basked in darkening gray sun. The ceiling was a massive dome of tinted glass and offered an incredible three hundred and sixty-degree view of Pratus. The walls of Control were lined floor to ceiling with computers, read-outs displays, radars, weather sensors, and nine hundred other forms of tech that Ada would never begin to understand. The space itself was wide and vast with rows of stations lining the round room in neat little isles. In the middle of the room, surrounded by at least thirty Control personnel, all working furiously, was Reston, Ada, and Marah's father.

Ada and Marah marched through the rows of blinking stations, past the crews of personnel, and stopped directly in front of Reston who turned to them and blinked in complete surprise.

"What...what are you two doing up here?" He asked, his voice low. He wasn't a tall man, but his thick gray brows and smooth bald head gave him a constant irritated look, accented by his dark eyes that creased at the edges.

"What did you do?" Ada asked aggressively. "What the hell is going on out there!?"

Reston waved to his crew chiefs and they gave their commander a little room. Reston pulled his daughters close and his voice growled beneath his brilliant snowy mustache.

"I don't have time to do this right now, girls. I'm extremely busy, as you can imagine, and would really appreciate it if you both just went to your rooms for now."

"Who did you shoot down, Papa?" Marah asked quietly, searching her father's eyes. "Is someone attacking us?"

Reston grit his teeth and then forced his shoulders to relax some. "We're not in any danger. It was just one...ship. Craft. Something..."

"What do you mean 'something'?" Ada pressed, her voice low.

"Why don't you just go to your rooms and I'll come by a little later once I've calmed the situation down a little-"

"Pap, what the hell did you just shoot down?!" Ada barked, catching the attention of the crew chiefs.

Reston gripped Ada's arm hard and brought his face close. "Keep your voice down." He looked around and then continued after a moment. "We don't know exactly what it was. We've never seen anything like it."

"What do you mean?" Marah whispered, her voice filling once more with fear.

"We requested its access codes a dozen times over." Reston continued, keeping his daughters tight to him. "We tried to communicate with it every way we knew how as soon as it broke through the atmosphere. God knows we did."

"So what happened?!" Ada hissed.

Reston's voice dropped. "It began to talk to us. Except, it was...nonsense. Garbled. And the things we could understand were..." his face paled some. "Listen to me. Whatever the hell that thing was, it's better buried in the sand. The last thing I ever wanted was to activate those awful cannons, but what we heard...what it was saying between the static..." His throat tightened. "When morning comes, I'm going to send teams out to investigate the crash site. We're going to make sure that thing is dead and destroyed. I'd send teams now, but I don't want anyone going out during the Negative."

Ada felt her stomach slowly roll over as her father's words pressed into her head. She felt her own fear begin to prickle her skin.

"What did it say to you? What did you hear?" Ada asked, her voice barely a whisper.

Reston shook his head. "Go to your rooms. Stay there until morning. I have a lot of work to do and a long night ahead of me. I'll be able to manage and calm our people better if I know my two girls are safe."

"Pap-" Ada began to plead, but Reston cut her off.

"Go. I'm not asking. Please. For me."

And then he reached out and cupped his daughter's faces in his hands, his features softening.

"Please."

Ada suddenly felt exhaustion overwhelm her. She looked into her father's face and felt her heart soften some. She looked at Marah and then nodded.

"Come on. Let's give Pap some room."

Reston smiled wearily. "Thank you."

"Be careful, Papa," Marah said before they left, and for some reason, hearing her sister say that filled Ada with dread.

Ada lay on her cot in the dark, idly flicking through her com pad. All the news channels were running stories on the afternoon's events, but it was all just speculation. The theories about what happened ran from a full-on invasion to a singular mad pirate attack on Typhon. Ada eventually turned her pad off and placed it on the nightstand next to her cot. No one knew what was going on and all the pieces she read weren't doing anything to calm or inform the residents of Pratus.

The halls outside her room were quiet, the late-night hour retiring most to their beds despite the earlier excitement. But in rebellion of the clock, Ada found she couldn't sleep and so she stared at the ceiling with her hands behind her head. She thought about what her father had told her and tried to decipher his words a hundred different ways. She knew his decision to fire the Glo Cannons was sure to stir up some controversy in the political rings and she hoped he had made the right call in light of the repercussions he was sure to face.

Sighing, she rolled over on her side and shut her eyes. As soon as she did, an internal alarm exploded in her mind, seemingly coming from nowhere.

Something is in the room.

She sat bolt upright and reached for her pistol, a small bolt action single shot that she kept at arm's reach. She grabbed it from its spot on the nightstand and quickly turned on the lights. The room bloomed with light and Ada sat poised at the edge of her bed, expecting to see something standing in the corner. But there was nothing out of the ordinary. Just her desk, chair, small dresser, and a mirror. No intruders. No monster in the shadows.

What was that all about? Ada thought as her heart slowed. She placed the pistol back on the nightstand and then covered her face with her hands, rubbing her eyes.

She paused. There. Something in the hallway. A noise.

Ada slowly stood up and gathered her pistol once more. She turned off her light and crept to the doorway which was sealed shut for the night. It was past curfew so any non-essential personnel were supposed to be in bed, which was most of this wing. She pressed her ear to the door and waited, her stomach-churning.

A beat passed. Then another. A second before she could reach for the door release, she heard it again.

It was a low mechanical sound as if some quiet engine was struggling in slow motion. It sounded like metal being carefully, awfully bent, a creaking chug that rolled into a soft, deep rumble. It was a noise unlike anything she had ever heard before.

Ada raised her pistol and thumbed the door's release. It wicked open quietly revealing the darkened hallway of the residential quarters. Low floor lights cast dim shadows against the walls as Ada stepped out, her heart crawling up her throat.

The sound came again, a groaning squeak of metal and then a low, choppy burst of static. Ada whipped around to face the hall to her left, ice filling her veins.

And that's when she saw it. The sight of it pulled Ada's mouth open in a terrified scream, but the breath was robbed from her lungs as her eyes tried to make sense of what she was seeing.

It was huge, its body filling the entirety of the hallway, its head scraping the ceiling as it slowly pulled itself along.

Whatwhatwhatwhat-

Ada's thoughts tumbled and crashed into one another as the thing's features were ignited by the low light. Two long pale arms pulled the bulk of the thing's mass across the floor, like a dog with its hind legs broken, its flesh almost completely white, its curved fingers tapping across the tile. Its torso was thin but expanded and thickened toward where its legs should have been. Instead of legs though, its body seemed to come together in a smooth, slithering sack, like the ass-end of a slug. Running from the tip of its base and up its spine was a twisting cord of wires and cables that seemed to be embedded in the thing's flesh, with parts pulsing with strange blue light. The cables ended at the thing's head, which was completely metal and looked like a massive box with a pattern of small holes like a speaker system embedded around the crown of its features. The square head was completely devoid of eyes, a mouth, or a noise. Instead, jutting from the base of the metal box head, were a pair of long white tusks that were at least two feet each. The metal head swung toward Ada on a thick neck, and the creature froze as if sensing Ada's presence.

Every ounce of Ada's being screamed at her to shoot the thing, but she was cemented in place, paralyzed by terror.

The creature tapped two of its bony fingers across the tile and then it emitted a chattering burst of static from the speaker lining its cubed head. Following the static was what sounded like a low horn that then tumbled into a turning of gears, each sequence of noise flowing together like some kind of mechanical language.

And then it moved toward Ada, dragging its slug-like body down the hall using its long arms to pull itself effortlessly along the tile.

Gasping, Ada dove back into her room and slammed the panel to shut the door. Inside, in the dark, she stood gasping, her eyes wide. What the hell was that thing!? Where had it come from!? She could hear it moving closer toward her door, its fingers tap tap tapping their way ever nearer, its awful head continuing to produce a wave of quiet, chilling noise like the sounds before.

Before she could decide what to do next, her thoughts were invaded yet again by an urgent alarm, more insistent than ever this time.

There's something in the room with me.

Enclosed in the black, she cast her eyes into the corners of the room, body shaking with adrenaline and fear.

And this time, she saw something. It was standing in the corner, facing her, its mass darker than the shadows surrounding it.

Ada brought her gun up, terror rattling her throat, but before she could pull the trigger, the mass of darkness spoke.

"You've done a *terrible* thing."

Ada hesitated for a microsecond, the soft, low voice stopping her trigger finger right before she squeezed it home. It was all the time it took for the darkness to leap at her, a horrible, heavy weight that smashed into her chest, bouncing her off the wall, sending her gun spinning away. She could feel hot breath on her face as the thing climbed on top of her. Screaming now, she struggled to get free and clawed at the shadowed mass. Horribly, in the chaos, she saw a pair of violet eyes staring down at her, almost human in shape, but not quite.

Whatever the thing was, it was strong and she could feel arms and hands, also human to the touch, grasping at her while a pair of legs tried to pin her in place. Howling, she raked her nails across the thing's eyes and was rewarded with a low, screeching hiss, like steam being released from an overheating valve.

Ada bucked and threw the thing off her, scrambling to her feet and throwing herself at the door. She slammed it open and went sprawling out into the hallway without thinking, knowing that moments before the other monster had been out there as well.

But mercifully, the hallway was empty now and Ada hauled herself up, panting, gasping, as the world around her began to seep back into her panicked head. She heard others screaming now, horrible shrieks of fear and terror, the sound of death and pain echoing down the wing.

Ada spun around to face her open doorway and saw a human-shaped shadow staring back at her from the archway of darkness, its violet eyes gleaming.

"You have no idea what's coming for you all," the voice said from the maw. "Now that we know what's inside of you."

The shape stepped forward and reached for Ada and she felt her back and hit the opposite wall, fear exploding up her throat.

And then a gunshot deafened her. She turned away from the blast, shrinking into herself, and heard the purple-eyed shadow let out a groan and then fall heavily to the floor. Blinking, Ada opened her eyes, ears ringing, and felt a pair of hands pull her upright.

"Pap?" Ada gasped, her eyes filling with tears as her father's face filled her world.

Reston's face was splattered with blood and his nose was split across the bridge. He looked terrified, but alert and in control of himself.

"Are you ok?!" he practically shouted at her. "Did it hurt you!?"

Ada felt tears begin to run down her face. "What was that thing!? What is happening!?"

More shrieks filled the hallways and the sound of thundering feet echoed all around them, joined by the blast of the Orbital Clerk's .45 cal auto repeaters.

"We're under attack," Reston said, his voice strained but firm. "I don't know how they got in, but there's a lot of them and we need to get you somewhere safe NOW!"

A crew of Orbital Clerks rounded the corner at Reston's back, coming to a stop at his side. They were all breathless and a few of them were stained with blood.

"We've driven most of them out and the rest we've killed, at least on this level." The Orbital Captain announced, keeping his copper faceplate down. "Our teams are sweeping the lower plates now, but they already got a few of us before the alarm was raised. It isn't good."

"How many?" Reston barked.

"Too soon to tell. But sir, they weren't killing us."

Reston's eyes narrowed. "What do you mean?"

"They were taking captives, dragging them down the halls like they were nothing. I think they were taking them out of the city—back with them."

"What?" Reston hissed. "Alive?"

"Yessir." The Captain said. "But that's not all."

"What is it?" Reston asked in a whisper.

"Sir, your daughter was one of the captives they took. She's gone."

Reston's eyes widened and he slowly turned to stare at Ada.

Ada felt her mind fold in on itself and her throat let out a pitiful gasp. "*Marah…*"

CHAPTER 2

G rayson slid into the alley like a shadow passing between mountains. The heavy rain and dark skies helped mask his sudden departure off the busy streets, cloaking his presence like a miserable veil. He hoisted his pack across his shoulder and ventured deeper into the dirty slit of pavement. The chatter of the city became muted as he crept away from the main street, the neon lights at his back pouring into the shadows to illuminate the puddles around his boots, casting greens and pinks in muted bursts.

Thunder rumbled overhead and Grayson craned his neck to stare up at the strip of sky, an inky ribbon that ran between the towering buildings. A flash of lightning added a flare of white to the bright, busy streets below, but the populace of Malice ignored the weather. They were used to the rain and thunder. It was said that the neon aesthetic that dominated the city was constructed in order to contrast the near constant gloomy downpour that the planet seemed encased in, but Grayson didn't care about color or light. Not tonight.

He continued down the alley, wiping his face of rain. His fingers prodded the black strips of tape he had placed beneath his eyes, hiding the glowing crescent scars that marked him for what he was. He found the tape still held, hiding the light beneath it.

A little further down the alley and he found the ladder. He checked to make sure he wasn't followed and then hoisted himself up, careful not to slip on the slick metal rungs. He took them quickly, his confidence growing, the bag across his back clinking gently in his ears. Another peal of thunder broke the sky as he reached the roof, a bullwhip crack that raised the graying hairs on the back of his neck.

The roof was empty, save for a couple of metal power boxes and the odd ventilation duct. He had scouted this location a couple of days prior, marking it to memory as the perfect spot for what he needed to do. He checked his wrist reader and saw that it was almost midnight. He walked to the edge of the roof and stared down at the sprawling, towering city of Malice that crawled out from his location in all directions. Skyscrapers lined the horizon, massive constructs outlined in brilliant neon strips of light. The streets below him bustled with people, despite the late hour, and the hum of vehicles filled the air with a mechanical whir. Above him, hovers whistled by, a hundred feet over his head. Their traffic pattern mirrored the gridlocked streets down below, a constant rumble that never ceased no matter the hour.

To his left, dotting the bordering rooftops of the commercial district, were dozens of billboards, each one glowing and adding to the rainbow glow of Malice. The one closest to Grayson displayed a short, eight-second loop of a woman and man grinding against each other, half naked, with a flash of text and a brand logo at the end.

Grayson turned away from it all and took a knee along the edge of the roof. He was at least two hundred feet above the street, high enough where no one would spot him, the rumble of traffic from above muting his movements. He slung his bag off his shoulder and began to work, casting a glance at the towering building directly in front of his position. It was a mega scraper, one of the corporate ones, rising so high into the rain that he couldn't see where it ended. Its borders were edged with pulsing pink strips, marking it a residential building.

Grayson continued to work, his hands moving with practiced discipline. When he was finished, he raised the sniper rifle and inspected his assembly, knowing he didn't need to but doing so anyway.

It was a DR-50L, a titan of a gun, pure titanium with glo-fused rifling along the barrel, and a hair trigger you only needed to breathe on. The stock nestled comfortably into his shoulder, the soft padding along the crook practically sighing at his touch. He checked the clip, a twenty-four round aluminum custom piece he had specifically made, and confirmed that it was loaded with coring rounds. It slid into its receiver and the rifle accepted it with a soft, satisfying click. Grayson thumbed the scope cover off its hinge and adjusted the calibration to x32.

With a grunt, he hoisted the gun and stared down the barrel through the night vision magnification. Satisfied, he adjusted his position and lay flat against the roof, feeling the cold, wet surface seep into his clothes and skin.

He hated that.

His target was in the high rise across the street, the pink borders humming silent light across the dark air. He knew which window to aim for from the encrypted doc he had received a week prior. It only took him a few seconds to spot his target. The magnification of his rifle brought Grayson directly into his target's living room. The target was a middle-aged man whom he could see lounging on his couch watching the late-night news vids on his television. He was alone and sprawled out beneath a thick blanket with his head poking out, his face awash with the light of the tv. Grayson thumbed the magnification and brought his target closer, his vision now filled with the man's head and upper body. He looked tired.

Grayson quickly pulled his eye away from the scope and activated the SD card that was slotted into his rifle, ensuring that his kill would be recorded and documented for his client.

The rain beat down on him and Grayson pulled in a breath, placing his eye to the scope once more. He could feel the beat of his heart in his ears. He counted them.

When he reached five, he squeezed the trigger.

The rifle bucked violently against his shoulder as the coring round was discharged, a blast of power and violence that trembled across his prone form.

The man on the couch died in an instant, the bullet boring through the thick window, turning his head into a gory stump. Blood exploded as his head and skull evaporated, spraying a fine mist across the blanket and onto the tv screen.

And the job was done.

Grayson quickly cut the recording feed from his rifle and slid out the SD card, crawling into a kneeling position. He pressed the small chip into his wrist reader and uploaded the kill shot. A second later it was sent.

"Sorry pal," Grayson muttered beneath the rain-soaked sky.

He disassembled his rifle and vanished once more into the night.

He entered his small apartment and locked the door behind him, ensuring that the deadbolts were secure before allowing himself to relax. He took his bag into the bedroom and placed the disassembled rifle back into its titanium case. When that was finished, he went to the bathroom and turned on the faucet.

When did I get so tired? he thought as he stared at his reflection. The wrinkles around his silver eyes seemed deeper tonight, more telling. He ran his hands through his gray hair, watching as it spilled across his eyes and down just past his chin. His fingers scraped across the equally gray stubble lining his jaw and he sighed.

When did I get so old?

He reached up and carefully peeled the strips of black tape from beneath his eyes, wincing. When he looked back at his reflection, his features hardened.

Looking a little dim tonight, big guy.

The scars beneath his eyes glowed gently, the blue light soft. He traced the crescent moons beneath each eye and then let his hand fall away. He squeezed his eyes shut and splashed himself with cold water, hoping to shock himself into alertness. As a rule, he refrained from sleeping for twelve hours after a job had been completed. Just in case. But tonight, he knew, was going to be a challenge.

He stripped his clothes off and then looked down at the glo regulator infused into his thigh. The small metal rectangle protruded an inch from his skin, the twin tubes on either end extending outward before slotting into his flesh.

Maybe I'll just up myself a tick.

Grayson turned the tiny knob on the regulator and he saw the tubes on either end flare with blue light before mixing with the red of his blood. He let out a small gasp as the balance of glo in his bloodstream increased, heightening his senses. When his vision stopped shimmering a moment later, he exhaled.

That's better.

He took a shower, the small isometric bathroom filling with steam as he washed the night from his body and his memory. When he was finished, he clothed himself and then checked his wrist reader to see that the funds for the job had been transferred into his account. Two thousand U-creds and five hundred salt chips.

"Looks like cause for celebration," Grayson muttered to himself, striding across his apartment and into the kitchen. Like all things in his living space, the kitchen was simple, dynamic, and functional. Nothing more and nothing less. He poured himself a glass of water and then went to his balcony, the thin glass slider opening to let in the night air. The awning above sheltered him from the rain as he stepped out, breathing in the wet scent with a sigh. His apartment was on the thirty-seventh floor, giving way to a spectacular view. The city of Malice sprawled out beneath his vantage point, an expanse of noise, light, and metal. He had lived here for forty-seven years now, the planet of Lighton his birthplace, the city of Malice his home. He traveled frequently, sometimes for months at a time, but this planet, this city always eased the tension in his shoulders whenever he returned to it.

Grayson took a sip of water, feeling the glo tingle through his body, and raised his silver eyes to the sky. He watched the patterns of traffic above, the low rumble of hovers crisscrossing between the buildings, skimming between the splashes of brilliant neon.

His wrist reader chirped, snapping him from his trance, and he glanced down at it, slightly annoyed to have his peace and quiet interrupted. His mood evaporated in an instance when he saw who was calling him. A smile tickled the corners of his mouth.

He thumbed his reader. "Hey, sweet pea."

The small screen filled with his daughter's face, an image of youth, life, and a purity he had long outgrown.

"Hi, Daddy!"

Grayson put his water down and kept the wrist reader raised. "Hi yourself. You look fantastic, Claire. Did you change your hair color or something? You look different."

Claire smiled at him through the screen. "I got it cut a couple months ago. You never call me anymore, Dad, I've been worried!"

Grayson exhaled through his nose, feeling guilty. "Has it been that long already? I'm sorry, honey. I've had my hands full. You look great though. How are things? How are you?"

Claire shrugged and grinned, her short blonde hair complemented by her large brown eyes, giving her a radiant look that Grayson missed.

"I've been well. Keeping busy with the new job, learning all the stupid ins and outs of the office politics. And then Jace fills all my free time when I have it, so I guess we can blame him for the gap between our calls."

"How is he?" Grayson asked. "Did you two ever move into that new place?"

"We did! About a month ago now. We have to have you over for dinner."

"I would love that."

"Maybe you can bribe Titus to come too."

Grayson leaned against the railing of his balcony, nodding. "That'd be good. I'm sure he'd like to see Jace—see how his son is treating my daughter."

"Have you worked with him lately?"

Grayson stiffened some. "No. Haven't seen him in a while. I'm sure he's fine though."

"And how have you been, Dad?" Claire asked, a little more cautiously now. "Work...going ok?"

"Sure. Yeah."

Claire nodded, her expression eager for more. "Yeah? You haven't stopped yet? I mean... you haven't tried anything else since the last time we talked? I mean like...other work."

Grayson snorted. "What on earth would I do? Come on. Who would hire me? I wouldn't be able to pick up the city's *trash* looking like this." Grayson waved to the blue crescents beneath his eyes.

"Well, you could try-"

"Hon, we've been down this road before, and honestly I'm too tired to re-pave it. Can we just leave it?"

"I just worry about you, Dad," Claire said, her eyes filling with concern. "If you keep pumping that crap into your system and taking on these shady-"

"You know what happens if I stop, Claire." Grayson cut in. "This is just the way things are. If you're worried about money, there will be a pretty sizable sum coming your way the second I croak-"

"Dad!" Claire squeaked. "I don't care about money! I care about you! I care about your health and what you're doing to your body! Jesus, every time I call I worry you won't pick up because something terrible has happened!" Claire calmed herself a little and ran a hand over her face. "Shit. I'm sorry. I just wish things were different. I wish I could see you more. I miss you. You're the only family I have left."

"I don't think Jace would appreciate that," Grayson said with a small smile.

Claire huffed. "Hey, we don't get married for another year. I love that boy, but we haven't tied the knot just yet." And then her eyes fell away. "There's actually something else I wanted to talk to you about."

"Ah, here comes the meat and potatoes."

"Dad, I'm serious."

Grayson cleared his face. "I'm all ears, kid."

Claire bit her lip and then finally looked into the screen. "Dad. I'm pregnant."

Grayson felt nothing at all for a moment, the news blasting through his brain like a blank shell.

"Dad?"

Grayson blinked and then his face warmed. "Holy hell, Claire. That's amazing. Wow. Are you sure?"

"Oh, I'm sure."

"A kid?" Grayson said, shaking his head. "A little Claire?" He smiled. "I don't even know what to say. Congratulations, baby. That's exciting. Wow."

Claire's face lit up. "We don't know the sex yet, but yeah, you're going to be a grandpa. How's that feel? You're going to be a grandpa!"

"I guess I really am getting old," Grayson said. "I should come see you guys. Soon."

"Please! We're dying to see you! Are you back on Lighton?"

"I am. I'm in Malice, at my place."

"That's perfect! You have to come over then to see the new place and have dinner. I'm sure Titus will want to come too."

"Has Jace told him yet?"

"No, he wants to do it in person, but I just couldn't wait."

"How far along are you?"

"Three months."

Grayson whistled. "You certainly know how to keep a secret."

Claire looked at something offscreen and then back at her father. "I know, I know. Ok Dad, I gotta run. Promise me you'll come over soon!"

"I promise. I love you, Claire. Tell Jace I said hi."

"I will."

"And keep yourself out of trouble," Grayson warned. "You're living for two now."

Claire rolled her eyes. "Thank you, Doctor Dad. I should be telling *you* to stay out of trouble. At least stay safe, ok?"

"Always."

"Bye Dad."

Grayson switched his wrist reader off. He stared out at the rain for a couple of minutes in complete peace, letting the news wash over him in warm, glowing waves. He picked up his glass of water and drained it.

"Good for you, kid." He whispered.

And then his body trembled, a terrible jolting pain that ripped up through his spine and exploded into his head. He gasped and dropped the glass, hearing it shatter, but not seeing it. His vision blurred with blue fog as the pain spiked. He opened his mouth to scream, but before he could, the agony passed like smoke in the sun.

Panting, he fell to one knee and put a hand to his head. Tears leaked from his eyes and he wiped them away, his fingers coming away streaked with blue.

It's getting worse.

He took a deep breath and hauled himself to his feet. He pulled at the waistband of his pants and twisted the dial on his glo regulator, lowering the amount coursing through his bloodstream. After a moment, the world righted itself and he went inside.

As he gathered a broom to sweep up the glass, a thought pulsed at the forefront of his mind. A thought that seemed to grow more present with every passing day.

How much longer do I have?

When he finished cleaning up, he went inside and collapsed on the couch. He flicked on the tv and began to scan the news vids. Nothing seemed to hold his interest as he flipped through the channels. Crime was spiking in Malice, the mining corporations continued to push for off-world exploration, a couple of hovers collided and killed twelve people along with six more that were crushed down below on street level. Nothing but bad news and greed.

He wondered how long it would be before the assassination made it to the airwaves.

As he was about to give up and turn the tv off, his wrist reader chirped once more. He glanced down at it and grunted.

"Speak of the devil."

He accepted the call and his old friend's face filled the screen.

"Titus," Grayson smiled, "I was just talking about you."

The big black man grinned, his white teeth complemented by the white stubble lining his scalp.

"Grayson," He acknowledged. "How in the hell are you my friend? Did I catch you at a bad time?"

"I wouldn't have answered if you did," Grayson said. "Jeez man, it's been ages. I was getting worried about you. You look good."

But he didn't. Titus looked old, weathered, the lines creasing his face running long and haggard. There was a weariness in his eyes that Grayson didn't like. The scars beneath the big man's sockets glowed softly, the blue light curving up the flesh like tiny, sick moons.

"Didn't catch you sleeping, did I?" Titus asked.

"I don't sleep much anymore."

"Too busy chasing ass at this hour, huh?"

"Ass is a young man's game. I'm more interested in being alone these days. With my *own* ass."

"Now why would you want to hang around that wrecked thing?" Titus asked.

"At least I always know where it is." Grayson snorted. "What about you? Where are you these days? Shit, it's been over a year now hasn't it?"

Titus got a faraway look in his eyes. "Damn, has it? I can't keep track anymore. It's either night or day, I've given up on anything beyond that."

"Are you back on Lighton?"

"Yeah. Got in two days ago. I'm in Malice. You at your place?"

"Sure am."

"Well, then it seems like my luck is holding out."

"And why do I feel like mine's about to run out?"

Titus grunted. "Always the pessimist, aren't you? Maybe I just wanna buy you a beer."

"Do you?"

Titus flashed his bright smile again. "No."

"You're insufferable."

"True, but I do want to see you. Tonight, if possible."

Grayson sat up a little. "Seriously? You know how late it is?"

"What, is it past the old man's bedtime? You gotta be up early for a cheap breakfast somewhere?"

"I just finished a job. A couple hours ago."

Titus's face dropped. "Shit. You for real?"

Grayson nodded. "Yeah. A local thing. Only took a week's time, but it was serious, a black ink hit."

"Was it a Vagabond contract?"

"Course it was."

Titus seemed to mull this over for a moment before speaking. "You ok? It go well?"

"I'm fine. It's done. Funds were deposited. I'm in the clear."

"Good. Damn. Seems as if my timing isn't as perfect as I had hoped then."

"What do you mean?"

"I got something for you. For us."

"A job?"

"Yeah. Something off-world. I need to talk to you about it in person though."

Grayson rubbed his eyes. "And it has to be tonight?"

"It does. This one came through the system last night. It was flagged red."

"Time-sensitive. Perfect."

"Can I trouble you for a drink with your old pal? Please?"

Grayson raised an eyebrow. "Please? Now I'm getting nervous."

"I'm going to be at the Silver Sin in thirty minutes. Meet me there? I'll explain everything then."

Grayson let out a heavy sigh, feeling exhausted. "Sure. Ok." He leaned forward a little. "Hey, Titus?"

"What's up?"

"Are *you* ok?"

Titus showed his teeth, but his eyes were hollow and the blue crescents beneath them flared like ghosts. "Course I am. You can't put this old bastard to bed. Not yet at least. See you soon."

And then he was gone.

Grayson leaned back on the couch and closed his eyes. "Goddamn it."

He rubbed his eyes again, the events of the past week filling his bones with lead. Finally, he pulled himself off the couch and went into the bathroom. He retrieved his roll of black tape and cut two strips, fixing them beneath his eyes to hide the glow of his scars. It was still obvious to the general public who he was, what group he belonged to, but the tape sent a message.

Leave me alone.

Next, he went to the bedroom and pulled out his revolver. It was another custom job, one he had made himself. The barrel was ten inches of power cut steel with an optional laser sight attached to the bottom. The wheel was an eight-shot that hummed like an angel as he fingered the release and spun it on its well-oiled hinge. He loaded it quickly with armor-piercing poison rounds, each silver kissed tip coated with a deadly brew he had bought two years ago off-world. The grip was chiseled black iron with steel cord roping that perfected the balance and made up for the extra inches on the barrel.

He slid the gun into his hip holster. After a moment's consideration, he popped the side out of his glo regulator in his thigh and removed the nearly empty blue cartridge from its designated slot. He reached into his bedside drawer and pulled out a small copper case. He popped it open and took out a fresh glowing capsule which he replaced back into the slot of his regulator, clicking it into place. He made a mental note to be more mindful in the future of his glo levels. Usually, he needed to replace the dosage every six months, but lately, it was becoming more frequent, a detail that he'd rather not think about.

I wonder just how much of this crap I have in my system, he thought as he went to his closet. *Thirty-two years since initial injection.* He stamped into his boots. *I'm probably more glo than human at this point.*

He reached for his jacket and then paused. His fingers hovered over his Vagabond-issued overcoat, a black leather cut with an electric blue V stitched into the sleeve at the bicep.

Wouldn't make much sense to tape up my eyes and then put this old thing on, he thought. Instead, he grabbed his long brown leather coat and stepped out of his apartment.

The rain beat down on him like a million tiny fists. It plastered Grayson's graying hair to his face as he stood impatiently at the kiosk outside his building, waiting for a taxi. He preferred ground-level travel whenever he could help it, despite the long wait time for a ride. Hovers made him nervous. He had seen too many vids of them colliding mid-air. You couldn't crawl out of a wreck if you plunged a hundred feet first. Not without a world of luck.

The city of Malice bustled around him, every rain-soaked person pushing past him with an annoyed urgency. The glow of billboards and neon striped residential buildings pulsed like a heartbeat, the rainbow of pinks, blues, and yellows magnified by the water-soaked asphalt. The rumble of traffic along the streets filled Grayson's ears and the smell of diesel and vapor smoke invaded his nostrils, tickling the inside of his skull.

After a couple of minutes, an old taxi pulled up to the kiosk, its rubber tires squeaking as it came to a stop. Grayson ducked into it and shut the door, grateful to be out of the rain.

"Silver Sin." He instructed the driver who was a young woman twenty years his junior.

"You got it." She mumbled, barely giving him a look.

The bright city of Malice began to rumble past the rain-streaked windows as the taxi pulled away from the curb. The dark sky overhead continued to clog with heavy clouds and a peal of thunder boomed down over the indifferent stream of traffic that filled the roadways. Grayson stared out at it, his face glowing as the colors of the district illuminated his face as he passed them by.

"Oh shit, you're one of them aren't you?"

Grayson looked at the driver, his eyes meeting hers in the rearview mirror. They were wide and young and very, very worried.

"Pardon?" He asked.

"You're one of those juicers aren't you? One of those lunatics filled with glo?"

Grayson felt tired all over again. "Yep."

The woman tightened her grip on the wheel. "Shit. You're not going to like...blow up or something are you? Look, I'm just trying to make ends meet here and I don't want to put my job or my life on the line tonight ok?"

"Then just get me to the Silver Sin." Grayson muttered.

The woman's eyes continued to dart from the road to the rearview, unconvinced.

"I'm not going to blow up," Grayson stated flatly. "I have my regulator and it's working just fine. Not like you need to know."

"So you're not going to cause any trouble?"

Grayston rubbed his eyes, feeling his headache returning. "If I really wanted to, I could crank the thing, overcook, and ruin everyone's night but I'm a little sleepy right now and don't feel like getting arrested or spending the few remaining years of my life behind bars, ok?"

The woman blinked and then nodded rapidly. "Yeah, sure. Sorry. Ok. Right. I've just never met one of you people before, not in person at least.

I always see stories about your group. You're part of that group, aren't you? The Vagabonds?"

Grayson looked out the window again. "Yeah, kid. Vagabond. But I'm just going to have a drink with an old friend right now. I'm not on a job. You won't get in trouble." He looked back to greet her worried eyes in the mirror again. "And I'm not going to overcook. So relax."

The woman seemed to ease her death grip on the wheel a little. "Ok. Cool." And then she smiled. "I mean, this is fucking *cool*. I can't wait to tell my friends later that I actually met one of you people. They're going to freak."

Grayson closed his eyes and considered stuffing the barrel of his revolver into his mouth.

THE RAIN HAD LESSENED some by the time he reached the Silver Sin. The bar was nestled between two sky rises, their pink outline glowing brightly, marking them as residential. The Silver Sin had a strip of blue outlining its borders, marking it as an entertainment location and the object of his outing.

He pushed inside, his fingers absently checking the tape beneath his eyes. The bar was only half full, a low electronic beat thumping in the background to mix with the low growl of conversation and pooling vapor smoke. Keeping his head down, he strode toward the bar searching for Titus.

He spotted the big black man without much difficulty. His old friend was sitting at the corner of the long counter, nearly impossible to miss. At nearly fifty, Titus was a mountain of a man. His cutoff shirt revealed bulging muscle that rippled as he tipped his beer back and drained it, the tendons in his neck straining as he swallowed. His knuckles were wrapped in black cloth and a silver chain hung from the man's neck with a small V pendant attached to it.

As Grayson approached him, he noted that Titus had nothing to cover the scars beneath his eyes, the twin crescent gouges alight with a blue glow, marking him for what he was.

When Titus saw Grayson, his face pulled into a tight, wrinkled smile.

"There he is. I knew you'd come."

Grayson reached his side and smiled. "Hey, pal. Long time."

Titus stood up, nearly knocking his stool aside. "Get in here you old fart. Give papa a hug."

Grayson grunted but embraced his friend, grateful to see him. When they pulled apart, Grayson took a seat next to the big man and ordered a round for them both.

"Not feeling particularly shy tonight are you?" Grayson said after a moment, tapping his cheek with a finger.

Titus shrugged. "Let 'em stare. I've done enough good in my life to feel ashamed about what I am."

"Is that so? If I recall, it ain't all been good," Grayson noted, tipping a beer to his lips as it was placed before him.

Titus touched a finger to the tip of his nose, "True. But times are a changin'. I'm not the wild boar I once was, buddy."

Grayson curled his lips. "Well pardon me."

Titus raised his hands defensively. "Alright, I was a little lost back when we started, but I've lost my taste for those kinda contracts. Especially over the past couple years." He grinned openly. "I'm a changed man. I've dulled those edges you love so much."

"A little late to be reborn in the light of morality, isn't it?"

"It ain't ever too late. But you know I've always veered away from the real nasty requests we get. Hell, the worst ones I ever did were with you."

Grayson nodded slowly. "I guess you're right. Well, good for you then. What caused the change of heart?"

Titus took a swig of beer before answering. "Just getting old, man. Really been thinking hard lately. The Vagabonds get a lot of listings through the network, but they ain't all greed-filled vendettas. There's a lot of people who just need a helping hand. Figured if I'm going to keep working then I might as well take the jobs that make the universe a better place. Real decent of me, I know, you don't gotta say it. And hell, if there's an afterlife then I'd like to start tilting the table in my direction if you catch my drift."

"Oh I catch it," Grayson muttered, his head filling with the scent of vapor smoke as it plumed around him, the patrons at the bar huffing away with indifference. A couple of them were staring at Grayson and Titus, but Grayson ignored their wide eyes and wary looks.

"So how you been man?" Titus asked, leaning forward. "How's Claire? You talk to her lately?"

"Yeah. She's good. Her and Jace seem happy. They seem to be making it work."

"Course they are," Titus smiled. "It's 'cause I raised my boy right. I take full credit for his dedication to your daughter."

"Well that's just weird," Grayson said. "Just how many drinks am I behind at this point?"

"Not as many as I'd like," Titus answered with a grunt. "We got some business to discuss."

Grayson put his beer down. "Already? I haven't seen you in ages, Titus, what the hell have you been up to? Where have you been?"

Titus's mouth tightened some and then he scratched at the white stubble lining his scalp. "Sorry. You're right. It *has* been a long ass time." He sighed, his large form drooping over the bar. "To tell you the truth, man, it's been tough."

"That halo on your head not fitting quite right?"

Titus bit his lip and looked down at his hands. "Go easy, Gray."

Grayson straightened some. "Sorry. Did something happen?"

Titus lowered his voice and stared at the drink between his hands. "I got into some shit during my last job. Bad shit. But the contract was good. I was helping out some decent folk way out past Black Orbius."

Grayson whistled softly. "That's a long way away from home, pal."

"I know. But these poor people needed help and so I took the contract. Me and one other Vagabond. We figured two of us would be enough to deal with their troubles and then we'd split the payout."

"So what happened?"

Titus closed his eyes and pressed his fingers to them. "We got the job done, but I had to overcook."

Grayson sucked in a breath. "*Fuck.*"

"Yeah. Fuck. You know how that shit affects me, man. I take it harder than the rest of us Vagabonds for whatever reason. It really messed me up. Nearly took out the people I was trying to help, but we were being attacked and I panicked. Didn't think there was any other way out of the situation."

Grayson looked sideways at his friend. "They knew who they were hiring. It's not like us Vagabonds are some great universal secret. People know what we do and how we do it. I'm sure they sent the contract through the network because no one else would help them. But you did. Right?"

Titus pulled his hands away. "Yeah. I did. For better or worse." He looked at Grayson then, his dark eyes meeting Grayson's silvers. "I just hate that I had that one, awful moment of uncertainty. I *panicked*. I lost my shit and I coulda hurt a lot of people."

"We're paid to hurt people," Grayson said quietly.

Titus gripped Grayson's arm. "Yeah, but not the good ones. Least not anymore. Not for me."

Grayson's mind wandered back to earlier in the evening. In his mind's eye, he saw the man beneath the blanket. He saw his head evaporate as the bullet pierced his skull.

"A job's a job. We do it to get by. It's all we're good for. It's all we *chose* to be good for."

"You gotta stop thinking like that," Titus cautioned. "Won't do you any good in the long run."

"Yeah, well, I think my run is reaching its end."

Titus cocked an eyebrow at him. "How do you figure?"

It was Grayson's turn to feel uncomfortable. He shifted on his stool and clasped his hands together, his voice soft. "I've started to fringe, I think."

The light in Titus's eyes faded some. "Aw hell. You sure?"

Grayson nodded. "Yeah. Think so. I get these...attacks. They hurt like hell. Feels like someone is pulling my bones out through my back."

"How often you gettin' them?"

Grayson rolled his shoulders. "I don't know. It's only happened a couple of times over the past year. But I know what it means. And they're getting way more frequent."

Titus knotted his brow. "I had no idea, man. I'm sorry. I'm sure I'm not far behind you. Especially seeing how I just overcooked again. Sometimes I think I can feel the glo in my veins eating away at what's left of me. Tearing me down. Breaking me, one breath at a time. Almost like it's alive." He squirmed on his stool. "You ever hear your bones creaking? Like they're trying to talk to you?"

Grayson gave him a quizzical look. "No. Can't say I do."

Titus blew out a breath. "Figures. This shit is so unpredictable. You would think someone would have figured out all the nasty little tricks glo is capable of by now. Hell, we don't even know where it comes from. We just blindly mine it when some breaks through the atmosphere like some kind of mysterious care package. You know they found two thousand gallons at the bottom of a crater on Pathallilic last year? No one has any idea how it got there or where it came from. But did we scoop it all up? You bet your ass we did. I mean, where is this shit falling out of the sky from?"

"I don't know, man," Grayson said, shifting the conversation, not in the mood for conspiracy. "Someone will figure it out. Look, what's this job you wanted to talk to me about?"

Titus finished his beer and then wiped his mouth, and took a long breath before answering, his voice gaining volume. "Right, right. Well, like I said, it's an off-world gig. There's this mining planet, Pratus—it sent out an urgent request through the Vagabond network. Seems like they're having some trouble lately."

"What kind of trouble?"

"The listing wasn't terribly specific, but it sounded like they were having a bit of a marauder problem. Hit and run type of thing. People getting taken. People disappearing. That kind of deal."

"That sounds pretty amateur," Grayson observed. "Why can't they just take care of it?"

"Beats me. They must be desperate."

"Pratus…" Grayson said, reaching into his memory bank. "That name sounds familiar."

"It's a fairly new settlement. Big salt mining operation. New money, only a couple generations old. There's a city there called Typhon. They were the ones who sent up the flare."

Grayson scratched the stubble along his chin. He ordered another beer while he considered the job. Titus kept quiet and let his friend mull it over. When his beer came, Grayson spoke again.

"Why pick this one? There's dozens of active jobs right now. This seems a little below our pay grade."

"Trust me, the pay is good. Did I mention their main export is salt?"

"I heard you. But I wasn't talking about the payout."

Titus sighed. "I don't know man. These people need help and they're pretty far out there. If we don't help them, I don't think any of the other Vagabonds will."

"Yeah, cause it sounds pretty lowkey. Not really something we'd waste our time with. That's a lot of travel and a lot of effort to deal with a problem that's as common as a rainy day on Lighton."

"Not every Vagabond is a thrill seeker like you, Gray," Titus said around a smile.

"I'm not a thrill-seeker, I just don't see why you'd want to go all the way out there for something like this."

Titus exhaled, a slow groan from deep in his chest, and he leaned forward. He suddenly looked very tired.

"Look man," he said quietly. "If you're going to make me come out and say it then I'll say it. I need an easy one. Something we can breeze through and collect without a problem. I know we're not getting any younger, I know this shit in our veins is going to have its way with us soon, and that's exactly why I need this."

Grayson took another drink. "You haven't started to fringe yet, have you?"

"No, but it'll be soon. And it'll be bad. I need to work some easy jobs. I want to leave something for Jace. And for Claire."

"You and me both."

"So let's do this one. Help me out. It sounds like we're both working for the same thing anyway." Titus leaned into Grayson. "I need this, man. Please. After this last job, I feel like I gotta get right again. That's why I need you there. We've been friends for a long time. You know me. I'd feel better with you there."

Grayson looked at Titus, their eyes meeting. He could see the desperation in his friend's face, the need.

Grayson let out a long, shaking breath. "Fine. Ok. I'm with you."

Titus smiled, relief flooding his face now. "Thank you. I owe you one, Grayson. I appreciate it."

"You don't owe me anything," Grayson said, waving a hand.

Titus leaned back in his stool. "There *is* one other thing."

Grayson closed his eyes. "Course there is."

"Don't get huffy," Titus snorted, smiling. "You'll like this. There's one more coming with us. Another Vagabond. A young kid, pretty fresh."

Grayson turned to Titus, looking incredulous. "Are you serious? Why on earth do we need a third? Two of us should be more than enough to handle something like this."

Titus laughed. "Keep your pants on. Like I said, he's young and he could use some help getting used to the club. He's a good dude. A little strange, but solid."

"Strange? Strange worries me."

"I'm going to keep an eye on him, don't worry," Titus assured. "And he'll be useful, I'm sure. If this job turns out to be a real pain in the ass, we'll be glad to have another with us."

"I guess so," Grayson said, still unconvinced. "What's this kid's name?"

"Shinji."

"And what's his deal?"

Titus shrugged. "He grew up in a rich family, didn't feel like he belonged, so he bounced and joined the network."

"That sounds a little clean cut."

"His parents didn't care for him much and he returned the feeling with an extra helping of disgust. From what he's told me, the kid despises the upper class. Thinks they're lazy. Uninspired. He's just looking for a chance to find his own way."

Grayson nodded. "Right. Ok. I guess we'll make it work. If you vouch for him, then I guess he can come."

Titus grinned. "Cool. He's meeting us at the docks tomorrow morning."

"Tomorrow morning!?"

"The money waits for no one," Titus chided.

Grayson drained the rest of his beer and looked down at his hands. They were shaking slightly. He closed them into fists and sighed. He felt like he could sleep for a week.

"Tomorrow it is then."

CHAPTER 3

When Grayson arrived at the docks the following morning, he felt completely drained. He hadn't slept and the night had felt eternal. He had spent the dark hours in his apartment with one hand wrapped around his revolver. The assassination had finally made it onto the news, but there didn't seem to be an indication that he was a suspect. The talking heads on the news vids speculated that this was a Vagabond job, but there weren't any leads to back up the claim. The usual debate had followed the proclamation, arguments cast back and forth about why the "glo juiced freaks" were even allowed to walk free. Grayson watched with half-lidded eyes as a pair of women screamed at one another on the tv, one on the defensive, the other attacking her every word. To the general public, the Vagabonds were a two-edged sword, both helping and hurting society. Everyone had an opinion on the matter, but an actual confrontation was rare.

Hate us until they need us, Grayson had thought, trying not to fall asleep. It was an old saying within the network, a common disdain among the Vagabonds toward the public.

Where's the real crack in morality? He had thought idly as he watched the debates. *Is it in the person who pulls the trigger or is it in the draftee of the contract?*

His mood had worsened as he watched the debate. One of the women was arguing that the entire Vagabond network needed to be blacklisted, claiming that the free-market approach was a deadly threat to society.

As if that'd stop anything.

The other women countered and began listing off all the good the Vagabonds had done to protect the deep space colonies when no one else would answer the call. This was met by more frothing at the mouth by her opponent and the circus continued on its loop until he had shut off the tv.

Everyone thinks they have it all figured out, he thought quietly as morning birthed across the sky.

How pathetically linear we are.

Grayson pulled himself from his thoughts as he shuffled through the busy loading bays, a bustle of activity roaring around him. The rain had ceased overnight, but the sky remained a thick carpet of gloom above. A dozen ships spanned the area around him as he made his way toward export-c where Titus's craft was prepping. It was early enough that the off-world traders hadn't left yet, still in the midst of loading their shipments. The stink of glo reactors filled the air as engines ignited and rocket fuel vaporized, clouding the crowded dock with a nauseating haze.

Grayson bumped into a pair of techs loading pallets onto a Class C hauler and they turned to bark at him but slammed their mouths shut when they saw his face.

He hadn't taped his eyes today and his black leather coat boldly portrayed the electric blue V on the sleeve, marking him for what he was. Since he was on a job, a public service contract, he had decided to dress appropriately and show the client exactly what they were buying.

As the techs scurried off, Grayson jumped away from a small ship as its engines burned blue, the exhaust flaring a moment before he stepped into its path. Cursing, he took the long way around and told himself to wake up and pay attention. He hefted his pack higher up on his shoulder and gripped his weapons case in a gloved fist. Everything felt heavy and sluggish and he wished he were in bed instead of here, dodging blazing death fumes.

"Grayson! Over here!"

Grayson headed toward the voice, concentrating on it over the din of noise. A ship took off to his left, sending a blast of air across the spaceport. His hair whipped across his eyes and he squinted and turned away from the rising craft, his mood souring even further.

"You look like you could use a caffeine vape this morning, buddy," Titus said, striding into view, his voice booming. Grayson approached him, noting how cheery and well-rested he appeared.

He found it incredibly annoying.

"Let me take that for you," Titus offered, sliding a hand around Grayson's pack.

"Thanks. You're looking awfully chipper this morning," Grayson said moodily. "Bet you got a tight six hours last night."

"Oooh, someone's grumpy," Titus snorted. "You can sleep on the way if you need to. I ran diagnostics already and pre-set our course. It's going to be a four-day trip so you'll have plenty of time to rest those silver puppy dogs of yours."

"Four days?" Grayson asked as another ship launched across the dock, sending a second blast of hot air rippling through the congested space.

"Four days."

"That's with a glo jump?"

"Yep. I told you it was a ways away."

"Guess you did."

"Come on, let's get on board," Titus soothed with a soft smile, leading them through the throng toward his ship.

It was a Class B rig, which meant it had an exterior weapons system and glo jump capabilities. Titus had paid good money to keep the ship updated and despite its age, he had always opted to fix any problems that arose instead of trading up for a newer model.

The ship was small, only seventy-six feet in length, with a singular glo drive attached to a triple rocket engine mounted to the aft end. The nose of the ship was two-pronged with twin mounted gunner cockpits installed in both sections. They were rounded orbs and the exterior plates were tinted gold to reflect blinding fire. Titus had lovingly named the ship "Afterburner" but Grayson had always referred to it as "ol' goldy eyes" because of the twin gunner spheres, a fact that annoyed Titus to no end.

They made their way up the extended ramp and into the belly of the ship, leaving some of the dock's noise behind them.

"I thought you said someone else would be joining us," Grayson noted as Titus closed the ramp at their backs, sealing the ship.

"I did. He's stashing his stuff in one of the bunk rooms," Titus said, striding past Grayson down the tight metal hallway toward the cockpit. Grayson followed him, keeping his rifle case locked in his grip. His boots echoed off the steel glassed floors and he turned to look down an adjoining hallway, toward the small living quarters and thought he heard movement from one of the four bunk rooms.

Titus shot a look over his shoulder at Grayson. "What, were you expecting him to be waiting for you on bended knee?"

"Absolutely," Grayson responded. "With a pillow and blanket in hand."

"You really are tired aren't you?"

"Obviously."

"You have any problem with the contract last night? Any unexpected visitors or calls?"

"No. I've ghosted out. Don't worry about it."

"Dandy," Titus said as they entered the cockpit. He turned around and handed Grayson his bag back. "Here, take this to your room. Go say hi to the new kid, too. I'm going to take off and get the ball rolling here."

Grayson slung his pack back over his shoulder. "What was his name again? The new kid?"

"Shinji."

"Right. Shinji. I'll wave to him before I pass out. Don't bother me for the next twenty hours, please. And keep the ship steady for me."

Titus slid into one of the two pilot seats, throwing a thumbs up in Grayson's direction. "You got it, princess. Go get your beauty sleep before you turn into a goddamn pumpkin."

Grayson slumped back down the hallway and turned toward the bunk rooms. When he reached his own, he turned toward the door opposite the hall from him. It was sealed, but he could hear movement from inside. He thought about knocking and introducing himself to the new kid but found he was just too tired. Instead, he opened the door to his room, tossed his stuff down, and collapsed onto the small cot.

He was asleep in seconds.

HE WASN'T SURE how long he slept when he finally opened his eyes again. He could feel the steady, familiar hum of the ship around him and knew they had already left Lighton's atmosphere and were in deep space. He scrubbed his eyes and allowed his mind a moment to catch up.

He found that he felt a lot better. The ache in his neck had all but vanished and the weight in his chest had been removed. His exhaustion had been cured and he was thankful to wave it goodbye. He checked his wrist reader and blinked.

I've been asleep for twenty-six hours?

He double-checked the time and date again to confirm.

Guess that job took more out of me than I realized.

Slowly he sat up on the edge of his cot and wiped the sleep from his face. The ship was silent around him, besides the low hum of the glo jump drive. After a moment, he stood and changed out of his clothes and put on a fresh set. He was feeling better the longer he was awake, more conscious and alert, ready to take on this contract and all that it entailed.

A second before he opened his bunk room door, his head exploded in pain. It came without warning and with all the brutality of a lightning strike. He let out a sharp gasp and sank back down onto his cot, grabbing at his skull, eyes squeezed shut. A bolt of electricity rocketed up his spine in a fiery coil of agony and then detonated in his brain, sending stars rocketing behind his eyelids.

And then it was gone, leaving him reeling. Slowly, he lowered his hands from his face and took a measured breath. He mentally checked his motor and mental functions and found everything seemed to be working. The pain he had felt melted away like snow beneath the sun as if it had never been there at all.

Another one? He thought, his breath returning to his lungs. *Already?*

It sent unease wriggling through his guts. He checked the glo regulator in his thigh and saw that it was still functioning at its normal setting. He almost wished it wasn't. It would be a lot easier to fix it than to confront what was actually happening.

No use worrying about it now. I still have time.

He found that he was extremely parched and his stomach rumbled for attention. He wasn't sure if he should eat just yet, but decided that water was probably a good idea. He thumbed the door open and stepped out into the dark hallway. It was lit by pulsing red floor lights, the crimson shadows flaring along the metal walls.

Titus must have switched on the auto-drive and gone to sleep, Grayson thought as he made his way down the far end of the hall toward the small kitchenette.

When he entered the room, his heart nearly stopped.

"Jesus," he sputtered, putting a hand to his chest. "You scared the hell out of me."

The man at the small table smiled around the shadows, his features illuminated by the red lights.

"Sorry. I couldn't sleep," the younger man said, his voice soft.

Grayson stared at him from across the table, sizing him up. "You must be Shinji."

"I am. Nice to meet you, Grayson."

"I see Titus has already told you-" Grayson started, but the words died in his throat as the red lights pulsed once more.

He stepped toward the table, squinting. "What the hell...?"

The young man, Shinji, didn't move. He didn't say anything. He stared at Grayson with dark eyes, his black hair tied in a knot at the nape of his neck. His skin was smooth, almost like plastic, and his frame was slender, but not thin. Beneath his right eye was a small, singular crescent scar, a glowing blue cut that was still in its infancy.

But that wasn't what robbed Grayson of speech. It was the large metal box strapped to the kid's back. It was the size of a footlocker with two pairs of thin tubes on each side that extended into the young man's biceps. The tubes glowed red and blue, the liquid inside swirling and streaming together.

"What the hell did you do to yourself?" Grayson asked. He leaned against the kitchenette, his hands gripping the sink at his back, his knuckles white.

Shinji's face remained neutral. "It's my regulator."

Grayson shook his head. "Son, I've met a lot of Vagabonds in my day, but I've never met one strung up in a contraption like that."

"I would imagine not," Shinji said, leaning forward on his elbows, the metal coffin on his back groaning slightly. "Not many Vagabonds have the capabilities I do. For better or worse."

"Do I even want to know?"

"Probably not," Shinji said quietly. "But this device is necessary. If you're worried about me slowing you down, I can promise you I won't. I've conditioned myself to counter its weight."

Grayson continued to stare at the younger man, at the rectangular piece of machinery that loomed slightly over Shinji's head.

"Titus vouched for you," he finally said. "That's good enough for me."

Shinji nodded. "He's a kind soul, that one."

"I wouldn't go that far."

Shinji folded his hands neatly in front of him. "What do you know about our contract?"

Grayson slowly turned and retrieved a glass from the metal cabinet behind him. "Just what Titus told me. A mining planet needs our help with some local trouble."

Shinji produced a small data chip and slid it across the table. "Pratus, a salt-rich world filled with sand and heat. If you want to read up on it, I've put together a file. It might be useful."

"Thanks. I will," Grayson said as he filled his glass from the water reserves.

Got ourselves a regular student here.

Shinji stared across the table at Grayson. "Is there something you want to say?"

Surprised, Grayson turned back to Shinji. "What?"

"I asked if you wanted to say something."

Grayson took a slow sip of water before responding. "How old are you, kid?"

"Twenty."

Grayson grunted. "How long have you been in the Vagabond system?"

"Four months. Initial injection was five months ago."

"And how many jobs have you taken on in that time?"

Shinji smiled, but it was all teeth. "Twenty-two."

Grayson let out a low whistle. "You certainly don't like to sit on your hands."

"I would like to enjoy my life before this shit kills me," Shinji said, spreading his hands to display his massive regulator. "And that takes u-creds and a lot of work. So no, I don't like to sit on my hands. I wouldn't know what to do with them, honestly."

This kid is nothing but business, Grayson noted.

A beat passed and then Shinji sighed. "Look. I'm not here to be a pain in the ass. I realize you probably didn't want me coming. I know I'm new and you don't know me, but Titus made me an offer and I took it. I'm not here to step on anyone's toes. I just don't like to laze about. That's how people get fat and die and I can't think of a more disgusting way to go."

Grayson set his glass down and wiped his mouth. He didn't know what to make of the strange young man before him, but he figured he would have plenty of time to acclimate himself with his behaviors.

"Glad to hear it," Grayson said after a moment and extended his hand. "I know you already know my name, but I'm Grayson. It's good to meet you."

Shinji paused, as if surprised by the gesture, but then he clasped Grayson's hand with a fingerless glove. "I'm Shinji. I look forward to working with you."

Grayson let his hand drop after they shook. "You hungry? I think I'm going to make something. Feel like I haven't eaten in about a year. I'm sure Titus has something good I could whip up if you're not picky."

But before Shinji could respond, a low wave of noise rippled through the ship, snapping their conversation apart. Grayson cocked his head to the side, alert, and waited.

Another low wave of noise rumbled beneath the deck as if the ship itself were going to sleep. Shinji didn't move. He just watched Grayson.

Something's wrong, Grayson thought, jaw tightening. *Wonderful.*

The low hum of the ship sputtered then—once, twice, and then went silent. The lights along the floor continued to pulse red across the walls, but the remainder of the ship seemed dead.

Without a word, Grayson rushed to the cockpit, his heart beginning to race. From somewhere behind him, he heard a door open and then hurried movement. Titus came stumbling into the cockpit a second later, knocking past Grayson who was surveying the control dashboard.

"What'd you do?" Titus demanded, still half asleep. His eyes were heavily bagged and he was shirtless, his bare chest tight with muscle and more than a few scars.

"I didn't do anything," Grayson muttered, staring past the blinking control board and out into the emptiness of space. Stars dotted the vast black canvas, millions of them, all twinkling silently.

"We've stopped," Titus said, scrubbing sleep from his eyes. He slid into one of the seats and began tapping at the controls. Nothing happened. Nothing changed.

"What in the hell…?" He mumbled.

"What is it?"

"Everything here seems to be working fine, but nothing is responding to my input."

"Did a circuit blow?"

"No, everything is green across the board."

"What don't we have access to?"

"The weapons system and the glo jump drive. The thrusters aren't responding either. We're dead in the water without a water pistol." Titus shook his head, fully awake now. "It's almost like-"

The cockpit windshield suddenly filled with movement, snatching Grayson's attention away from Titus.

"We got company," Grayson announced. Titus looked up and then his hands closed into fists.

A mid-sized ship coasted past, an older model that had clearly been modified. It drifted ahead of them, then readjusted its course and began to swing alongside them, its long prow aimed to fit snugly against the Afterburner.

"That's what I was afraid of," Titus growled. "It seems like someone's been fishing out here and we just happened to be swimming by."

"Marauders?" Grayson asked. He already knew the answer.

"Buncha dirty space pigs," Titus spat, disgusted.

"What'd they do to the ship?" Grayson asked, staring down at the illuminated control board. At his back, Shinji darkened the doorway, his metal regulator nearly filling the space.

Titus tapped a few buttons, getting no response. "They must have used emp worms."

Shinji squinted out the window at the ship as it slowly approached. "What's an emp worm?"

Titus leaned back, exasperated. "They're nasty little devices that target specific ship functions." He tapped at the controls again, as if proving his point. "Like the weapons system and our motor functions. It's a hell of a lot cheaper than building an all-out emp bomb, but they don't last as long."

"When will we regain control of the ship?" Shinji asked quietly, never taking his dark eyes off the approaching threat.

"Not soon enough," Titus said angrily.

Grayson looked down at the big man. "We're going to have to deal with this."

"Obviously. I'm not letting some star whores take the Afterburner. Not in a million years, bud."

"Do our coms work?" Shinji asked.

Titus tapped at the control panel and then blinked. "Yeah. But there's no one out here with us. We're not getting rescued if that's what you're asking."

Shinji looked at Titus. "It wasn't."

A rumble shook the floor and Grayson steadied himself from falling. "It seems as if they've parked."

Titus stood up and pushed past them. "Grab your guns. They're going to be coming in through the repairs room where the outer dock door is. Hopefully, there aren't many of them."

Grayson followed Titus down the hall and back through the kitchenette. "They'll most likely lead with shock charges. We should hole up across from their entry point so we don't get our teeth rattled loose."

"Good idea," Titus acknowledged. Grayson hurried around him and went to his room. He retrieved his revolver and grabbed a handful of extra shells. After making sure it was loaded, he went back to the kitchenette.

Shinji stood next to the table, his bulk taking up more space than Grayson felt comfortable with.

He's a big target with that thing on his back.

Shinji reached down and pulled out a long knife from his boot and then unstrapped a small automatic pistol he had strapped to his thigh, something Grayson hadn't noticed.

Titus joined them in the small space a moment later, holding a shotgun that was almost as big as he was. Sitting beneath the twin square barrels was a cylindrical ammunition clip that slotted tightly next to the double black iron triggers. The fire waxed, the steel-plated stock was nestled beneath the crook of Titus's arm as he checked to make sure it was loaded.

Down the far hall, the repairs room was visible from their vantage point. Grayson didn't care for close-quarter combat and he felt a slight tickle of claustrophobia along the base of his neck. As he shook the sensation away, the outer door in the repair room began to glow and a line of fire began to form around its seal.

"I'll teach them to ruin my door," Titus said thickly as he positioned himself behind the kitchenette entrance. Grayson took the opposite side and checked to make sure he had a direct line of sight down the hallway and into the repairs room where their visitors were slowly breaching the ship.

Shinji stayed where he was by the table. Grayson shot him a look and noticed that the young man had his hand around his regulator's dial, located along the side of the large metal box. Shinji clicked it four times and then let out a shuddering gasp as his system flooded with an influx of glo. The small, singular scar beneath his right eye flared and Grayson wondered how long it would be before the kid had a matching scar beneath his other eye.

Not long if he's using four clicks for a fight like this.

Grayson reached down to his own regulator and juiced himself. Two clicks. Immediately, he felt the familiar rush of adrenaline explode through his veins, heightening his senses, tightening his muscles, hardening him for the coming skirmish.

Titus didn't touch his regulator and Grayson noticed he was making a point not to make eye contact. Grayson shifted his attention back toward the door and saw that it was almost completely breached, the line of fire completing its circuit.

A moment later and the door was kicked inward, clanging loudly onto the floor. Grayson stayed put, held his breath, and waited—heart thumping. He gripped his revolver and shut his eyes as something was tossed into their ship, a metallic pair of cubes that bounced halfway down the hall.

A heartbeat passed before the shock charges detonated. Even from behind cover, Grayson felt the blast of super-compressed air and electricity roar through the throat of the hallway and erupt all around them. Heat washed over his face and he winced against it, sparks dancing off the floor and across the ceiling above them. Shinji's form sparkled with it, the blast hitting him full in the chest. He planted his feet against it and he grit his teeth, unmoving, the contraption on his back groaning.

And then the first of their attackers boarded the ship, only seconds behind the shock charges. It was a man dressed in shoddy metal-plated armor. His eyes were alight with eagerness and he raised a pistol and sent a pair of bullets tearing past Grayson's cover. Titus pivoted from his vantage point and brought his shotgun up. He pulled both triggers and the blast tore the man apart at the waist, shredding through his armor to splinter and tear at his flesh. Blood sprayed the hallway as the man's insides erupted, his spine caving. He fell apart and splattered onto the floor.

Three more men flooded the breached door then, two with automatic rifles, the third holding a primed shock charge. He let it fly toward the kitchenette and Grayson saw it land at his feet, blinking once before detonating.

The shock charge exploded across his body and he flew backward, crashing hard into the table and then falling to the floor. Electric sparks licked at his arms and legs, sending heat coursing through his body.

But beneath the pulse of glo, the pain was a distant thing, something to be dealt with later. Grayson pulled himself quickly to his feet as the three men charged down the hallway, automatic rifles screaming. Shinji crouched low, the bullets pinging harmlessly off his regulator. He cocked his arm back, stood once more, and then threw his knife with all his might.

The blade thudded into the lead man's eye, flipping him onto his back, to the floor, killing him instantly.

Grayson stood as the remaining two entered the kitchenette, barrels swinging toward his face. He ducked as one of the riflemen discharged his weapon, the blast howling past his ear. Grayson grabbed the barrel and jerked the rifle away, simultaneously shoving his revolver beneath the man's chin and blowing his brains out the back of his skull.

The remaining man jumped back and pointed his rifle directly at Grayson's head. A second before he pulled the trigger, Shinji spun, smashing the man against the wall with his regulator, pinning him in place.

Grayson raised his revolver and ended the man's life, the bullet shattering his victim's teeth as it entered his mouth and exited out the back of his head.

"Titus!" Grayson yelled, spinning to see his friend pulling himself off the floor, the shock charge rattling him. "You ok?"

Titus picked up his shotgun and nodded, looking dazed.

Why didn't you juice? Grayson thought urgently.

But before he could assess his friend's health, two more gunmen entered the breached door. Grayson sensed them before he saw them, his glo charged mind screaming to duck. He dropped to the deck as a volley of fire pocked the far wall, whistling through the air he had just been occupying. From his prone position, he aimed at them and fired off a pair of shots. One of them went down screaming, clutching his thigh, but the other one ducked out of the way and continued to empty his clip in their direction.

Shinji suddenly leapt forward, sprinting down the hall toward their attacker with all the fury of hell behind him.

What is he DOING!? Grayson thought frantically.

A bullet caught Shinji in the shoulder, but it only seemed to fuel his aggression. He burst into the repairs room where the man was pinned, his automatic pistol raised. Shinji let out a stream of fire from point-blank, drawing a line of red holes across the screaming man's torso. But before he dropped to the deck, Shinji grabbed him with one hand and slammed him against the wall. He shoved the barrel of his pistol into the man's gurgling mouth and pulled the trigger. Blood erupted and bone shattered, painting the floor with a gush of gore.

Panting, Shinji finally let him go and the corpse slumped at his feet.

Grayson blinked. He could feel his heart hammering in his chest. He could hear his pulse in his ears.

But the rest of the ship was quiet, save for the man he had shot in the thigh who lay moaning across the room from Shinji.

"Titus, you good?" Grayson asked, pulling himself up.

Titus held his shotgun loosely, still appearing shaken. "I'm fine. That last shock charge caught me off guard is all. I'll be alright."

Grayson reloaded his revolver and then snapped the cylinder shut. He strode down the hallway and into the repairs room, keeping an eye on the exposed breach. Shinji had the remaining man pinned to the floor, a boot on his squirting thigh. Blood coated the floor and the man groaned as Grayson approached.

"Now that we have a little breathing room I think it's time you told me who you people are," he growled, leaning down into the man's face.

The man was about the same age as Grayson, his face contorted in pain as Shinji's boot pressed against his wound. His voice was thick and heavy.

"Let me go. Please. We're just trying to get by, same as you. We'll leave. I promise."

"How many more are still in your ship?" Grayson demanded.

"Six. I can call them off. Please."

"You really think they'll listen?" Shinji said from behind his teeth. "In my experience, people like you don't seem to know when they've been bested."

Grayson took a knee and leaned into the man's face, his shadow enveloping the wounded victim. "What are you doing all the way out here?"

The man whined beneath Shinji's boot, his eyes pleading. "We were chasing a ship. We weren't even baiting you! You just happened to fly across our trajectory and our captain thought it would be profitable to board you and see if you had anything worth scavenging! I didn't even want to! Most of us didn't! You have to believe me!"

Titus approached them from behind, his voice rumbling over Grayson's shoulder. "What ship? Who were you chasing?"

"I don't know," the man croaked. "We'd never seen anything like it before. It was massive. We thought it might be worth something if we caught up to it."

"Where did it go? Where is this ship?" Grayson pressed.

The man squirmed, gasping as more blood leaked from under Shinji's boot. "We couldn't catch it! I don't know where it is! It was en route to Pratus though! Maybe it landed there! We lost it a couple days ago and thought we could pick up its trail again!" The man let out another moan and then looked up into Grayson's face. "Look man, we had no idea you guys were Vagabonds. I'm sorry. Please, let me go!"

Pratus? Grayson thought. He turned to Titus who met his eyes.

"Wonder if this has anything to do with our contract," Titus said quietly.

"Could be. That's a hell of a coincidence if it's not."

"What do you want to do with him?" Titus asked, distracted.

A sudden clatter of noise from the breached door drew their attention and Titus raised his shotgun toward it.

"Sounds like your friends in there are preparing for another assault," he muttered.

Shinji stepped off the man's leg suddenly, his voice a low slur. "TItus, you said the coms are still working, right?"

Titus kept his eyes on the hole but nodded.

Without warning, Shinji reached into his opposite boot and pulled out a long knife. He grabbed the wounded man by the hair and dragged him away from Grayson.

"What are you doing, kid?" Grayson asked warily, standing.

Shinji shot him a dark look, his scar flaring blue. And then he leaned down and began to saw their prisoner's head off.

It was a brutal splash of violence that caught Grayson off guard and he stepped back in surprise as Shinji's knife dug back and forth into the gurgling, horrified man's neck. Blood drooled from the growing incision, the flesh parting with ease.

"Hey, stop!" Titus yelled, stepping forward, his eyes wide.

But at that moment, Shinji's blade hit bone, and he grit his teeth and carried the knife through the screeching spinal column, ending the sputtering man's life. It wasn't until the blade tore through the other side that Shinji spoke.

He stood, holding the severed head in one hand. "This'll get them to piss off I think."

Titus just stared at the younger man, his face bunched in disgust and shock.

Shinji stepped away from the headless body. "The coms. Come on, we don't have much time."

Grayson ran his tongue along his teeth, his voice a whisper. "Right. I'll take you. But Shinji?"

"What?"

"Don't you ever do something like that again. You got that?"

Shinji cocked an eyebrow. "What do you care? This man tried to kill us not two minutes ago."

Titus finally found his voice. "While you're on my ship, you do as I tell you. And kid? I'm telling you to *never* pull a stunt like that again." He shot a disgusted look at the headless corpse. "Now go with Grayson. I'll stay here and make sure they don't poke their heads out."

Grayson strode past Shinji and heard the younger man follow, his giant regulator groaning across his back. They reached the cockpit and Grayson slid into one of the pilot seats. He brought up the coms readout and selected a public channel so that his broadcast would be picked up by their assailants.

"Make sure the video feed is on," Shinji instructed.

"Yeah, I know how this works, kid," Grayson said thickly.

The small screen before them lit up and a red light blinked on, indicating that they were live. Shinji stepped forward and raised the severed head toward the display, a snarl on his face.

"This is the Afterburner. Everyone you sent to kill us is dead."

He shook the dangling head at the screen. "This is how it's going to end if you send anyone else on board." He stepped closer to the display so that his glowing scar could be plainly seen.

"This is a Vagabond ship. If you don't leave in the next thirty seconds I will board you and I will *massacre* you. The clock starts now."

Grayson ended the transmission and turned to stare up at Shinji. "I think they got the message."

"I wasn't kidding. They have twenty-five seconds."

Grayson let out a long breath. "Take it easy, will you? They'll leave, especially after that performance." He reached down and adjusted his regulator, returning his blood levels to normal as if to prove a point. He pointed to Shinji's dial.

"You might want to do the same."

"They haven't left yet."

"Not exactly patient, are you?" Grayson observed. He looked at Shinji's shoulder, the one that had been shot. He jutted his chin at it.

"How is it?"

"It's fine," Shinji said, distracted. "Barely broke the skin."

Grayson chewed on his lip for a moment before answering. "Be sure you ingest a lot of water over the next twenty-four hours. I saw how many clicks you juiced. That's really going to cramp you up if you're not careful."

Shinji shot him a pestering look. "I know how to take care of myself."

Grayson stood and pushed past him. "Course you do. You're invincible."

"Hey, I saved your ass today," Shinji called.

"And I'm sure I'll save yours before this job is done."

From outside, the attackers began to pull their ship away, stealing Shinji's eyes from Grayson's retreating figure.

"Told you they'd leave," Grayson yelled down the hall. He entered the repairs room once more and saw that Titus was just finishing resealing the cauterized door back in place.

"Good timing," Grayson said as Titus shut off a blowtorch and tossed it aside.

Titus looked around the room full of bodies. "Once I heard their engines ignite I figured it'd be best if we all weren't spaced."

"Speaking of which…" Grayson said, looking at the corpses.

"I'll have Shinji dump them out the waste chute," Titus said. "And then he can scrub all this blood off my damn floors."

Grayson looked down the hall toward the cockpit and then back to Titus. He kept his voice low.

"That kid has a violent streak in him a mile wide, Titus."

Titus sighed and nodded, looking tired all of the sudden. "I know. I'm going to keep an eye on it."

"See that you do," Grayson warned. "That could spin out of control real fast."

"I know, man. I know."

Grayson ran a hand over his face, his fingers scraping his graying stumble. "I'm going to take a shower and get out of these clothes."

"All right. Hopefully, the ship regains power here in a few-"

As if on cue, a loud shudder went through the floor and up the walls, the familiar hum returning.

Titus smiled. "Good girl. I'll have us back on track before you know it, Gray."

Grayson turned to head for his room. "Can't wait. Come get me when we reach Pratus."

CHAPTER 4

Ada stood and watched the ship approach from her place on the docking plate. The hot sun beat down on her and the twelve Orbital Clerks at her back. Her father, Reston, had planted himself by her side, immobile, with his hands clasped behind his back.

Help is coming, Ada thought wearily, craning her head toward the pale blue sky. Heavy bags hung beneath her eyes, a result of the past week. It had been a terrible slew of days, a panicked, uncertain time full of terrible questions with no answers along the way.

After the initial attack, Reston had sent out crews of Orbital Clerks to search for the people, her sister Marah among them, who had been taken by the strange invasive force. Three teams, ten men each.

None of them had returned. And the attacks kept coming. They usually happened at night or during the Negative, though one had come at dawn, three days after her sister and the others had gone missing.

They had learned little about their attackers and it wasn't enough to stop or even hinder the aggressive threat.

As Ada continued to observe the ship as it grew closer, she thought back to her first encounter with them. She remembered its violet eyes, the way it had spoken to her in that awful voice, warned her that they had done something terrible. After her father had saved her, they inspected the bodies of the creatures they had managed to kill and found that they resembled humans, save for a few troubling features.

But the thing in the hallway that she had seen, the massive two-armed slug and its horrible metal head and machine-wired spine...that was something else entirely. They had taken to calling those creatures Tusks, due to the two bone white tusks that jutted from the bottom of their square metal heads. They weren't seen as frequently as the more human-looking attackers and seemed more impulsive and reactive compared to the calculated, stealthy thing that had been in her room.

The incoming ship slowed, the roar of its thrusters sending sheets of heat across the expansive docking plate. Ada shielded her eyes as the craft swung around and then began to lower. As it did so, she felt her stomach plummet as well.

I can't believe it's come to this, she thought uneasily.

When the crews of Orbital Clerks hadn't returned from their mission, along with the consistent attacks on Typhon, her father, Reston, had sent out a desperate plea. Ada knew how much he hated the thought of turning offworld for help, but it was clear to everyone that they were dealing with something they had no power or understanding over.

I don't care who they are so long they get Marah and the others back, Ada thought beneath a blanket of fatigue. *They'll find them. They have to. Alive.*

The ship finally touched down, sending another wave of heat and grit across the exposed docking plate. The Orbital Clerks around her didn't move, the sand particles bouncing off their copper battle armor. Reston had insisted they suit up to greet the newcomers, stressing how important it was to maintain their image despite the circumstances.

Reston himself was dressed in his command suit, pressed to perfection, the white fabric bleached to a snow-white crisp, matched by his mustache.

Ada didn't care how she looked. She didn't see the point. They weren't here to impress the new arrivals, they were here to instruct and inform. People had died and dozens had been taken. There were more important things than a clean shirt and boot polish.

"Please mind your mouth," Reston said quietly, looking at Ada out of the corner of his eye. "It's important we don't tick these people off. We need them."

Ada blinked and felt a stir of irritation swell inside her. "Screw manners, these people need to get out there and find-"

"I know that," Reston hissed. "Don't think for a second that all this fluff means I don't care. I'm worried sick about our people, about Marah, and I want them back more than anything. But these people, they're different than us. Human life holds little value to them. They don't have families or people they care about. Money and blood are the only two things they understand so keep that in mind when you feel something inappropriate about to slip out your mouth."

Ada clicked her teeth shut, deciding this wasn't the time to snap at her father. She knew how stressed he was, how the entire city of Typhon was relying on him to solve this new, horrible problem they faced. The past week had seemed to age him a year. She could see it in the way his shoulders drooped now, the way his eyes appeared distant and dull whenever he addressed her. So she kept quiet.

The ship dropped its ramp with a hiss and Ada felt her stomach churn once more. She had never met a Vagabond before, but she had heard plenty of stories. There was a cloud of disdain that encircled their reputation, a violent, almost mythical element encasing each tale she had heard of them. When her father had posted their plea into the open Vagabond network, she had been shocked. They represented everything her father loathed, from their cold, impersonal ways to their glo filled veins. It also spoke to how desperate he was becoming and that filled her with dread.

A moment after the ramp hit the docking plate, three men emerged down the exit. Ada felt her gut twist once more as the stories of her youth became real before her very eyes.

All three were dressed in black, their leather coats sporting an electric blue V along the sleeve, tagging them for who they were. Two of them were older, nearly thirty years her senior. One of the two was a large, barrel-chested black man who oozed confidence with every booted step he took toward her. He was ribbed with muscle and was exactly what she had envisioned a Vagabond to look like. A tower of power, a titan with immeasurable strength.

The second one was tall, but not nearly as built. He had a lean, tight look to him that spoke of talents discovered in the shadows. His graying hair hung past his silver eyes and his jaw was lined with stubble. He was pale, as if he lived in darkness, and she noted the way he walked as if each step was run through a series of calculations. He looked at her once and then continued to sweep his gaze over the rest of the welcome party with disinterest. Strapped to his back was a massive sniper rifle, the biggest Ada had ever seen.

The third man was younger, appearing to be around the same age as herself. But the sight of him sent a tremor of unease through her. A contraption was strapped to his back, a large metal box that Ada first mistook for a coffin. Running out of the box were a series of wires and tubes that were embedded into the man's upper arms. His hair was pulled back into a knot and he walked across the docking plate with a casual confidence that she didn't care for.

The trio of men stopped about six feet away from Reston, Ada, and the line of Orbital Clerks, sweeping their eyes across the platform as if they were taking in every little detail. At this proximity, Ada noticed another feature about them that she hadn't noticed when they landed.

It was the scars beneath their eyes. They each had a single cut beneath their sockets, a glowing blue slice of hardened tissue that gaped neon light from within. The two older men had a scar beneath each eye, but the younger one, the one with the metal coffin on his back, only had it beneath his right eye.

Reston stepped forward with all the professionalism of sixty years behind him. He stuck out his hand to the large, towering one and cleared his throat.

"Welcome to Pratus. I'm the commander of Typhon, the city you see before you. I appreciate you coming on such short notice."

The big man smiled then, surprising Ada, and pumped her father's hand. "Good to meet you. I'm Titus."

"Welcome to Typhon, Titus," Reston said formally. He then shifted down the line to the tall, lean man.

The man gazed at him with silver eyes but didn't offer her father his hand. "I'm Grayson."

Reston dropped his hand, but nodded, unfazed. "Welcome to Typhon, Grayson. It's a pleasure."

"Thanks."

And then Reston reached the last man and Ada saw the muscles on his neck tighten some as he swallowed.

The younger man's face was unreadable as he stared at Reston. When he opened his mouth and spoke, his voice was much softer than Ada would have guessed it to be.

"I'm Shinji. Your planet is very hot, Commander Reston."

Reston tried to smile, but it came out forced. "Yes, well, I'm afraid you're right. Welcome to Typhon, Shinji. It's an honor to host you."

"Course," Shinji said quietly, turning away to stare at the Orbital Dome behind Reston, along with the host of towering redstone pillars that hosted the heightened city around it.

"Quite a place you got here," Shinji said, almost to himself.

Reston flashed another manufactured smile. "Thank you. It's the pride of our generation."

Titus stepped forward then, his voice loud, yet calming. "It's quite an accomplishment. I understand now why you're so desperate to keep it safe. This place could be spectacular one day."

Ada felt her jaw tighten. *One day?*

But Reston continued, unbothered. "It could indeed. I must apologize though, I've never sent out a Vagabond contract before and I'm not quite sure how your organization works. Do you need anything? Water? Food? A place to put your things?"

The one with the metal box on his back, Shinji, shifted where he stood. "How about we get out of this damn sun and you tell us what you need?"

Ada noticed the quiet one, Grayson, shoot Shinji a hard look.

Reston bobbed his bald head. "Of course. Let me take you inside the Orbital Dome. I've set up a room for us to discuss the details of our contract."

Titus offered a smile. "That would be great. Thanks."

Together, the small party walked in silence across the docking plate and back into the dome, the host of Clerks taking up the rear. Reston led them through a series of small hallways, keeping the brigade away from public spaces and away from prying eyes.

They entered a small room with a single long table that stretched the length of the space. It was surrounded by metal chairs and the far wall looked out into the desert plains of Pratus. Sunlight poured in through the thin, high window, spilling orange light across a host of food and drink that had been set up in advance on the table.

Shinji went for it immediately, grabbing a plate and filling it with an array of items. Grayson and Titus didn't touch it. Instead, they pulled out their chairs and sat down at the end of the table. Reston waved the Orbital Clerks away, leaving only a few of his captains to sit in on the briefing. Ada took a seat opposite Grayson and watched him carefully as her father took his place at the head of the table. His captains flanked him on either side, alert and ready in case the new arrivals turned malicious. Ada didn't think it was necessary but found herself glad to have a few more of her people in the room.

"I got to say," Titus began, folding his hands in front of him, "the contract you posted was a little light on details."

Reston cast a glance at Shinji, who was standing by the window, eating, before answering. "Yes, I apologize for that. I'm afraid it's because we don't know much about what has been happening here."

Grayson leaned back in his chair. "Why don't you start from the beginning then."

Reston nodded. "Of course." He took a moment to gather himself and then he began to recount the events of the past week.

Ada listened intently, never taking her eyes off the three men. They displayed no emotion as her father described the strange ship that had come into orbit and the awful transmission he had received after failing to hail them on the coms. He described the dread he had felt when he heard the voices in the static, garbled, terrible things that he explained made no sense. He stressed that he knew, in his gut, that this ship was a threat and why he had ordered the Glo Cannons to fire upon it.

And then the attack. He described the Tusks and their strange, alien appearance. He went over in detail how his people had been captured, taken, and dragged off to wherever the creatures had come from. Ada saw the pain in her father's eyes as he revealed that Marah, his second daughter, had been taken as well.

"How many times have they come back to take your people since that first night?" Titus asked somberly.

"Four," Reston said. "Each time they come we lose at least a dozen more."

"You ever manage to kill one of them?" Grayson interjected.

Reston nodded. "Yes. Just one on the first night. It was in Ada's room."

Grayson turned his silver eyes to Ada and she felt an urge to squirm in her seat. Instead, she grit her teeth and returned his gaze.

"It was one of the other ones," she explained. "The human-looking things. There was a Tusk in the hallway that night as well, but that wasn't what was in my room. This thing spoke to me. It could think and communicate. The Tusks seem more animalistic. Impulsive. Reactive."

"Can you describe what it looked like?" Titus asked. "The thing in your room?"

Reston waved a hand to two of the captains behind him. "We can do better than that. We kept the body in cold storage to study. If you'd like, I could have it brought up here."

"That would be helpful," Titus agreed.

The two captains left the room and Reston turned his attention back to the men at the end of the table.

"I need to make it clear that we're a mining operation," he said wearily. "The Orbital Clerks have been trained to mostly police the public, but we're a peaceful settlement. We don't have a lot of lawless troublemakers here. What we're facing now…"

"It's a little out of your league," Shinji finished, setting his food down. "We get it. We're usually not someone's first choice."

Reston offered an apologetic smile. "I suppose you're right. I'm sure you're all used to dealing with situations like this, but to us this is all new and a little frightening."

Ada felt a twinge of shame at that. She looked at her father and he met her eyes, giving her a tired smile.

Shinji leaned against the wall and crossed his arms. "So what do you need us to do? Go and wipe these things out?"

Reston looked at him apprehensively. "I don't care how you get rid of them, but I need these attacks to stop. My people are scared and my operations have been delayed. I can't afford either. I need this threat dealt with. I'm not a proponent of violence, but I will always put this city's safety first. If there's no other way, then yes. Kill them. Send them away. Burn them out of existence." He leaned forward then. "Make Typhon safe once more. Please."

Grayson was the one who spoke next, his voice even and calm. "How sure are you that these creatures came from the ship you shot down? Your cannons blasted it out of the sky, right? What makes you think any of them survived? Maybe this is some new threat that's been unearthed by your mining operations."

Ada spoke before her father could. "We keep a lot of records here, dating back to the settlement of this planet. We have to. We do it so the next generation understands this place and are prepared to learn from everything that's been discovered. And in all those years, there hasn't been a single mention of something like this. I'll be the first to admit that this is a big planet and there's still a lot we don't understand yet. But these creatures? They're new. And I think you'd be pretty stupid to think they'd come from anywhere but the alien ship we just shot down."

Shinji snorted from across the room, but Grayson's face remained a slate of stone. He looked at Titus and then at Reston, his voice almost amused.

"Your daughter has a mouth on her."

Reston winced. "She's...passionate."

Titus spread his arms, trying to diffuse the tension. "It's understandable. Her sister was taken and more are vanishing every day. I'd be going out of my mind."

Ada stared at him. "I am. Which is why I'm going with you when you leave."

Reston nearly choked. "What? Ada, no, don't be ridiculous. I think the three of them are more than capable of dealing with this. They don't need you getting in their way."

Ada's eyes blazed into her father's. "I'm guessing they've never been to this planet before. They don't understand it and they don't know it like I do. I've been working with the survey crews for three years now. I know my way around. I know how to survive out there. I can help them."

Shinji placed his hands on the table, leaning toward her, his metal contraption creaking. "No offense lady, but you had your chance to deal with this issue and you failed. Why don't you let the professionals handle this one."

Ada's temper spiked and her eyes flared in anger. "No offense, but I don't think you'd last two days out there in the sun without my aid. You look like you burn easy."

Shinji grinned at her. "You have no idea."

Titus brought his hands together. "I actually think it's a good idea. It's true, we don't know this planet very well and having someone along who does would be highly beneficial. What do you think, Gray?"

Grayson said nothing for a moment. He stared at Ada as if weighing her worth. She wanted to reach across the table and throttle him just so he'd stop looking at her.

Finally, he nodded. "Sure. I think she'd be useful."

Shinji rolled his eyes and turned away from the table. "Wonderful."

"Be quiet," Titus lectured. He returned his attention then to Reston. "I'm going to need to see a map. I want to know where the ship crashed. I have no doubt that's where your people are being taken. I'm sure we'll find the source of your problem there."

Reston waved to Ada. "She can show you. If you think it's best that she go, then who am I to say otherwise." He looked at Ada then, his face pleading and fatherly. "Just promise me you'll be careful. I've already lost one daughter. I can't bear to lose another."

"I will. And we'll get Marah back," Ada said firmly. "She's alive. I know she is."

"Doubt it," Shinji mumbled.

Grayson's head snapped toward Shinji, his voice a hard whisper. "Why don't you grab another plate of food and let the grown-ups talk for a minute."

Shinji's eyes filled with darkness, his face souring, but he closed his mouth.

Suddenly, the doors to the room opened. A pair of captains entered, wheeling in a stretcher. Lying on the stretcher was a single body bag.

The captains pushed the stretcher over toward the table and then stepped back, returning to their position behind Reston.

Grayson slowly stood up, facing the stretcher. He exchanged a look with Titus who then joined him by the body bag.

"Let's see what we're dealing with," Titus said, reaching down to unzip the encasing.

Lying inside was a single body that appeared to be a human male. As Titus pulled the zipper down its torso, Grayson leaned down to inspect the corpse. A dark bullet hole spotted the left cheek where the kill shot had been delivered. Its hair was dark and seemed feathery, almost airy, despite the frost that clung to it. Grayson reached down and pulled at the eyelids to inspect the sockets.

The thing's eyes were bright purple and larger than a human's by half the size, giving it an eerie, alert appearance despite its stillness. Grayson pulled its mouth open and after a moment, he pointed at its teeth.

"Look at the canines. Notice anything?"

Titus leaned closer. "You mean besides how huge they are?"

Grayson tapped one of them and then the other, the set twice as long as a human's and sharpened to a point.

"Look at the tips."

Titus brought his face closer and then he grunted. "Looks like they're hollow. There's a little opening here at the bottom. On both of 'em."

Ada came and stood next to the stretcher, crossing her arms. "We noticed that too. We don't know what purpose they serve, but we think they might be able to secrete something out of them. We didn't find any traces of residue on the teeth though."

"Did you test their blood?" Titus asked.

Ada nodded. "We did. We have no clue what it is they have in their veins, but it's unlike anything we've seen before. The composition doesn't match any of our known biological records. We have no idea what's pumping through their organs, but it's not human blood."

Titus grabbed the thing's head and pulled it up slightly, inspecting its ears, neck, and shoulders. "What have you been calling these creatures?"

"We've been calling them Canines," Reston said from his place at the table. "So far we've only seen two variations of our attackers. The Tusks and these Canines. There could be more, but we have only been exposed to these variants."

"You have any Tusk corpses?" Shinji asked.

"No, I'm afraid not."

"Shame."

Titus furrowed his brow as he continued to lift the Canine's head up, revealing a small, puckered hole in the back of its neck. It was black and crusted over, almost like a deep cut that had begun to scab.

"Is this a ballistic wound?" He asked.

Ada shook her head. "No. Whatever that is, we didn't do it."

Grayson studied the hole. "Looks like some kind of second sphincter almost. You see how the muscle puckers inward toward the center?"

Titus grimaced. "Gross." He let the head fall back down. "Maybe it's how they breathe. Or maybe it's some kind of second mouth."

"You obviously haven't done a full autopsy," Grayson observed, stepping away from the stretcher.

Reston slowly stood. "No. We figured we should wait until you got here so you could examine it without any tampering. I was honestly hoping you'd know what it is."

Grayson looked at Titus and then over to Shinji. "Nope. What about you two?"

"'Fraid' not."

Shinji shook his head. "No. I'd remember if I had."

"How many of these Canines have you encountered?" Grayson asked after a moment.

Ada frowned. "I don't know. Hard to get a read on just how many there are. Like we said earlier, they tend to stick to the darkness."

"What about these...Tusk creatures?"

"We don't know."

Shinji circled the table. "So we're off to fight an enemy whose numbers are completely unknown to us on a planet we don't know much about." He flashed a smile to Titus and Grayson. "Bet you guys are glad I tagged along, huh?"

Titus grunted. "Ada, do you have transport for us? I want to head out as soon as possible, but I'm afraid my ship would ruin any element of surprise we might still hold."

Ada nodded. "We'll take a pair of dusters. I'm afraid your friend's contraption is going to force us to take separate vehicles." She threw a thumb toward Shinji's massive regulator. "I can drive one of them. I know the terrain pretty well so if one of you pilots the second duster and stays close then we shouldn't have a problem."

"Perfect," Titus said, pleased. "I'm going to grab the rest of our gear from the Afterburner and we should be ready to head out within the hour."

Grayson held up a hand. "Hold on. We got into a bit of a tangle on the way over here and I wasn't able to read the file about Pratus. What's your day/night cycle like here?"

Reston looked toward the window. "We have six hours of daylight each day, followed by six hours of darkness. There's a thirteenth hour in between the cycle though called the Negative. Think of it as a really, really bad dusk. Ada can fill you in on the details during your journey." He turned away from the window then. "We're in the second hour of daylight now so you'll still have half a day to travel before the Negative and full dark."

"That works for us," Grayson said. He turned to Titus and Shinji. "What say we get moving?"

Titus nodded. "Just let me get the firepower."

CHAPTER 5

G rayson scanned the desert as the duster bounced and rolled across the dunes, the vehicle offering surprisingly good shock resistance despite its older design. He looked across at Ada as she drove, her eyes focused, her lips pursed. He could tell she was uncomfortable and before they left, he had considered taping his eyes to hide the glow of his scars. Instead, he left them as they were.

I'm not here to baby these people, he thought quietly as the world rolled by.

The bright sun was dimmed some by the tinted windows of the duster, offering slight relief as the dazzling sandhills reflected the golden light. Grayson swept his eyes across the rising redstone cliffs and valleys before them, flooded with the peaks and dips of swelling dunes. Titus and Shinji were trailing them in their own duster, a couple dozen yards back.

Grayson touched his sniper rifle which was slotted next to him against the door and then his fingers brushed the revolver strapped to his thigh, opposite his regulator. The briefing had gone as expected, though the reveal of a strange pair of unknown foes had been somewhat of a surprise to him. He didn't know what to make of the situation quite yet and so he held most of his speculation to himself.

After a half-hour of terse, silent travel, Grayson's wrist reader chirped, breaking the fragile ice inside the cab. He looked down at it, frowned as he brought up the incoming message, and then smiled slightly. It was from his daughter, Claire.

Still hoping to have you and Titus over for dinner soon! Jace said you can tell his father about the pregnancy so make sure you deliver the news with the appropriate level of excitement! Love you and let me know when you can make it!

Ada glanced at Grayson and noticed him smiling.

"Your friend's talking shit about us?"

Grayson looked up, surprised that she was finally speaking. "What? No. It's personal."

Ada grunted and resumed her attention on the terrain, but she didn't seem like she was convinced.

Grayson quickly typed out a brief response and then sent it back to his daughter.

Offworld on a job with Titus. Shouldn't be gone long. I'll call you when we're back and set up that dinner. Love you, kid.

"If you think you can drive better than me, I'd love to see you try," Ada said after a moment.

Grayson glanced at her. "You're pretty defensive aren't you?"

"Just don't like people talking behind my back," she snapped.

Grayson looked out the window. "No one's talking behind your back. Relax. It was a message from my daughter. Not like it's any of your business."

Ada's eyes widened a little with surprise. "Your daughter? Seriously? I thought you people didn't have families."

Grayson waved a hand. "Well I guess you thought wrong."

"How old is she? Where does she live?"

"How about you just get us where we need to go and we keep this job strictly professional."

Ada soured. "It was just a question. I was getting sick of the weird silence. You're not a very conversational person."

Grayson shrugged. "Hey, if we don't have a connection then you won't get all weepy-eyed if I bite the dust during this job."

Ada barked a laugh. "Oh is that it? I thought you people were damn near immortal."

It was Grayson's turn to grunt. "Hardly. Though it takes a hell of a lot more to kill us." He frowned then. "And stop saying 'you people'."

"Did I hurt your feelings?"

"It's irritating," Grayson said. "The medics say I have a low tolerance for it."

Ada cocked an eyebrow. "Is that so? Alright, I take it back then. Sorry."

"Whatever," Grayson said, leaning forward in his seat to stare up at the sky. He pointed to the strange, milky disk that seemed to be inching closer toward the sun with each passing minute.

"By the way—what the hell is that thing?"

"That's the Negative. When that disk of...whatever it is...crosses over the sun, things get all wonky for about an hour."

"Wonky how?"

"Disorienting. The light changes, everything flips and gets real crazy. It's like looking at the world through a photo negative lens, hence the name."

Grayson leaned back in his seat and touched his revolver. "Sounds like a dangerous time to be out."

"It is. We try to find someplace safe to hunker down once it's started; wait until full dark when we can use light again."

"You haven't found a way to counter it yet?"

Ada offered him a grim smile. "It's worse than it sounds. You'll see."

Grayson returned his eyes to the blurring landscape. "Wonderful." And then he sat up sharply, his attention drawn to something in the distance, across the dunes.

"Stop the duster," he said quickly.

To her credit, Ada compiled without question, bringing the vehicle to a screeching halt as clouds of sand billowed up around the tires. At their back, they heard Titus stop as well, their engine idling.

"What is it?" Ada asked.

Grayson's eyes pierced the landscape. He reached down and twisted the dial on his regulator. He grit his teeth against the surge that followed, but forced his attention back to the sandy redstone rise, about half-mile away. Aided by the glo in his veins, he confirmed his suspicions.

"Something's out there. I can see it moving toward Typhon. You see the sand deposits in the air? Over by that cluster of rock?"

Ada squinted. "No...?"

Grayson grabbed his sniper rifle and pushed his door open. "Trust me, it's there."

The sun hit him like a copper fist and he winced against its glare. He slung his rifle over his shoulder and began to walk toward a small rise. Titus and Shinji exited their duster and caught up to him with Ada in tow.

"What is it?" Titus asked, already wiping moisture from his brow.

Grayson stopped and pointed. "Something's headed toward Typhon. Could be our guests. You see them?"

Titus squinted in the sunlight before shaking his head. "I don't see anything but sand and scraggy underbrush, bud. You sure?"

Shinji reached up and twisted the dial on his regulator. After a moment, he nudged Titus. "He's right. Looks like they're burrowing just beneath the surface, headed right for Typhon. Juice up and you'll see it."

Grayson looked back at Ada. "Does Typhon have vehicles that can move like that?"

Ada shielded her eyes against the sun. "We have mining equipment that can burrow into the salt deposits, but they're extremely cumbersome and don't go very fast."

Grayson exchanged a look with Titus and then stared out across the flat, shimmering ocean of sand and redstone.

"I think it's safe to assume whatever's out there isn't friendly." Grayson got down on one knee and pulled his sniper off his shoulder. "Let's say hello, shall we?"

"You sure about this?" Titus asked quietly.

Grayson raised his rifle and shut one eye. "No."

He thumbed the magnification and found the clouds of dust. With the aid of his scope, he could see about a dozen small mounds of sand moving at a high velocity as if something was swimming just below the surface. He drew in a breath and tracked the lead mound. The glo in his veins sharpened his vision and his heartbeat fell into perfect harmony with the pulse in his head. When he pulled the trigger, he knew the bullet would go exactly where he wanted it to land.

The report of the DR-50L was nearly deafening without its silencer and the gun kicked into Grayson's shoulder like a hammer blow. A tuft of sand erupted a foot in front of the lead mound, a warning shot meant to catch his target's attention.

Without slowing, the twelve odd mounds immediately altered their course as one, streaming directly toward Grayson and the others. Grayson watched this through the lens of his scope and noted that they were picking up speed as if enraged by the interruption.

"Well, that did it," Grayson announced. "We got a dozen targets headed this way."

"Shit," Ada hissed, clearly alarmed.

Shinji grinned. "Why don't you just wait in the duster and let us handle this. Won't be but a second."

Grayson kept his rifle raised and tracked the lead target once more. When he had a beam on it, he pulled the trigger again with an intended kill shot.

The sand erupted in a splash of dark liquid, mixed with particles of sand and grit as the bullet struck its mark. The mound rose some, exposing a fleshy, metallic thing that Grayson couldn't quite make out, but was relieved to see it flop to the ground and stop moving, save for a few twitching spasms. He aimed for the next one, noting how close they were getting.

"Shinji, get my ballistic case out of the duster," Titus instructed, his voice grim. "Hurry up."

Still grinning, Shinji did as he was told, nearly bounding for the vehicle, his regulator swaying on his back.

"Is it them?" Ada asked, her voice laced with anxiety.

Grayson squeezed off another round and watched as his second target slammed to a bloody, gory stop as the bullet blew it to bits.

He looked at Ada from the corner of his eye. "I think so. You better do as Shinji says and get in the duster. We'll handle this." He downed a third target before standing, a clock ticking down in his head.

They were getting close.

"I see them now," Titus said as Shinji returned. He handed Titus a massive metal case and Titus dropped it, unlatching the release to open it. Inside was a vast array of weapon parts, explosives, and ammunitions. He grabbed a trio of small, metallic-glossed boxes and then sprinted ahead of Grayson and tossed them in the sand, spread out along a line.

Shinji glanced at Grayson. "Why are we wasting our time with this? How about I just overcook and then we can be on our way?"

Grayson shot Shinji a hard look. "For this? Don't be ridiculous."

Shinji shrugged and then grabbed a wide, rectangular blade from the weapons case. He slotted the grip into place and then juiced himself another two clicks. He tested the weight of the weapon and then unstrapped his auto-pistol from its holster. Next, he loaded incendiary rounds into the small clip with practiced ease.

Titus returned to the weapons case and quickly pulled out the pieces to his shotgun, snapping the fire waxed metal into place.

"We have about thirty seconds before they're on us," Grayson said, casting a look over his shoulder to see Ada climbing into one of the dusters with a worried look. He shrugged out of his coat and unstrapped his revolver. He locked his sniper into the slot across the back of his polycarbon, light combat armor and then readied himself. Ahead of them, nine large mounds of sand continued to burrow straight for them like emp worms in deep space.

Grayson clicked his regulator twice more and then shot Titus a look. "You might want to do the same."

Titus's eyes never left the mounds ahead of them, a trickle of sweat running down his face. "I'll be fine. This is kid's stuff."

"We don't exactly know what we're dealing with here," Grayson warned, feeling his heart begin to race as the glo surged across his contracting muscle fibers.

Titus cocked his massive shotgun. "Yeah, but I know how to kill 'em."

The first of the mounds reached the line of metal boxes that Titus had planted, fifteen yards from the dusters. An explosion billowed out as the sensors to the explosives tripped, sending a shower of sand, flesh, and dark blood raining across the heat-stained sky. Grayson saw something erupt beneath the sand, a meaty sack and a long, white arm that looked alien to him. A terrible, mechanical screech filled the air and then silenced as body parts scattered beneath the blast.

The second and third boxes detonated, sending another blast of earth and dark liquid into the sky. A moment later and the remaining creatures were through, emerging from the sand with a roar, exploding from the surface with a violent fury.

At first, Grayson had no idea what he was looking at. Surging straight for him was a pair of creatures he had never seen before. They were big, nearly twice his size, and each had a pair of long, thin arms that ended in sharp, dangerous looking claws. Their torso expanded out below the waist, but instead of legs, the creatures had large, bloated sacks of flesh that they dragged behind them with alarming ease. Lining their spines were metal studs and wires that ended at the nape of their necks to reveal box-shaped metallic heads that sprouted a pair of long, viscous-looking teeth, almost as long as his arms.

Grayson dove to the side a second before the two creatures crashed into him, his mind thundering instruction.

Tusks, was all he had time to register before the rest of the creatures exploded out of the sand and lunged for them. Shinji took the brunt of the frontal attack head on as three of the creatures plowed into him, their weight pushing him backward in a brutal assault. Instead of toppling over though, Shinji raised his arms to protect his face and then spun, smashing the trio with the bulk of his regulator, allowing him space to raise his blade and pistol. He snapped off a burst of fire into one of the Tusk's faces and then ducked low, bringing his blade up to cleave the creature's metal head off. The metal box released from the neck with ease, bringing with it a fountain of dark blood.

Grayson jumped back as the two Tusks that had lunged for him resumed their attack. He underestimated their long reach and he felt claws rake across his shoulder and down his combat armor, causing him to nearly trip. Instead, he planted his feet and felt the glo in his veins surge with power. He skidded backwards on his heels, away from the two Tusks, allowing him the space to raise his revolver and squeeze off two shots. The bullets took one of them in the throat, sending a screeching, gurgling transmission exploding out of the strange creature's boxed head, sounding as if it were coming through some kind of speaker system.

The blast of Titus's shotgun shook the air, a constant stream of high-powered detonations that rattled Grayon's teeth.

Titus was backpedaling frantically as four Tusks slithered and clawed toward him, swooping and sliding across the sand like pregnant worms, their movement precise and quick. Titus deposited two rounds into one of their chests, ripping it open to expose a dark, dripping cavity of ruined organs. The Tusk dropped to the sand as the three others slithered into Titus's reach, lashing out at him with their long claws. Grunting, Titus dropped to one knee as a trio of angry red lines lacerated his arm. The Tusks loomed over him, preparing to strike once more and Grayson felt his heart surge in a panic.

Shinji was on the Tusks a moment later, his dripping blade carving a long, bloody arch across their torso's, his auto-pistol spitting heat-laced rounds that detonated blue fire on impact. It was enough to allow Titus to scramble to his feet and blast the wounded Tusks away with a pair of bone crunching shotgun rounds.

Grayson turned to the last of the Tusks, heart hammering, every detail of the battle pulsing around him in stark, bloody clarity. He could feel his pulse screaming as he planted his feet, raised his revolver, and shot the last of the attackers dead.

The air stank of death, gunpowder, and sweat. It took Grayson a moment to realize that the battle was over as perspiration poured down his face. His breath tasted rotten on his tongue as he swept his eyes across the litter of corpses before him, their alien, grotesque bodies bleeding a hundred different ways.

Grayson forced his heart to slow as he cautiously righted himself out of his battle posture, making sure none of the creatures were playing dead. He wiped sweat from his face and looked at Shinji and Titus.

"You guys ok?"

Shinji grunted a response and kicked at the Tusk lying dead at his feet. "Bastards are quick." He looked at Titus, at the trinity of oozing red lines dripping down his arm. "You good, man?"

Titus snorted and wiped the blood away with a gloved fist. "It's nothing. Barely broke the skin. I'm fine."

"You should have juiced," Shinji said, exhaling. "If you had, you wouldn't be bleeding right now."

"I ain't afraid of bleedin', kid."

Grayson knelt before a dead Tusk and prodded its large, metal head with the barrel of his revolver. "At least we know they die now." He tapped the metal once more, noting the strange beehive pattern of holes crowning the head. "You guys see this?"

Shinji wiped his blade across one of the carcasses. "Hell, I heard it. Sounded like some kind of transmission. I'm not quite sure these things are totally biological."

Grayson stood with a grunt. "Reston mentioned hearing some kind of transmission when he hailed their ship. I wonder if it was one of these things that responded."

Titus began to wrap his bicep with an anti-infectal medical cloth, his voice low. "Starting to think he was right in shootin' these things out of the sky. They don't seem very friendly."

"Grayson did pop em, though," Shinji pointed out as he reloaded his auto pistol.

"I got their attention first," Grayson corrected. "Then they hauled ass our way. Don't think they were coming to see if we wanted a good-night kiss."

"True," Shinji finished, slapping his clip back into place.

As Grayson was about to turn around, a handful of the Tusk corpses began to shudder and shift. It happened so suddenly that he almost didn't have time to react. He spun, pistol raised, as four of the Tusks peeled open at the base, their fleshy sacks parting like banana peels with a wet squelching sound.

To his utter disgust, four human shaped figures scrambled out of them with lightning-quick speed.

"Canines!" Grayson bellowed, his mind reeling.

One of the creatures emerged right at Shinji's feet and it lunged at him, teeth bared. Grayson raised his revolver and squeezed off a round, heart hammering.

Click!

Grayson cursed his carelessness as the gun dry fired, leaving Shinji completely exposed. The Canine grabbed Shinji by the leg and sunk his teeth into it, its fangs piercing through the combat fatigues with ease.

Shinji howled in pain and anger, kicking away, half falling as the Canine held on, blood gushing around its jaws.

Two others sprang toward Titus who let out a cry of shock, fumbling for his shotgun as they closed in with terrifying agility.

The last leapt for Grayson. With his revolver dry, Grayson's glo charged mind reacted without thought. He took one step back and reached behind his head to grip the barrel of his sniper rifle. In one fluid motion, he disengaged the lock and brought the weapon over his shoulder like a golf club, the butt of the weapon crunching into the Canine's jaw, chipping teeth, and shattering the thing's nose. It fell onto its back with a thud, dark fluid leaking from its ruined face. Grayson stomped hard on its chest and then flipped his rifle around, bringing the barrel straight down into the creature's eye, into its brain, and then exiting out of the back of its skull with bone-crunching finality.

The boom of Titus's shotgun rippled through the air and Grayson looked up in time to see the pair of attackers fly backward, their heads reduced to spurting stumps.

"Shinji!" Titus yelled as the younger man continued to battle the Canine attached to his leg.

Shinji finally toppled over, his blade swinging wildly in an attempt to strike and dislodge his assailant, but the sharpened steel whistled harmlessly through the air as he forfeited his balance and went crashing to the sand.

Without hesitation, Grayson raised his rifle to his hip and squeezed off a round. The bullet blasted into the creature's knee, pulverizing it, and sent the creature skidding away from Shinji in a cloud of sand and dark blood.

"Jesus *Christ!*" Shinji screamed, clambering to his feet. "What the fucking *hell!?*" He hobbled toward his dropped pistol and Grayson saw that blood was dripping out of the young man's leg.

He was juiced, Grayson thought. *That shouldn't be possible.*

Shinji snatched his pistol up and pointed it at the still groaning Canine as it clutched its stump. "Stupid, sneaky bastard," he snarled as he took aim.

"Wait!" Grayson yelled. He strode over to Shinji and placed a hand on the pistol, lowering it. "Don't kill it yet. I think it's time we had a chat with these things and find out just what the hell they want."

Shinji looked enraged at the idea, but he consented a moment later. "Fine. But it dies as soon as it stops being useful."

Grayson nodded. "Right." He looked at Titus then. "They get you?"

Titus lowered himself slowly to the sand where he sat, looking exhausted and bewildered. "What? No. No, I'm ok, Gray. Just wasn't expecting that." He let out a throaty bark then. "I mean what the hell?"

After making sure he really was ok, Grayson then strode over to the squirming, human looking creature with Shinji at his back. The creature looked up at them with hateful, piercing purple eyes, its face contorted in a snarl. It held its ruined leg as dark blood gurgled over its fingers.

"Shit, they really do look a lot like humans, don't they?" Shinji observed with a grimace.

The Canine opened its mouth and a stream of garbled sound came out as if it were trying to communicate with them.

Or curse us, Grayson thought. He pulled his knife out of his boot and waved it in front of the thing's face. He noted that it looked almost exactly like the dead body Reston had presented earlier. Male, dark feathery hair, purple eyes.

This could be that thing's twin, he noted. *Do all these psychos look the same?*

"What did you do to me?!" Shinji yelled down at it, pointing to his leg. "What the hell kind of teeth do you have to puncture through glo-juiced skin? Huh? Why don't you smile for me, you ugly bastard? Here, Grayson, give me that damn knife and let me extend his mouth a little."

Grayson kept the knife to himself and ignored Shinji. The Canine continued to spew a garble of noise at them, none of which was decipherable.

"I thought these things could speak our language," Shinji snarled. "Isn't that what Ada said? Didn't they talk to her or something?"

"It did."

Grayson and Shinji both turned to see Ada striding across the sand toward them. Her face was flushed, but her eyes held nothing but hatred for the creature squirming in the sand.

"You sure?" Grayson asked when she reached his side.

Ada stared down at the creature, into its burning purple eyes. "It's not something I'd forget. They can talk. Believe it."

Grayson ran his tongue along his teeth and then he squatted down in front of the Canine. He motioned for Shinji. "Hold it on that side. It's going to buck something wild here in a second."

Shinji did as he was told, his rough hands pinning the Canine's shoulders to the sand. It snarled and spat, but the fight was clearly bleeding out of it. Grayson then took his knife and waved it in front of the creature's face.

"I know you can communicate with us. I suggest you start."

And then he grabbed the thing's hand and began to slice off its fingers as if he were cutting pieces off an apple.

The creature shrieked and bucked, its eyes rolling, but Shinji pressed his fists into its shoulders from above, holding it in place. When Grayson had carved off three of its five fingers, he stopped. He looked down into the Canine's panting, sweating face and tapped his knife against its forehead.

"You ready to open up? If not, then I'm going to start opening you up one tiny cut at a time until we see all the strange organs you got inside that body of yours."

The creature opened its mouth then, almost desperately, and Grayson saw the muscles in its neck tense and then shift, almost as if it were rearranging its vocal cords. The thing coughed violently once, twice, and then it spoke.

"You...are all...dead," it rasped, its voice rough and wet. "You have no idea what's coming for you."

Grayson swapped a look with Shinji before responding. "I think we have a fairly good idea, but that's not what I'm interested in discussing." He flashed the knife again. "I need to know where you're taking everyone."

The Canine grunted, wincing. "You people...created this mess. We're just fixing it."

"Where's Marah!?" Ada yelled then, leaning down. "Where did you take my sister!?"

Grayson stared up at her and she backed off after a second, clearly infuriated. A moment later, Grayson continued his inquisition.

"You say we created this situation. Are you talking about your ship? The cannons that destroyed your transport?"

The Canine stared into Grayon's face and its mouth slowly twisted into a sneer, revealing its long, sharp teeth. "Ship? You think that's just a ship you shot down?" And then it laughed, a gasping, gurgling expression that set Grayson's teeth on edge.

"*Where* are you taking the civilians?" He pressed, grabbing the Canine's ruined hand once more. He lined the blade of his knife against the stump of a remaining finger. "I'm going to continue to dismantle you piece by piece until I get what I want, so I suggest you cut the shit."

The Canine's mouth closed with a snap and it looked at the knife with angered fear. "Yes, we took the civilians to the...the *ship*...as you called it," it answered, never taking its eyes off the bloody blade.

"Why?!" Ada yelled from over Grayson's shoulder.

"Because Voratarium needs them," The Canine spat. "To fix what you fools have done." It sat up against Shinji's grip then, the tendons in its neck straining. "And when this is all over, there won't be any of you left. We'll keep coming and coming and coming until we have what we need." It smiled then, another nasty reveal of its teeth. "Even now, they come. Thousands of them. They know what you've done here. They know where you're going. It's only a matter of time."

"Where's your ship?" Shinji rumbled, shoving the thing back down into the sand. "Where did it crash?"

"You really are clueless filth, aren't you?" the Canine growled back.

Grayson cut off another finger. He did it quickly and without warning and the Canine's reaction brought about the intended obedience he sought.

"North!" The Canine howled. "We crashed at the foot of a mountain range, just beyond a valley!"

Ada pulled out a cloth map and studied it for a few heartbeats. "If he's telling the truth then we're headed in the right direction, just like we suspected. Beggar's Valley is another couple of hours north of here. The Northern Salt Range isn't far beyond that."

Grayson nodded, satisfied. He guessed they had gotten as much useful information out of the creature as they could, but a lingering, itching question still burned in the back of his mind.

"Where did you come from?" He whispered, staring intently down at the wounded creature.

The Canine's face went slack, its voice a slurring exhale. "You couldn't possibly fathom the answer to that question."

A gunshot exploded right next to Grayson's ear then, causing him to stumble back in surprise, his heart surging in his throat. In the same instant, the Canine's head exploded in blood and fire, silencing it forever.

"I've heard just about enough shit out of him I think," Shinji said darkly as he lowered his smoking pistol.

Grayson sprang to his feet and turned on Shinji, their eyes clashing. "The next time you discharge a weapon that close to my ear, I'll cut *yours* off and use the oil from your skin as weapon grease," Grayson growled, sweat dripping down his face. "And the next time you kill our prisoner before I'm done talking to it-"

"You'll what?" Shinji interrupted, his face blank, his voice unimpressed. "You'll do what, Grayson?"

"Stop it," came Titus's rumbling voice, booming like thunder over the sandy hills. Grayson and Shinji looked to see the big man approaching, his arm and shoulder wrapped now. He looked tired and worn out, his eyes wet and hollow.

"Bickering like idiots is a fast way to get ourselves killed out here," Titus said, coming to a halt before them. "And frankly, I'm too damn tired to listen to you two measure your dicks. So shut up and let's get moving. We don't have that much daylight left and I want to put some more dust in our tailpipes before we stop and rest. You think you two can handle that?"

Grayson let out a long sigh and forced himself to calm down, chiding himself for letting the younger man get to him. He closed his eyes and wiped the grime of battle from his face, his pulse slowing.

"Let's get out of the sun before I sweat myself to death," he said finally. He reached for his regulator and returned his blood levels to normal as if signaling that physical and verbal combat had come to an end.

Shinji's face remained impassive, but he did the same, his regulator creaking against his sweat-soaked back.

Ada shook her head at the three men. "I was honestly expecting a little more professionalism."

"Well that was your first mistake," Grayson said, a headache on the horizon. He began to walk back toward the dusters. "Come on, let's get going. Titus, I'm riding with you."

CHAPTER 6

The pair of dusters bounced and rolled across the hard-packed sand, the sun frying all life out of the soil beneath. Clusters of dead trees huddled beneath the burning glare, withered and wilting against its heat. The dunes swelled and rolled across a plate of rocky outcrops and small mountains, the world stretching out in a spread of red, gold, and brown. The sky above remained a bluish-white canopy, cloudless and empty save for the glowing orange orb of the sun and the strange, milky disk that continued to slide closer toward its counterpart.

Grayson sat opposite Titus and watched as the bland landscape slithered by, his thoughts lost in the skirmish they had just left.

"You're awfully quiet," Titus said from the driver's seat.

"I'm thinking."

"Well, that's a nice change. We going to talk about what just happened?" Titus asked, accelerating some in order to keep up with Ada's duster a dozen yards ahead.

Grayson looked down at his dusty gloves. "I'm just trying to figure out what we killed back there. Those Tusks, they were transporting the Canines inside of those flesh sacks."

"Pretty gross," Titus agreed. "But efficient. Something I noticed though—Ada said the attacks on Typhon happened at night or in the early hours of the morning. We just fought them in broad daylight. What do you make of that?"

"I think it's easier to steal people in the dark," Grayson said. "I don't think they're biologically averse to sunlight."

Titus chewed on this for a moment before nodding. "You're probably right. Did you notice those Canines we killed had pucker holes in the back of their necks too?"

Grayson raised his eyebrows. "I didn't see that, no. You mean like the one Reston showed us in Typhon?"

"Yep. While you and Shinji were playing tough guys, I inspected a couple of the corpses. They all had it. And they all looked the same, too."

Grayson grabbed his seat as the duster bounced over a rocky hill. "That I did notice. It also mentioned its ship not being a ship and something or someone called Voratarium. You make anything of that?"

Titus ran a hand over the white stubble lining his head. "I think we're walking into a conflict we know nothing about." He grunted. "Ain't pretty, but it is what it is. We've dealt with a lot of bad in our day, but this one makes me a little hesitant. There's a lot of them and only a couple of us."

Grayson scratched his chin, recalling his conversation with the Canine. "If we're to believe what that thing said, then it sounds like there's a whole army of them waiting for us."

"Yeah, I caught that part," Titus said. "You having second thoughts about this job yet?"

"No."

"Course not. You never do. Just thought I'd ask anyway," Titus said, returning his attention to the wheel.

Grayson looked at him sideways. "What's up with you by the way?"

"How do you mean?"

"You haven't juiced once this trip."

Titus kept his eyes away from Grayson's. "And? I ain't dead am I?"

"No, but you're going to end up dead if you don't start. This isn't just about you either, Titus, this is about Shinji and me."

"Didn't know you cared so much for the kid."

Grayson set his jaw. "It's about *me*. I don't care much for that impulsive psychopath, but he's a valuable asset and he knows how to fight. But you? Honestly, I'm going to have a hard time relying on you if you keep this up. I mean look at you. You're all bandaged up. *We* shouldn't need to do that."

Titus stretched his face south. "Don't tell me what I need to do. Hell, you of all people should be more careful with how much glo you're pumping into your system."

"And why's that?"

"You're startin' to fringe some, ain't you?"

Grayson stared hard into his friend's face. "What I'm doing is staying alive and gettin' the job done. I'm doing that so I can collect my pay, fuck off this miserable rock, and make sure my daughter has everything she needs when I die. Hell, we were dead the second we injected ourselves with this shit and we knew it. You remember what you said to me when your gang found me back on Lighton all those years ago before we were Vagabonds?"

Titus's shoulders slumped some. "Get strong so this won't happen again."

"And then you beat my ass."

"I was holding back."

"Tell that to my broken rib."

Titus let out a long breath. "Well, I felt bad afterwards. That's why I took you in. That's why when you injected yourself, I did it with you."

"Bet you wished you hadn't now," Grayson said.

Titus shrugged. "I don't know. We only get one life. I can't say where mine would have gone if we hadn't joined the Vagabond network. But I'm glad we stuck together. I mean that, Gray."

Grayson turned to look out the window. "So am I. That's why I need you to start juicing again. I can't have you dying on this job. We have to get back to Malice."

"Oh yeah?" Titus asked, cocking an eyebrow. "What's waiting for us back in the city? You got a little surprise planned for me? A little cake or some shit?"

Grayson turned to him and their eyes met. "Claire and Jace are having a baby."

Titus almost flipped the duster but managed to keep it under control long enough for him to collect his jaw.

"The HELL you just say?"

Grayson felt a smile touch his lips. "I found out just before we left the city. She's a couple months along already."

Titus's eyes bulged. "And you didn't say anything?!"

"You've been kind of bitchy lately. Figured I'd wait until the right moment."

Titus slowly shook his head back and forth, his mouth opening and closing furiously as he tried to express his growing grin.

"Hot DAMN that's incredible, Grayson!" he finally whooped, pumping a fist into the air. "Our kids are going to be *parents*! Hell, you and me are going to be grandpa's! What do you make of THAT!?"

"It's pretty wild," Grayson admitted with a smile. "But I'm happy for them. Jace is a good guy. They're going to be great with the kid."

"A freakin' kid," Titus echoed. "I'll be dipped in gold. Wow."

Grayson's smile dropped. "Do you understand now why I've been riding your ass so hard about being smart on this job?"

Titus's spark dimmed a little at that. "Shit…"

"I know you don't want to juice," Grayson continued. "But at least stay alive long enough to meet your grandson."

Titus lit up again. "A grandson…how about that." He blustered out a heavy breath then and nodded. "You're right Gray, like usual. You don't have to worry about me. I'll take care of my end and make sure we get back to Claire and Jace. I promise."

"I'm glad to hear it."

Just at that moment, Grayon's wrist reader chirped with an incoming audio call. He accepted the transmission and Ada's voice filled the duster.

"We have to stop. There's something wrong with Shinji."

Grayson and Titus swapped a grim look and then Titus slowed the duster to a halt behind Ada as she did the same. Grayson climbed out of the vehicle, shielding his eyes from the setting sun as it fell toward the distant horizon, the milky disk only a fraction away on its intercept course.

Ada and Shinji exited their duster at the same time and when Grayson saw Shinji, he felt his heart sink into his stomach.

Oh great.

Shinji was pale and his face was slick with sweat. His hair was damp and the cord holding his hair back had come undone, spilling strands of black across his dark eyes. The scar beneath his eye glowed dimly, the blue light barely visible.

"What's going on?" Titus asked, striding over to the younger man. "Shit kid, you look terrible."

Ada walked to Grayson, keeping her voice low. "I don't know what's wrong with him, but he's burning up. His condition started to decline as soon as we got in the duster."

Wonderful, Grayson thought. *Just wonderful.*

Shinji waved Titus away as he tried to inspect the youth, his voice haggard and angry. "Don't touch me," he spat, stumbling backward. "I don't need your help. I'm fine."

"You don't look fine," Titus observed with concern. "In fact, I'd say you look like hell warmed over."

"I just need to sleep it off," Shinji said, leaning back against the duster, his breath coming in labored pulls. "I just caught something on the way in. No need to call the morgue."

Grayson's eyes traveled down to Shinji's leg to where the Canine had bit him. His stomach dropped.

"I don't think that's just some viral thing," he said, pointing. "That looks nasty. Why don't you let Titus take a look at it?"

Shinji looked down at his leg and his eyes grew wide. The bite mark was an angry purple, fading to a nasty green around the punctures. It oozed a thick yellow puss and the flesh was swollen and tight, as if ready to burst.

"Goddamn it," Shinji growled, his voice wet and dazed. "What the hell did that thing spit into me?"

Titus took a knee and reached for the small med box on his belt. Shinji looked furious but said nothing as Titus gingerly cleaned the wound and then wrapped it with anti-infectal medical tape. When that was done, he sprayed the bandage with a cooling solution that doubled as protection once the gel dried.

Titus stood and wiped his hands. "That should help some, but I don't like the way that looks." He turned to Grayson. "We don't know the severity of the wound which makes Shinji's situation dangerous. We might want to consider heading back to Typhon for a bit until we know how this is going to affect him. We don't have the medical equipment with us if this turns grim."

Shinji heaved himself off the duster, his pale face alight with defiance. "Absolutely not. Don't be ridiculous. I'll be fine. We're not going back."

Grayson looked at Ada and then at Titus. He shrugged. "I'm indifferent. The kid knows his limits. If he says he's fine, then I say we continue on."

Titus strode across the sand to Grayson's side, his voice low. "Gray, we have no idea how bad that bite is. It looks infected to hell and back. If we don't get that under control then he could lose his leg. Or worse."

"We can't go back," Ada said suddenly. Her voice was hard and her eyes harder. "If we go back then we waste time and a lot of it. There are people out here depending on us to rescue them. If we turn back then we might as well kill them ourselves."

"We don't even know if they're alive," Titus countered.

"Of course they are," Ada defended fiercely. "I wouldn't be here if I didn't believe that."

Shinji hobbled over, chest heaving, dribbles of thick, sickly sweat running down his face. When he spoke, his voice was hoarse. "Stop talking like I'm not here," he rasped. "This isn't up for discussion. We keep going. Let me sleep this off and I'll be fine in the morning. It's just a fever. If I'm not ok by dawn, then we can go back. Deal?"

Titus chewed his lip for a moment and then sighed. "Fine. But you're coming with me. I want to keep an eye on you."

"Whatever man."

Grayson looked at Ada. "Guess you're stuck with me again."

Ada craned her neck back to look at the setting sun. The sky was beginning to bruise and the strange, translucent disk had almost made contact with the setting sun.

"We only have about a half an hour until the Negative," she announced. "Begger's Valley is just up ahead, beyond that next rise. If we can get to it and put our back against the cliffs, then I think we'll be ok until nightfall. At least then we can use our duster's lights."

"You said the Negative lasts an hour?" Titus asked with concern, stabbing his eyes toward the setting sun.

"More or less."

"We better get going then," Grayson said. He followed Ada back to her duster with Shinji's sickly growls at his back. Titus told him to keep quiet and then they were seated and the small posse was on the move once more.

It only took ten minutes to get to the valley, the landscape rising and then dipping dramatically, tipping the dusters down into a wide, rocky basin. The sand gave way to hard packed clay with clusters of massive boulders littering the mile-wide expanse between the cliff walls. Across on the other side, Grayson noted the sharp rise of broken stone that marked the parameter and border of the valley. It was almost as if a colossal river had once run through this part of Pratus, only to dry out beneath the relentless sun.

When Ada finally found a spot she was satisfied with, the shadows had grown long and the world was turning gray. Grayson felt as if the air itself had begun to shimmer like it was waking up and starting to move, a sensation he found he didn't care for.

Ada backed the duster up against a cliff face and Titus navigated his own duster and did the same. Rolling out across the windshield was the expanse of the valley, a flat plain of darkening red, pimpled with clusters of equally crimson boulders. It was a solid mile across to the other side and Grayson wondered if maybe they should risk crossing over before the darkness came in full.

Ada shut off the engine and her face became noticeably pale. She looked at Grayson in the dusty silence.

"It's been a while since I've been out in the Negative," she admitted. "I'm not a fan."

"We'll keep you safe, don't you worry."

"Don't make me gag. Come on, we should get out there and keep watch until this passes. We're not going to be able to see much and it's all going to look very strange to you, but we have a better vantage point out there than in here."

Grayson grabbed his sniper rifle and followed her outside. He went to Titus's duster and peered inside once Titus lowered the glass panel.

"How's he doing?" Grayson asked quietly.

Titus looked over at Shinji who was crammed into the passenger seat. He was dead asleep, his face damp, his cheeks flushed. His regulator groaned as Shinji shifted, muttering to himself, shivering.

"He juiced himself and then fell asleep," Titus said quietly. "He shouldn't be able to do that. Not with glo pumping through his veins."

"Maybe it'll help."

"I hope so. He looks awful."

Grayson stood, looking over the roof of the duster at the growing dark. The space just in front of his eyes swirled a little and he swatted at it, surprised, but there was nothing there.

Some kind of illusion...?

"You and Ada going to keep watch for a while?" Titus asked.

"Yeah. I have no idea what to expect here, but let's just wait this out until dawn. We can worry some more then."

"Right."

Titus rolled up the window and Grayson returned to Ada who was now sitting on top of the duster's roof, legs crossed. Grunting, Grayson put a boot on the bumper and hoisted himself up next to her.

She looked at him with mild surprise as he lowered himself down beside her. "You don't have to be up here, you know."

Grayson laid his sniper across his knees. "Yeah, well, neither do you."

Ada huffed a breath. "Whatever. How's Shinji look?"

"Terrible."

"What are you going to do if he isn't better by dawn?"

Grayson stared out at the darkening world. "I have no idea."

"You're not one for planning, are you?"

Grayson looked across at her. "Why don't you take him back then?"

"You need me out here," Ada said testily. "You don't know this world."

Grayson pointed across the valley with a gloved finger. "I know there's a crashed ship over that way. I think we'll be able to find—"

The words died in his throat as the air shifted, catching him off guard. As if the cosmos were drawing a curtain, the light faltered and then faded, bleeding into something different.

"Here it comes," Ada whispered, the inflection in her voice changing as quickly as the sky.

Grayson clutched his gun as the world continued to alter, the landscape dimming and then igniting as if the sandy cliffs had been dipped in neon white. He blinked and scrubbed his eyes, the sky shivering and swirling until it became pitch black, a void that swallowed all light and reflection.

"Easy now," Ada warned, looking at him. Grayson turned to her and saw that her form had taken on a haunting aura, her eyes inky wells while her skin and face were swallowed by the neon white. When she spoke, her mouth looked as if it were a bottomless pit.

"You might want to close your eyes for a moment or you'll get sick. Let your body adjust."

Grayson squeezed his eyes closed and then opened them again. The air in front of his face swirled as if it were caught in a vortex, and then it realigned. It did this all across the glowing white valley, the earth devoid of lines or definition, each piece of the terrain lumping together to form a wash of phantom paste. He looked to the sky again and felt his stomach twist. The air above was completely empty, as if the world ended just above his head. There was no light, no stars, no depth to it. He felt like if he reached up his hand might vanish from his body. Instead, he looked down at himself and saw that he emitted the same eerie glow as Ada. It was as if his retinas had been replaced by dirty thermal scopes.

"This is going to take some getting used to," he said quietly, turning to look down the glowing throat of the valley.

"It's only for an hour," Ada assured him. When she spoke, she looked like some kind of demon, her features blurring and washing together as if drenched in an acid bath.

Grayson scrubbed his eyes again. He was beginning to feel extremely claustrophobic and he forced his pulse to steady.

"Take a deep breath," Ada said softly, breaking her usual sharp-edged tone for a moment. "If you want, you can talk to me. It may sound stupid, but it always helps me adjust whenever I get stuck in this."

"This lasts a whole hour huh?" Grayson said a little unsteadily. The air in front of his face kept warping and righting itself, causing a knife of nausea to stab at his gut.

"Yeah and then the moons come out."

"Moons?" Grayson asked. "How many do you have?"

"Just two. But they're pretty spectacular. They're a welcome relief after the Negative passes."

"I *really* don't care for this," Grayson said matter of factly. Begrudgingly, he did find that talking to Ada was helping him adjust. It was something normal and familiar, something to center himself with.

Ada folded her hands in front of her. "I don't like it either. But it's harmless. It's ironic, but the first time I got caught out in this, I was with Marah."

"That's your sister, right? The one that was taken?"

"Yeah. We were young and had snuck out to see what all the fuss was all about." Ada admitted quietly. "Marah started screaming and stumbling around, calling out for our parents."

"I get that," Grayson said uncomfortably.

"I wanted to scream too, but I didn't want to freak her out even more," Ada continued. "I pretended like it was no big deal and tried to make a game out of it. Marah didn't want any part of it, but she did calm down a little. When we eventually got back to our beds an hour later, she insisted she sleep with me. She was afraid it would happen again and she wouldn't be able to find me."

Grayson gripped the barrel of his gun and remained silent.

Ada looked down at her hands, her voice low and strained. "I know I keep saying it, but we have to find her, Grayson. She's alive and she's all alone right now without me."

"We'll find her," Grayson said quietly, not believing a word.

Ada looked up at him suddenly, her tar pit eyes accented by the neon white of her borderless skin. "Thank you for coming here. I'm sure there's a million other jobs you could have taken."

"Don't sweat it," Grayson said, her somber tone catching him off guard.

Ada looked out across the silent valley. "I know you probably think I'm some crazy bitch who-"

"I don't," Grayson said sharply. He looked down at his gun. "I get what you're doing and why you're doing it. You don't need to explain yourself to me."

Ada remained silent for a moment then, letting the dead quiet fill the space between them. Finally, she glanced at him, her voice cautious.

"What's it like?"

"What's what like?"

Ada pointed at him with her chin. "Being a Vagabond."

Grayson wiped a grain of white sand off his gun before answering. "I thought I told you I wanted to keep this relationship professional and focused."

Ada sniffed. "I'm not asking you to marry me, I simply asked you a question about yourself."

"A personal question."

"And…?"

Grayson sighed and looked at her. "How do you think it is?"

"I don't know. Freeing, in a way?"

Grayson grunted out a laugh. "Oh boy." He pinched the bridge of his nose and exhaled. "It's brutal. Lonely and brutal. But it's better than what it could have been."

"Why?" Ada asked carefully. "How could it be worse?"

Grayson craned his head back to stare up at the empty slate of darkness above. "My parents died when I was very young. We were very poor and I grew up in a city that was run by drug-crazed animals. When the gangs realized my parents had passed, they took over the shack we lived in and I was forced to run and live out on the street." Grayson looked at her. "I was five."

"Hell," Ada said quietly. "Didn't you have anyone else? Someone to take you in? Another family member?"

"Oh sure," Grayson said, the memories beginning to seep back in. "I had an older sister. She was thirteen at the time."

"Well…at least you had each other?" Ada ventured.

"My sister was a *cunt*," Grayson said venomously.

Ada blinked in the strange light. "Oh…" She paused then and lowered her head. "I'm sorry. Is that why you chose to inject yourself with that…that stuff?"

Grayson's mind continued to tumble backward, memories and images rising like corpses. "No. I injected myself because I killed my sister and needed to protect myself from the authorities."

Ada's sharp hiss of breath was all Grayson needed to know what she thought of that. She stared openly at him, her mouth slightly agape.

"Why the hell would you do something like that?" She asked, abhorred. "I know you said she was awful, but she was *family*. The only family you had, at that."

Grayson's memories bared their teeth and his voice dropped almost to a whisper. "She sold me a hundred times over to men and women so that she could eat."

Ada said nothing, the words pounding across her skull.

"I can't tell you how many times I was raped before I turned ten and decided I had had enough," Grayson continued, his voice a razor's edge. "When I realized I could stop it, I didn't even hesitate. I waited until she was asleep and then I cut her throat with a piece of broken metal. I took her money, *my* money, and fled. I didn't know where I was going or what I was going to do and I didn't give a damn. I knew I was in deep shit though."

"Where'd you go?" Ada asked, almost a whisper.

"To the other side of the city." Grayson cocked a thumb toward the second duster. "That's where I met Titus. He led a gang of kids back then, all about our age. He beat the shit out of me and took my money."

"What?"

Grayson nodded. "I know. But then he did something I didn't anticipate. He picked me up off the ground and told me that if I worked for him then I could have my money back. And so I did. I hated him, I wanted to kill him, but I didn't have much choice." Grayson leaned back some. "We developed a weird friendship over the next couple years. We were always a hair away from getting locked up and I decided that I was tired of living like that. I found someone who had glo and I bought it off him with the money I earned working for Titus's gang. When I told him I was going to inject and join the Vagabond network, he insisted he do it with me. So we did." Grayson paused for a moment and then spread his hands. "And here we are, all these years later still trying to stay one step ahead of the reaper."

"I had no idea," Ada said after a long silence. "That sounds...terrible. Sorry you went through that."

"I don't think about it much these days," Grayson said quietly. He looked at her then, almost annoyed. "And don't go getting all sympathetic on me. I like you better when you're frowning and irritated. Hell, I have no idea why I even told you all that."

Ada smiled slowly then. "I told you talking helps."

Grayson grunted. "I guess you did."

"Do you think—" she stared but stopped suddenly. The words hung in the air between them, dead, and then she stood up sharply.

"What is it?" Grayson asked, alert, springing to his feet. But as soon as the question left his lips, he heard it.

Howling.

Static.

Electronic screeching.

He threw his eyes down the length of the valley, his heart surging. When he saw the white mass of alien bodies rounding the bend, two miles away, his mouth went dry.

"We got company," he hissed, leaping off the duster, rifle raised.

CHAPTER 7

A da watched as Grayson stumbled over to Titus's duster and pounded on the door. She could tell he was worried and that made her stomach flutter. He wasn't used to the Negative and it was clear that the weird light was throwing off his confidence, a fact that pressed into Ada's skull like a knife. As Titus emerged from the duster, Ada cast her eyes down the length of the valley and watched as the mass of movement continued to flow closer. It was nearly impossible to make out the details because of the Negative, but she could tell that the approaching horde numbered in the hundreds. Electronic transmissions echoed across the walls of the long basin and she knew what was coming.

Tusks. And a lot of them.

Titus, disoriented, dragged a chest out of his duster and began assembling something with hurried practice. Grayson climbed onto the roof of the duster and had the scope of his rifle pressed to his eye. He shouted something at Titus who nodded, their glowing white figures in stark contrast to the empty, flat darkness above.

"Can we drive in this?!" Titus yelled, still piecing something together from the munitions chest.

Ada gripped her pistol. "Not a chance. We'd end up flipping the dusters or ramming into the rocks. There just isn't the clarity for it."

Titus said nothing as if expecting this.

"There's got to be at least three hundred," Grayson called down from the top of Titus's duster. "Maybe more. It's hard to tell in this damn light."

"They still headed this way?" Titus asked.

"Yeah, we have maybe five minutes. Looks like Tusks and Canines."

"Canines too?" Titus asked, hoisted something tubular over his shoulder.

"They're on foot, running alongside the Tusks. Guess they didn't feel like riding shotgun this time."

Ada felt her nerves flare as another screeching blast of electronic noise reached them, a howling discharge of static and eerie vocal rage.

There's too many, she thought, watching as Titus positioned himself next to the duster. Her mind whirled with limited options and she started to wonder if they should take their chances in the vehicles. But before she could settle on a singular idea, Shinji emerged from the duster.

He was hunched over, clutching his head, the massive contraption on his back pushing him down as he moaned.

"What the hell are you doing?" Grayson barked, glancing down at the younger man. "Shinji! What's wrong!?"

Shinji continued to stumble forward, his hands pressed flat against his temples.

"Make it STOP!" He screeched suddenly, his voice frantic and pained. "For chrissakes, make them stop TALKING!" He fell to his knees in the dirt, one hand now clutching the bite wound. "Shut UP!" he snarled, his voice rising.

"I can feel them *inside* me!"

In the strange light, Ada's eyes flickered to Shinji's leg, then his head, and then she registered another blast of electronic noise from the fast charging horde. As soon as the transmission sounded, Shinji wailed even louder.

"They're triggering the wound!" Ada yelled, pointing, as the pieces clicked into place for her with perfect, awful clarity. "We have to drown it out! It's killing him!"

Shinji rose to his feet on shaking legs, one hand reaching for his auto-pistol.

"I can't take it," he moaned. "They're inside my goddamn head." He howled again and started to bring his gun up. But before he could do anything, Ada leapt for him. She grabbed his hand and pulled it back down.

"Block it out!" Ada yelled into his face. "They've poisoned you! The transmission is fucking with your head, you have to fight it!"

Shinji swatted her away, his mouth a snarl of teeth. "Don't touch me!" And then another blast of static howled down the valley, closer than ever. Shinji's eyes rolled back in his head and his mouth dropped open. Slowly, he brought the gun toward it.

"ADA STOP HIM!" Grayson bellowed from the top of the duster. Ada sprang forward and wrestled the gun back down, her voice a hoarse exhale.

"Titus do something!"

Titus was already taking aim, the colossal metal tube resting on his shoulder.

"Stay with us, son!" He roared as he centered the weapon's trajectory into the path of the storming force. A moment later, he activated the weapon.

A burst of noise hissed from the tube as the explosive was launched, a perfect white line that streaked across the length of the valley. It struck the front line and detonated into the charging force. An explosion rocked the valley and a web of snow white fire spread like a spiderweb into the mass of Tusks and Canines, a dozen detonations fanning out to erupt in hammer-thunder succession. Bodies were blown airborne along with a shower of dirt and rock, the front line parting like a gore soaked sea. Roars and screams of pain could be heard amongst the echoing explosions and the mass of flesh appeared as if it had been punched by a giant, burning fist.

But a moment later the hole closed, the ranks reforming as if nothing had even happened. The tide continued its death charge, slowing only to regroup before redoubling their speed.

Grayson's sniper roared in the chaos, each shot laced with acid tipped coring rounds, the bullets striking the frontline before ripping through their targets to strike two more bodies, each blast traveling three deep.

A wave of shrieking static struck them again as the Tusks sent their signal, the wall of noise pounding into Shinji's head. He screamed, his eyes bulging in the Negative's awful light. He threw his gun to the ground, wrestling for control of himself, and started to run, all sense of preservation lost as he battled against the roar in his head and the burn in his leg.

"SHINJI NO!" Titus yelled, lowering his weapon, his voice panicked.

Shinji didn't slow as he answered, his voice thick with desperation and anger. "I have to *stop it!*"

He reached for the dial on his regulator, his boots kicking up dust as he charged the oncoming force.

Realizing what was about to happen, Grayson leapt from the duster. "Shinji WAIT!"

Shinji continued toward the horde, now horribly close. He gripped the dial on his regulator.

"STAY OUT OF THE RAIN!" He roared back at them.

And then he cranked the dial all the way up to its maximum setting.

The result was immediate and horrifying as Ada watched, heart pounding in her throat.

Instantly, Shinji stopped dead in his tracks as his system overloaded with glo, his body shaking and vibrating as if he were being electrocuted. Ada heard him scream, a terrible throaty bellow that roared from the depths of his chest.

"Get back! Go!" Grayson yelled frantically, waving at Titus and Ada, his feet churning. "RUN GODDAMN IT!"

Ada turned and sprinted away from Shinji, confusion and terror gripping her in a vice. The mob had almost reached Shinji as he continued to scream, his body violently shuddering as if he were standing in an electro pool.

A second before the wave of Tusks and Canine's reached Shinji, he vanished.

Grayson grabbed Ada by the arm, his glo-fueled muscles taking them quickly across the hard packed earth. They stumbled in the nauseating light, their boots cracking against rocks and dead roots, the roar of the mob rising at their backs. Titus was screaming something, his voice lost in the chaos, his figure sprinting alongside Ada with hurried desperation.

And that's when the sky began to flash. It arrived without sound, the black overhead bursting with intermittent flares of blinding white, as if marking a runway.

"HURRY!" Titus yelled, his voice washed out a second later as great, peeling thunderclaps shook the hills. Ada winced as they boomed down around them, each one coming like the roar of a thermal cannon.

"Over there!" Grayson pointed, his finger cutting through the light distortion toward a small dark hole in the side of the valley. Ada felt herself pulled along as another snap of thunder cracked the sky.

"Here he comes! GO!" Titus roared, half tripping, his eyes on the sky.

Ada looked to the heavens and felt her breath melt away.

A line of white hot fire was forming above the basin, a wide, blistering gash in the cosmos, titanic in size and scope. It raced across the roof of the sky, the heat already shifting the air. Another booming blast of thunder followed and then the fire began to fall, streaking down toward the earth in colossal waves of power and violence.

"He's carpet bombing the whole fucking valley!" Titus cried, still scrambling for the small cave.

The horde had slowed some as the sky continued to ignite and split apart. Their screams of rage turned to howls of terror as they realized what was happening.

"Inside! Hurry!" Grayson barked, shoving Ada into the small opening of the rock wall as they reached it. He hurried Titus in next and then dove inside as the world outside became a blinding hell.

The rain of fire hit the valley with all the force of a thermo-nuclear payload. The earth quaked as it was bombarded, each cluster of fire slamming into the dirt with the force of a nine-hundred kiloton hammer. The mob screamed as they were struck, their bodies evaporating instantly as the trail of death stretched over them. Dirt and rock were blown into the air, each impact punching the earth with enraged precision. The shockwaves followed, rolling over the mass of bodies like tsunamis, boiling and scorching everything in their wake, one after another in rapid succession as the fire continued to fall and kill and destroy.

Grayson continued to blindly push Ada and Titus deeper into the cave as the ground shook and rocked beneath their feet. The walls around them groaned and began to split apart, the bombing thundering across the valley outside.

"Deeper MOVE!" Grayson yelled over the screech of death outside.

A gale followed then, a great, sweeping push of dirt, rock, sand, and gore. It battered the walls of the valley and exploded across the face of the cave, sending debris hurtling toward Ada as if a grenade had gone off. Grayson stepped in front of her and wrapped himself around her figure, taking the brunt of the blow, the rocks and pebbles pelting his skin and armor.

"Dead end!" Titus cried suddenly from ahead. "There's nothing back here! We're trapped!"

Grayson pulled himself off Ada and pushed his way toward Titus, the ground still shuddering beneath him. Ada braced herself against the walls and felt them start to crumble as the hell outside continued its rampage.

She turned to Grayson and Titus, desperation filling her. Before she could cry out, the ground shifted with a massive, horrible crunch.

Ada fell backwards, the world rocking, the ceiling of the small cave cracking above them. She heard herself screaming as everything collapsed at once. Grayson was yelling at Titus, but it was lost in the wind and roar and carnage.

She tried to stand, but fell over again as the world continued to tremble, splitting open across the mouth of the cave and snaking dangerously toward them.

"Get back! BACK!" Ada yelled at the men, her voice shrill as the line of widening earth continued to grow and crack toward them. Her face was covered in sweat and grime, her throat dry with dust, her pulse thundering in her ears. She pushed herself away from the expanding crack, scrambling backwards on all fours, her mouth open in a cry of terror.

The world outside boomed once more and the crack found her. It happened in an instant, the walls of the cave splitting apart and then falling inward, throwing them all down into the maw of darkness below.

Ada felt herself go weightless as she fell, her world going dark as pain enveloped her.

She didn't know how long she was out. The first thing she noticed was the pulsing pain in her left shoulder. It flared like fire with every beat of her gurgling heart, her head a rattled wash of silence, fear, and panic. She opened her mouth, attempting to force air into her lungs, but a moan came out instead. Something pressed down on top of her, pinning her to the hard ground. She tried to move, but hissed sharply as her shoulder registered a massive spike of pain.

Ada forced her eyes open and found herself staring into empty darkness. She could feel rock all around her, on top of her, pressing in close, enveloping her.

The ground split open, she thought, gathering her senses. *And then we all fell.*

Claustrophobia reared its ugly head as her situation sharpened into focus, the walls of her prison pushing down on her.

Where am I?! What happened to everyone!?

She tried to push herself up again, but found that the pain in her shoulder wouldn't allow it. Something huge and heavy was pinning her in place and she felt her pulse quicken. Dust swirled up from the ground as she drew desperate breaths, the darkness squeezing her fractured composition like a fist.

Ada tried to move her other arm and found that it was mercifully free. She reached out and found purchase across the ground. She tried to pull herself away from the rocks pinning her, but it was impossible. Something shifted above her and she heard a rush of noise as something slid down and spilled over her legs, a deposit of gravel and dirt that had come free from her attempt. The weight covered her from the waist down and she felt what little composure she had begin to fray.

You're going to be buried alive if you're not careful.

She carefully explored the area around her again with her free hand. It seemed there was a little space to her right, a small flat area that was free of rock, a pocket in the collapse.

The thought hit her again: *Where am I?*

She prayed she wasn't lying under a mountain of rubble and that instead, she had fallen into some kind of underground ravine. The space to her right gave her hope and despite the total darkness, she thought she could feel a breeze from that direction, the slightest of winds.

She went back to the pile of rock pinning her left shoulder. She gingerly poked and scraped at it, registering the largest boulders and noting their position. The last thing she wanted to do was to pull one free and start another rock slide, burying her for eternity.

Where the hell are Grayson and Titus? She thought, still exploring the rock around her. *Are they down here too? Are they alive?*

She opened her mouth, coughed, and then called for them. Her voice sounded incredibly small and weak, the enclosed space swallowing her words. She paused, and when there was no response, she tried again, louder this time.

"Titus! Grayson!"

This time, her voice echoed slightly and traveled away from her to the right.

Tunnel, she thought desperately. *There's got to be a tunnel there.* She clung to the idea, begging for just a spark of light so she could see if her prayer rang true. The uncertainty and permanence of her situation rattled across her skull and she fought off another wave of claustrophobia. Dust fell around her, clogging her nose and throat, causing her to fall into a coughing fit.

There. A noise.

She snapped her mouth shut, waiting for the sound to come again. Her heartbeat crashed into her ears and she begged it to silence.

A moment later, she heard the noise again. It was to her right, where she suspected a tunnel. It sounded like something being dragged across stone, but it was far away, the noise bouncing off the walls like whispers.

"Grayson!?" Ada shrieked, feeling her sanity begin to crack.

Nothing. Absolute stillness. The darkness remained a relentless wall before her eyes and the weight continued to pin her in place.

"GRAYSON!"

There it was again. That dragging sound.

Someone is hurt and trying to crawl to me.

She opened her mouth to cry out once more, but something echoed across the darkness first. It was a voice thick with static and terribly, horribly deep.

"G-r-a-y-s-o-n!"

Her heart seized in her chest and she slapped her free hand over her mouth. Her eyes went wide and trickles of sweat streaked down her grime-stained face.

The dragging sound called once more, an octave higher this time. "G-r-a-y-s-o-n!"

It was getting closer.

Ada felt a knot form in her chest and panic rose in her throat. Desperately she began to claw at the mound of rock pinning her, her breath coming out in frightened, weak wheezes.

A chirp of electronic noise bounced off the walls around her, coming from her right. It sounded like a malfunctioning speaker system, a burst of static following.

And then her voice echoed back to her from the transmission.

"Grayson! GRAYSON!"

Her stomach pooled with fear and she began to cry, panting and tugging at her pinned arm and shoulder, knowing she shouldn't. Pain burst across her trapped limb like fire bombs, but she ignored it as the dragging sound drew closer and closer.

"G-r-a-y-s-o-n!"

The sound of her mimicked voice ignited her terror and she whimpered, clawed, begged to be free. The shadows pressed in, the darkness overwhelming, and the dragging sound slithered closer and closer, now just a few feet away. She could hear something tapping against the rock, metallic clicks that pulled nearer. The static was constant now, a low hum that whirled closer with every passing second.

"GRAYSON!"

The shrill call was right next to her now and Ada screamed as something reached for her, long clawed hands that wrapped around her throat with alarming power. She sputtered and began to choke, trying to kick her legs free of the debris that buried her. Her eyes bulged as the static continued to rain down over her, a chirping, beeping gasp that fueled the long, bony fingers around her throat.

She felt herself dying. Her lungs screamed for air and her head felt like it was filling with combustible gas, ready to detonate at any second.

Just as she was about to lose consciousness, the pressure around her throat ceased. Something grunted and roared above her and as her vision swam back into focus, she saw a wash of dim blue above her, casting shadows across the enclosed space.

The Tusk screeched in fury and squirmed away from its attacker, its massive body trapped in a bear hug as someone ripped it off Ada from behind. The blue light continued to move, splashing patches of darkness across the walls and illuminating others.

"Get...off...of...her!" A voice grunted as massive arms traveled up to the Tusk's neck, continuing to pull it backwards while also ripping its head opposite its metallic spine.

Titus...? Ada thought dimly.

With a roaring exhale, Titus stepped back and planted a boot into the Tusk's spine while still gripping its neck. Muscles bulging, he jerked the creature's head back and cracked its throat with a sickly pop.

Instantly, the Tusk stopped struggling, its body going limp in Titus's grip. He let it flop to the ground and wiped his face, the blue glow from his scars igniting his eyes and casting a low aura around him.

Ada stared up at him, her eyes filling with tears. "Titus? Is that really you?"

"I'm here," He said, sounding exhausted. He knelt next to her, the scars beneath his eyes spilling light over her situation. "Looks like the fall got you worse than me. Can you move at all?" He asked, his fingers already prying at the rocks around her.

"Just my right arm," Ada said, relief sweeping through her like a hurricane. It didn't matter if she died down here now.

At least I'm not alone.

"Alright, don't move," Titus instructed. "Let me dig you free."

Ada did as she was told, her heartbeat slowing. Titus circled her and began to throw rocks and dirt off her legs. He panted and grunted, pulling the larger rocks gingerly away from the pile. When he was finished, he went to her side and placed a gloved hand against the rock pinning her shoulder. He tested it and then threw his weight against it. Ada felt the massive weight leave her, only to be replaced by a dull ache.

"Go, go!" Titus gasped, holding the rock up. Ada scrambled out from under it and then Titus set the rock back down with a grunt. Ada sat for a moment and inspected herself, her fingers carefully exploring the tender flesh of her shoulder and arm.

Titus came and knelt next to her, his massive frame illuminated by the glow of his scars.

"Let me see that," he said gently, pulling her fingers away. He carefully pressed and squeezed her shoulder, noting her reaction to each probe.

"I think it's just bruised," he said finally, standing up. "You got lucky. That rock wasn't anything to joke about. Another couple of inches and your skull would have been crushed like hard candy."

"Thanks Titus," Ada said gratefully, reaching up to him.

He gripped her hand and pulled her to her feet. "Don't mention it. I'm just glad you're alive."

"Have you seen Grayson?"

"No. I was knocked unconscious when I fell," He said, pointing away from them. "There's a tunnel over there, a whole cave system in fact. When I woke up I heard you calling. Glad I got to you when I did." He eyed the dead Tusk. "I don't know how many more of these things fell down here with us. Shinji ripped the earth apart and I'd guess that we have more than a few unwanted guests down here."

Ada remembered then how Shinji had lost himself, running toward the horde like a madman.

"What did he do?" She asked after a second. "Where did he go?"

Titus slapped dust from his gloves. "He overcooked. It's a dangerous gamble and it's different for every Vagabond. The glo in our veins reacts to our biological composition in ways that's hard to predict. Until you over-cook for the first time, you don't know what kind of power it'll give ya."

Ada swallowed. "Can you do what Shinji did?"

Titus huffed. "No ma'am. Not like that. I've never seen anything like what Shinji did."

Ada tested her shoulder again, the muscle tender to the touch. "I'm not going to forget that show anytime soon. He just vanished. And then the sky opened up."

"Like I said, it's different for everyone," Titus rumbled, scanning the open mouth of the tunnel before them, the stone walls awash with blue light. "I've seen Grayson overcook once. It wasn't like that, but it was equally overwhelming."

"Why didn't he do it then?" Ada asked. "Why didn't you? Why did we run?"

"Because we still had a chance," Titus explained. "Overcooking takes its toll on us. Hard. It's not something you do lightly."

"Is that why you guys have shorter lifespans?"

Titus glanced at her in the dim light. He said nothing for a long moment and then he motioned toward the tunnel. "We should get going. There's got to be a way back to the surface. We just gotta find it."

Ada fell into silence and followed him. Together, they entered the narrow tunnel and began winding their way down its rocky throat. It twisted and dipped, widening for a few dozen yards before narrowing once more. Their boots echoed off the enclosed walls, scraping and testing each step. More than once they had to scramble on their hands and knees and after a while, Ada wondered if the tunnel had an end.

Finally, they reached another opening, the tunnel widening into a small cavern filled with stalactites, dust, and four more tunnels that snaked away from the one they had exited.

Titus eyed the different options. "Don't like this one bit," he muttered.

Ada went to each one and waited, testing the air with a wet finger. After some consideration, she pointed to the one directly across from the one they had emerged from.

"Two of them have airflow. This one feels the strongest, which tells me it's our best shot."

Titus nodded. "Sounds logical to me. I'll take the lead again, in case we run into any more friends."

"You don't happen to have a gun, do you?" Ada asked.

"Naw. But I've activated my regulator and I have a boot knife. It's not much, but it ain't nothin'."

Ada waved a hand. "Off we go then."

The tunnel was similar to the other one, its long, rock walls winding first down and then slowly upward. Ada noticed their slight ascension when her legs started to ache, an indication that they were headed uphill. As they walked, the darkness at her back became a constant source of anxiety. With Titus in the lead, Ada threw a startled look over her shoulder more than once, convinced she heard something. The glow of Titus's scars threw blue light ahead of them, bathing the walls in an eerie wash. The big man's form blocked most of the light from reaching her and so she stayed close to his back, nearly hugging him as they continued.

After some time, the tunnel opened up again, dumping them into yet another cavern. This one was bigger, but half the ceiling had collapsed in a pile of rubble. After some inspection, they found that the tunnel continued down at the far end.

As they were about to enter it, Ada held up a hand, listening. "Do you hear that?" She asked.

Titus cocked his head and then nodded. "Sounds like running water. Some kind of underground river?"

"I'd say so," Ada agreed. "Whenever my father's mining chiefs start a new dig, the first thing they do is burrow for water to keep the rock crushers' engines cool."

"I'd settle for keeping my throat cool right now," Titus said. "Not to sound dramatic, but I'm so thirsty I feel like I could drink an entire watercycle silo right now."

Ada had no idea what that was and so she simply nodded. "Yeah. I'm pretty parched too."

They pressed onward and soon found that the tunnel expanded outward, broadening their path and continued ascent. As they rounded a corner, Ada guessed they could drive six or seven dusters through the tunnel without ever bumping into one other.

What I wouldn't do for a duster right now, she thought, her feet aching.

Suddenly, Titus threw a hand up and ducked low, pulling her with him. He pressed them both against the tunnel wall, his actions urgent and alert.

"What is it?" Ada whispered at his back. She placed one hand across his broad shoulders and felt sweat stick to her fingers, bleeding through the edges of his battle armor.

Titus glanced back at her. "Something's up there. I can hear it. It's getting closer."

Ada paused in the silence. "I don't hear anything," she whispered.

Titus tapped his regulator and then his ear. "It's there, trust me. Keep your voice down." He then reached up and covered his glowing scars with his hands, snuffing all light from the wide, rocky tunnel.

Ada counted the seconds, waiting until her ears registered noise. It was a solid twenty seconds before she heard it.

Something scraped ahead of them, a clicking, slithering sound followed by a low gurgle of electronic chirping.

Tusk, she thought, her chest tightening.

Slowly, with one arm across his scars now, Titus reached into his boot and pulled out a massive knife, the blade as long as Ada's forearm. Together, they waited, listening to the noise as it slithered closer.

It stopped, a mere thirty or so feet from their position. With her eyes adjusted to the dark, Ada could make out the Tusk's large frame, its boxed head jerking left to right as a pur of static echoed around them.

Does it know we're here? Can it see us?

Titus remained pressed against the tunnel wall, knife held at the ready. He waited, unmoving, as the Tusk continued to test the air.

Suddenly, the shadows of its back half split open, blooming like a flower. A Canine crawled out of the fleshy sack with a squelching pull, rising to stand next to the Tusk. It's purple eyes glowed in the black, staring directly at them.

It sees us it sees us it sees us–

The Tusk garbled something then, a flurry of beeping notes directed at the Canine. The purple eyes swung away from them and the Canine answered the call, its own voice calm, icy, and speaking in a rolling, fragmented language that was completely alien to Ada. The two creatures seemed to converse for a few seconds, as if deciding what to do next. During the exchange, Ada noted that the Canine's shadowed form was slumped some, its left arm hanging uselessly at its side.

Must have been injured during Shinji's attack, she observed. *Good. I hope it hurts like hell.*

Without warning, Titus suddenly stood, looming over her. He planted a boot, cocked his arm back, and then threw his knife at the Tusk. It whistled through the air at a tremendous speed, end over end, and found its mark with a wet crack of metal and flesh. The Tusk screamed, a howling burst of static, anger, and pain, the knife buried to the hilt in its head.

The Canine leapt back, its eyes darting toward Titus's location, crouching low and emitting a hiss. The Tusk roared again and then tumbled over, its long limbs clawing at the air and then falling to the ground as its death rattle shook the expansive tunnel.

The glow of Titus's scars flooded the area in front of him and when the Canine spotted him and Ada, it let out a snarl and then fled, turning tail to dart back the way it had come. Ada noted how fast it was and thought for a second that Titus was going to pursue. Instead, he walked over to the dead Tusk and yanked his knife free. He wiped the blade and watched the Canine's shadow vanish back into the tunnel.

"I hope he's not the type to gossip," he said darkly.

Ada came and stood next to him, staring down at the dead creature at her feet. "You think they were looking for us?"

"Beats me," Titus said, sheathing his knife again. "But at least one of them knows we're down here now." He wiped sweat off his face. "Can't say that sits well with me, but I'm in no shape to go sprinting after that thing."

"Maybe it really is alone," Ada said, the image of the Canine's glowing eyes seared into her memory.

"That'd be a nice change of luck," Titus said. "Now come on, I can still hear water and all this killing has really chapped my lady kissers."

Together, they pushed further into the tunnel system. Ada's nerves remained on high alert, her eyes darting deep into the shadows as they went. At any moment she expected to see the Canine return with a dozen more at its back.

To her surprise, they reached the underground water source without incident. She didn't know how long had passed since their encounter with the Tusk, her sense of time lost beneath the claustrophobic walls. Titus was breathing heavily as they rounded a tunnel bend and entered a wide cavern, the sound of running water bouncing off the high ceiling.

"Looks like a river," he noted, his voice a husk. "Feel like we've been stumbling around in the dark for days now. Let's have ourselves a drink and a quick breather, I need to shut off my regulator for a couple minutes."

"Are you ok?" Ada asked as Titus clicked down the small device on his thigh.

"I'm fine. Just beat to hell. My head is killing me and I need some of that water. This shit dries you out like you wouldn't believe."

Together they strode across the rocky ground and over to the flow of water. It cut across the center of the cavern, running left to right, only a few feet wide. As they sank to their knees and drank, Ada noted that the river wasn't much deeper either.

We could wade through if we have to, she thought, filling her mouth with the icy cold. She looked up toward the opposite bank, water dripping from her chin. *We might even be able to jump it.*

"I could toss you over, if you'd let me," Titus said as if reading her mind. She shot him a frown and he grinned before dipping his face back beneath the surface, drinking deeply.

"Oh sweet stars in the sky," Titus said, pulling himself back up with a satisfied sigh. "That was just about the tastiest thing I've ever had." He wiped his face and sat back, resting his arms on his knees.

Ada pulled herself up the stony bank and sat next to him, her eyes scanning the cavern. It was illuminated by the glow of Titus's scars, the high ceiling soaring two dozen feet above them. Across the bank, the ground rose some and she thought she saw a slight twinkle of light. She pointed at it.

"Do you see that?"

Titus nodded. "Yup. Might be the way out. This is turning out to be one bitch of a cave system."

Ada checked her wrist reader for the time, suddenly realizing she had been wearing it the whole time. When she saw it was cracked, she let her arm drop dejectedly.

Titus grunted. "Mine's broken too. That's the first thing I tried when I woke up down here. Was hoping to raise Grayson or even your father.

Let him know our situation. I don't like calling on a client for help, but desperate times and all that."

Ada pulled her knees up to her chest and listened to the running water. "We shouldn't stay stationary for long."

Titus sighed. "I know, dear. Just give the old man a breather. I've been pushing myself and I'd rather not break my neck when we're this close to the surface. You young bucks don't know what it's like living on this side of twilight."

Ada looked over at him. "You're not that old."

"Maybe not in years," Titus corrected, tapping his regulator. "But this thing sucks the piss right out of you."

Ada was silent for a moment, allowing herself a second's peace. Finally, she looked back to Titus. "Why do it then? I talked to Grayson earlier, but I still don't understand why you'd forfeit half your life for that kind of power. It seems foolish."

"I am a fool, you're right about that," Titus admitted with a small smile. "But explaining to you the psychology behind my choices would take all day. So just keep thinking I'm an idiot and we'll leave it at that."

"I didn't mean anything by it," Ada said quickly.

Titus waved her off. "Ah, don't sweat it, kid. Just know that I never did this for power. Where I grew up, becoming a Vagabond was a means to an end. It got me out of some bad shit and that's all there is to it."

"Grayson told me you two were in a gang together," Ada said.

"Did he now?" Titus asked, surprised. "Look at you, getting him to spill his beans." Titus quieted some and then chuckled. "A gang...is that what he called it?"

"So it wasn't?"

"To him it probably seemed like a gang. But we were just a bunch of young fools running around trying to stay alive. Grayson had it harder than the rest of us and I came to feel like I was responsible for his well being."

"Was that before or after you beat him up and took his money?"

Titus snorted. "Damn, he spared no detail huh? Guess there's no saving face with you then. Yeah, it was after. And after a year of running from the authorities, I started to feel like we were family. There was just something about him that drew people in. Kids wanted to be around him. They wanted his opinion on things. I respected that, even envied it. But I came to love him like a brother just the same. He never talked much, but I knew he felt the same way about me. We needed one another, you know?"

"Didn't you have your own family to look after?" Ada asked.

Titus shook his head. "Never knew my family. Don't remember a damn thing about them. The only reason I know I had a mother is because I'm breathing. Unless I descended from the stars, but that's pushing it."

Ada stared at her boots, her thoughts going to Marah. "Do you have any family now?"

Titus smiled gently. "Sure. Got a son. Just one of those things that happened along the way."

"What's his name?"

"Jace. Him and Grayson's little girl Claire are together. Small world, I know." He grinned openly then. "They're going to have a baby."

Ada offered him a smile. "Congrats."

Titus crawled to his feet with a groan. "Thank you. Now how about we get the hell out of this tunnel? I'd rather not die in the dark before I get to see my grandchild."

Still thinking of Marah, Ada crawled to her feet, suddenly feeling incredibly alone. Titus looked at her in the soft light, noticing the change on her face.

"Hey, none of that now," he said quietly. "We're going to get your people back. That's why I'm here. I'm not leaving until the job is done."

Ada offered him a weak smile.

Titus placed a hand on her shoulder. "Anyone ever tell you you're like an egg?"

"Excuse me?"

"You're soft beneath that hard exterior."

"Now listen h-"

Titus chuckled and patted her on the back. "It's a good thing. I like that about you. I'm no composer of words so that might have sounded bad, but I got a lot of respect for you. You're not a Vagabond like us. You don't have the capabilities we do and yet you're standing here shoulder to shoulder with us and you haven't flinched once." Titus smiled down at her. "I can tell you got a lot of love for your sister. And I promise you we'll get her back, along with everyone else. So don't go gettin' gloomy on me, deal?"

Ada couldn't help but soften some. "Alright, deal. Jesus. Good thing it's dark down here or you'd see me blushin'."

"No shit?"

"You wish," Ada said. "Now let's cross this river and get out of here."

Ada went first, taking a running leap to throw herself across the waterway. She landed on the other side with a thud, nearly fell, but caught herself at the last second. She turned back to Titus and gave him a thumbs up. He grinned and made the jump with ease, his boots thudding into the rocky embankment next to her.

"Nothing to it," he said, taking the lead once more.

He froze almost instantly.

Ada bumped into him. "What the hell?"

"Ah no…" Titus whispered, his tone changing in an instant. Ada could tell something bad had just happened by the way the big man tensed, his whole body turning to stone.

She stepped around him. When she saw what had caused him to stop, she felt her stomach plummet. A cold finger caressed the back of her neck as she swept her eyes across the stony stretch before them.

At least thirty Canines were slowly crawling to their feet from where they had been hiding along the ground, backed by a dozen Tusks. Their eyes lit up like purple stars, igniting the darkness. The Tusks gurgled their static at them, menacingly, waiting for them to act.

They crept up on us, Ada thought, her heart racing. *How did we not hear them!?*

Titus put a hand across Ada's chest and pushed her back behind him. Slowly, he reached for his regulator and she heard the dial click up a couple notches.

"I don't like these odds," Titus said grimly. He pulled his knife out and held it tightly in a knotted fist. "Stay behind me no matter what."

"There's too many of them," Ada hissed.

"I know."

Ada looked back at the gurgling river. "Should we go back?"

"I don't think that's going to make much difference," Titus said, watching as the line of Canines began to advance. They hooted and barked at their prey, smiles lining their faces, brimming with confidence.

They have us trapped and they know it, Ada thought.

She tugged at Titus's arm. "Isn't there something you can do? Can't you...cook or something?!"

Titus shook his head. "Not down here. I'd bring this whole place down on our heads."

The Canines were only a few feet away now, the Tusks at their backs hissing and clacking their long teeth against the ground as they pulled themselves forward.

"Whatever you do-"Titus started, but he never had a chance to finish.

The Canines surged forward as one, a mass of bodies that leapt for them with a violent energy. Titus decapitated two of them with a swing of his knife, dark liquid blooming behind the arc of his blade.

Before he had a chance to reset, the rest of them were on him. They leapt and clawed, diving and scraping over him, teeth gnashing, claws gouging. The Tusks slithered to join the fray, slamming their bodies against the wriggling pile, knocking them to the ground. Ada felt hands grip her—cold, smooth fingers that dug into her skin the harder they gripped. Darkness rushed her and the pant and stink of hungry breath flooded down into her face as she was pressed to the ground.

Titus roared, his glo powered muscles contracting, and then he exploded outward, throwing his arms out, toppling the mass backwards. He punched and kicked against the tide, his knuckles fracturing bone, his boots shattering cartilage. The cavern filled with the howl of combat, a desperate, panting clamor of flesh pounding into flesh.

A Canine leapt for Titus's throat, teeth bared, but Titus grabbed it out of the air with one huge fist and collapsed its skull. Gore rained down across the other Canines, but it only seemed to enrage them. They bullrushed Titus once more, knocking him down, a pulse of two dozen bodies pushing him to the ground.

Ada screamed for him as three more Canines clawed at her, dragging her across the ground away from Titus. She kicked and punched, gouged and spat, but nothing seemed to slow her attackers. A Tusk loomed over her suddenly and a massive, bony hand reached for her throat, lifting her off the ground to throttle her. She gagged and coughed, the world shaking, her skull rattling.

"Titus!" She managed to wheeze, her vision dimming.

Titus saw her and roared. He snatched a Canine by the arm and pulled it off him with a vicious tug, never letting it go. Using it as a weapon, he began to beat the others back, crunching his victim into a bloody pulp in the process.

But then the remaining Tusks were on him, slamming their weighty flesh sacks across his stomach and legs, their long reach lashing out to strike him across the chest with their pointed claws. His armor sparked on contact and Titus fell back once more. The swarm of Canines rushed him then, seeing an opening. They wriggled over his body like worms, biting, slashing, raging to bring the big man down.

The Tusk holding Ada let her drop to the ground with a thud, her head bouncing against the rocks. In a daze, she heard Titus scream suddenly. It was a blood curling exhale of agony that brought a spike of clarity into her vision. She looked over to him and when she saw what had happened, she felt herself begin to scream as well.

A Canine had ripped Titus's regulator out of his thigh, the tangled nest of wires and tubes dripping with blood and bits of skin. It held it above its head and howled its victory, displaying its trophy for all to see.

The Tusk that had throttled her loomed back into Ada's vision, its fist aimed at her head. The last thing she heard before she was knocked unconscious was the sound of Titus screaming her name, his voice raw with terror.

CHAPTER 8

Grayson groaned and pulled himself from a pile of rubble. His head thundered and his muscles vibrated and throbbed beneath the flow of glo that pulsed through his bloodstream. Dust and dirt filled his lungs and he hacked violently, bending over to wretch. When the coughing fit passed, stars danced before his eyes and he rubbed at them with dirty gloves.

Where am I?

When his vision cleared, he saw stars above him, real ones, along with a pair of golden moons that glowed vibrantly across the ruined landscape.

Shinji, Grayson thought, his mind reforming and recalling the violent cave-in and rolling thunder. *Shinji bombed the whole damn valley.*

He looked around, assessing his situation, and found that he was ankle deep in a pile of gravel. He pulled his boots heavily from the wrecked earth and saw that to his left the landscape slid downward into a gaping abyss, the mouth of the hole partially filled with heavy rock and loose sandstone.

Where are Ada and Titus?

The thought came with an urgency that sent a bolt of worry though his skull and he cupped his hands to his mouth to call for them. He clicked his teeth together a moment later, realizing he had no idea if there were still Canines and Tusks around.

"Start screaming, that'll solve things," Grayson admonished. He forced himself to calm down, counting his heartbeats until he found his center. When he was steady, he looked around once more, tuning his eye to every detail.

The massive hole disappeared into the earth and he knew that if Ada and Titus were down there then they were either dead or beyond his help. When he realized this, he wrestled with his own helplessness for a moment before forcing himself to calm once more.

I hope you're both ok, he thought vainly. *Do whatever you have to, wherever you are.*

He balled his hands into fists and swept his eyes away from the hole and across the landscape, the world illuminated by the twin moons.

How long have I been unconscious? He thought, noting the dispersal of the Negative. *An hour? Two?*

The valley before him was a blackened stretch of complete annihilation. The earth was cracked and broken, charred to an almost cosmic darkness. The path of Shinji's trajectory was clear beneath the moonlight, a wide lane of ash and shattered rock that stretched down the length of the valley. It looked like a pulverized runway, a total destruction of everything in its path. There were no bodies to be seen among the wreckage and scorched earth, not even a stray limb or severed torso.

"What a mess," Grayson muttered, pulling himself down the slope before him and away from the gaping hole. Before he had gone two steps, he stopped and grabbed his head as a spike of agony lanced through his skull. He gripped his temples and grit his teeth, eyes bulging as the breath was robbed from his lungs. Gasping, he fell to his knees, eyes watering. A low moan bled through his teeth and tears sprang from his eyes to run down his grime stained cheeks. The world blurred and rattled, the pain rising and sharpening with every beat of his heart.

At the climax of his agony, the pain released him and he fell forward onto his hands, gasping. He dragged a couple lungfuls of air down his throat as the echo of the attack faded from his head.

"Goddamn it," he rasped, reaching to dial down his regulator to normal levels. How long had it been on now? How much glo had been pumped through his system?

He suddenly gagged and then threw up, his stomach revolting against the sudden change in his system. Wiping his mouth, he stood, knees shaking. He stared up at the twin moons and waited for his stomach to settle and his breath to return.

"Pull yourself together, Gray," he muttered, his voice cracked and dry. He could feel panic tapping on the window of his mind and he forced himself to turn his back on it. He took another couple of steps toward the flat of the valley in front of him and once he reached level ground, he began to feel a little better. He checked his regulator twice more to make sure he was back to normal levels before he stopped. He scanned the expanse around him and he suddenly felt very alone.

"What the hell am I supposed to do now?" he said aimlessly. He had no weapons, save for his boot knife, no transport, and no idea where any of his companions were. He was completely and utterly on his own in a world he knew next to nothing about.

His thoughts returned to Titus and Ada and the worry returned, a paranoid, anxious finger that poked deep into his chest. He forced it away and focused on his own situation. He was in trouble and he needed to start figuring out his next move.

As he did so, he noticed something in the distance. It wasn't far off and he walked toward it, his curiosity peaked. It was a small lump in the landscape, a dark shadow on the shadowed ground. When he reached it, his eyes widened.

It was Shinji's regulator. It lay in perfect order on the ground, the large metal box free of damage. The long tubes that ran out from it were neatly aligned next to it, as if someone had carefully placed them.

Puzzled, Grayson inspected it, circling the bulky contraption for some kind of sign as to what happened and why it was here. When he found no clues, he lowered himself down next to it and crossed his legs, taking a moment to think and plan out his next move. Should he bring the regulator with him? Where was Shinji? And if he did take it, where would he go? He knew the job was completely botched at this point, his mission a near complete failure. He had to regroup, find his allies, and get back to Typhon. He looked around for the dusters, but they were nowhere to be seen.

Probably got vaporized.

His head began to throb again and he braced himself for another attack, but none came. He took off his gloves and ran his hands down across his face, his fingers scraping against his stubble. He swept his hair out of his eyes and retrieved the knife from his boot. He stared down at it as if waiting for some kind of solution to his situation.

That's when he noticed his wrist reader was still functioning. The small screen was cracked, but not destroyed. With a flicker of hope, he thumbed it and tuned Titus's frequency.

"Titus you there? It's Grayson. You alive?" He waited for a return message and when none came, he sent another.

"Come on man, answer me. I know you're not dead."

Please.

Silence again. He tried Ada next and got the same response. He stared at Shinji's regulator and after a moment, he tried to raise him with the same result.

When's the last time a job went so wrong? He thought, cueing up Typhon on his wrist reader and selecting Reston's personal channel. Swallowing his pride, he sent a message.

"Reston, this is Grayson. We underestimated what we're up against. I'm not going to sugar coat it—it's bad out here and we need help."

It was only ten seconds before the message was read and his wrist reader chirped with a live incoming call.

"Reston?" Grayson asked, accepting it.

"Grayson, I got your message. How bad is it? Is Ada ok?" Reston asked, sounding strained, his voice pressed thin.

"We were attacked. Everyone is missing. I'm in Begger's Valley and I need transport back to Typhon."

"Missing?" Reston came back, his voice fraying.

"Yes, missing. Not dead. At least I hope not. Ada is with Titus. There was a...complication in the mission."

"What kind of complication? What the hell happened out there?"

"Three hundred Canines and Tusks is what happened," Grayson said. "We were able to eliminate them, but we were separated in the attack. Any chance you could send some dusters my way?"

A pause. Then, "Of course. But Ada, where is she? Was she harmed in the attack? Where did she go? My God, Grayson, just what *happened* out there!?"

"We got sucker punched," Grayson said. "There was a cave-in. Ada and Titus were together though and I can promise you that he'll take care of her, wherever they are. I'm not going to abandon them, but I need to regroup and gather some firepower."

"Jesus Grayson, when we hired-" Reston started, but Grayson cut him off.

"We're going to find them and I'm going to fix this. This job isn't over, but it's going to take a lot more than we originally assumed. Do you understand me?"

Reston was silent for a moment before answering. "I understand. I'll send a pair of duster's out toward Beggar's Valley. And Grayson?"

"Yes?"

"We're not going to stop until I find my daughters. Both of them. Along with the rest of my people."

"I wouldn't expect anything less. See you soon."

Grayson ended the call and stared back down at his knife. He felt a little less lost now, though the walls of his situation still pressed tight against his mind. He tried to raise Titus again, but got nothing. Standing, he stared down at Shinji's regulator and fought with what to do next.

Before he could, something shifted. Shinji's regulator let out a low groan of metal on metal and the entire thing shuddered slightly. Then, the top began to open.

Grayson took a step back as a pale hand emerged and gripped the edge of the regulator. It shook as it pulled upward, and a body followed like a vampire from its coffin.

"You gotta be kidding me," Grayson whispered, retreating another step.

Cloaked in shadow, Shinji grinned as he stepped out of the regulator, his eyes as dark as fire burned ash.

"Hello Grayson," he rattled, his voice low and dry. He pulled the rest of himself out of the regulator, his legs shaking some. He coughed into his hand, shivered, and then he lowered himself to the ground where he sat, catching his breath. His hair hung in loose strands across his pale face, his thin frame trembling from the sudden exit.

Grayson stood over him, staring down at the younger man, his mind racing. He struggled to speak, to release some of the shock that was clustered in his throat. Shinji looked up at him, his eyes heavy lidded.

"Neat trick isn't it?" He said quietly, his voice an exhausted drawl. "Glad to see you're still alive."

Grayson took a knee and studied Shinji. "What the hell did you do?"

Shinji looked around, scanning the valley. "I took care of our problem. Total annihilation from the look of it."

As he spoke, Grayson noticed that the skin around his left eye had begun to split, matching his right eye, revealing just the slightest of blue from underneath. He pointed to it.

"Looks like you finally got your wings," he said.

Shinji reached up with a shaking hand and probed at the new scar. He smiled grimly. "Now I look just like you, huh?"

Grayson shook his head. "I've never seen anything like what you did. I wasn't sure you would even come back from that."

Shinji slowly laid down on his back and stared up at the moons, his eyes indifferent. "I feel like shit."

"Do you want me to connect you back to your regulator?" Grayson asked.

"That'd be swell. Thanks."

Grayson stood and slotted the lid back over the large metal box, the hidden latches hissing back into place as he did so. Next, he dragged it to Shinji's side and carefully inserted the tubing into the young man's arms, the rubber nestling back into its familiar holes. When that was finished, Shinji leaned over and adjusted a pair of knobs along the side. An instant later, the tubes flooded with blue liquid and then red, his bloodstream accepting the familiar balance.

Shinji sighed and laid back down on the dirt. "That's better."

"Are you going to be ok?"

"In a little while. I need to sleep. Do you have any water?"

"No."

"Pity. I feel absolutely wrung out."

"I called Reston. We have dusters on the way."

Shinji's eyes found Grayson's. "Are we that fucked?"

"Look around. It's not pretty."

Shinji closed his eyes and sighed. "Guess I got a little carried away. Where's Titus and Ada?"

Grayson looked back up the slope toward the wide crack in the earth. "The ground opened up and I think they went down. I haven't been able to raise them since I woke up."

Shinji placed an arm over his eyes. "Well that's not good."

Grayson swept his gaze across the ruined valley, feeling exhaustion sink deep into his bones.

"I don't know why I keep signing up for this," he muttered, feeling helpless. He hated that. He wanted to wrap his hands around the feeling and strangle it out of himself. Instead, he dragged his hands over his eyes and stared up at the sky.

"How long until the dusters come?" Shinji asked from the ground.

"I don't know, kid."

"Have you seen any more of those sharp toothed freaks?"

"No."

"Then why don't you sit down and stop wringing your hands dry. There's nothing we can do but wait."

Grayson glanced down at Shinji and felt a roll of irritation coil through his stomach. "Why don't you just shut your eyes and put yourself back together."

"My eyes *are* shut."

"Then shut your mouth," Grayson said. "Let me think."

Shinji grunted. "Always thinking. Thinking, thinking, thinking. You know, I used to *think* you were one cool customer, you know that?"

Grayson said nothing, his eyes roaming the far slope of the valley.

"Now though," Shinji continued, his voice almost dreamy, "now I realize you're just as lost as the rest of us Vagabonds. Lost, lost, lost."

"Whatever you say."

"The man with the plan," Shinji muttered, folding his hands over his chest. "Always searching for his next move. Mr. Grayson the sharpshooter.

Staring up at the sky looking for answers. I guess we really are in too deep, huh?"

Grayson continued to sweep his eyes across the horizon. "For someone so wiped out, you sure are talking a lot."

Shinji opened one eye. "Talking keeps me from fringing out."

"You're too young to fringe."

Shinji snorted. "Don't act like you know what I deal with."

"Fine. Now please shut up."

Shinji propped himself up on his elbows, his eyes suddenly dark. "You know why I joined the Vagabonds?"

"I really don't care."

"It was to get away from people like you."

"Now you're just hurting my feelings."

Shinji shook his head. "I saved all our asses and you still act like I'm just some punk kid who doesn't know anything. You're just like my parents and all of their stupid, rich, stuck up friends. It's downright pathetic. When the shit comes for them, what do they do? They turn their nose up and let someone else deal with it. Someone low. Someone despicable in their eyes. God forbid they have to get their hands dirty."

Grayson looked down at Shinji. "Take a breath, kid. I'm not your daddy and I don't think I'm any better than you. I've just been through more. Now close your eyes and take a nap. Stop making so much noise."

Shinji glared at him for a moment before lying back down.

"Bitch," he muttered, shutting his eyes again.

He's right about one thing, Grayson thought as a cool wind blustered across the destroyed earth. *We're deep in it.*

He checked his wrist reader again to see if he had any more messages and when he saw that he didn't, he resigned himself to staring at the horizon.

He didn't see them at first. Not exactly. It was a flicker of movement that crested the far bank of the valley, high up on the cliffs. Grayson froze and lasered his focus onto the flitting shadows, the moons splashing soft light across the world.

"You have got to be kidding me..." he whispered, his words rising with the wind. Shinji opened his eyes and sat up, noting the urgency in Grayson's voice.

"What is it?"

Grayson pointed to the far bank. "They're back."

Shinji followed Grayson's finger and when he saw the mass of moonlit Canines standing along the cliff, staring down at them, his eyes widened.

"More of them?" He hissed.

Grayson felt a chill snake down his spine as the horde of Canines continued to line the edge of the cliff, a wall of purple eyes and shadowed bodies. Where the hell were they coming from? Just how many of these bastards were they?

A new Canine emerged from the ranks and stood centered along the cliff. Even from this distance, Grayson could tell that it was different from the others. Its eyes were golden, twin pinpricks in the night as its mass rose to stand over eight feet tall.

"I think we got their master's attention," Grayson said quietly, his mind racing.

Shinji tried to sit up, but his body wouldn't allow it, the force of his earlier onslaught draining him of strength.

"What are we going to do?" Shinji asked, his voice a hard edge.

Before Grayson could answer, the line of Canines began to run toward them. They streamed down the cliff face like a body of water, crashing and falling only to surge and pick up speed, headed directly for them. It was a silent charge, their intent clear even from this distance. Grayson watched, his blood pressure rising, his options horribly limited.

"Grayson!" Shinji snapped, alarmed now.

Grayson's fingers drifted across the dial on his regulator, his heart thundering in his ears as the stampede shook the ground beneath his boots. There had to be at least a hundred of them, maybe more. They were only a couple hundred yards away and gaining fast, each second passing like a frozen lifetime.

"Grayson do something!" Shinji yelled, trying to sit up and get his regulator onto his back, his body refusing to cooperate.

You have to do it, Grayson thought, knowing how dangerous it would be after so much exposure to glo in such a short time. He knew his body wasn't ready for it, but he didn't know what else could stop this.

"Get out of here if you can," Grayson barked at Shinji. "And no matter what happens, find Titus and Ada."

Without waiting for a response, Grayson took off, headed straight for the wall of Canines, the golden-eyed giant glaringly visible among the horde.

When he reached a full sprint, he shut his eyes, gripped the dial of his regulator and then cranked it to its maximum setting.

The result was instant and he felt the overcharge of glo flood his system like an ice bath, coursing through his veins with all the power of a full blown hurricane. He grit his teeth against it, his head exploding with pain, and then he crouched and leapt up into the sky.

The night air whistled past him, blowing his hair back as he ascended, the world growing smaller beneath him. As he rose, he could feel a tremendous pressure building in his chest, screaming to be released, to explode, to destroy, to kill and eviscerate everything in existence.

When he reached the height of his ascension, a hundred feet above the earth, he released it.

A blinding blue light enveloped him and he opened his mouth to scream, the glo erupting out of every pore, eating him in an electric charge that sparked and burned, a mix of ice and fire.

Grayson opened his eyes, the horde directly below him, and then he fell like a comet, the wind screaming in his ears, a trail of blue flame exploding out behind him like the afterburners of a massive warship.

He aimed for the golden-eyed Canine, the world rushing toward him at a tremendous speed, his head thundering, his chest heaving. He crossed his arms over himself, shut his eyes, grit his teeth, and then exploded into the mass of charging creatures with all the force of his fury behind him.

He felt himself strike the ground, heard the roar of Canines screaming around him, sensed the ripple of earth beneath his boots as it bowed to his power.

A second after he struck earth, Grayson snapped his eyes open and whipped his arms open, a scream bellowing from his mouth. In the same instant, the valley erupted, the ground ripping open as titanic shards of blue crystals shot up into the mass of bodies like fifty foot knives, all burning hot, their edges deadly sharp.

The span of crystals, each as thick as three men, exploded in a circle outward around Grayson, roaring from the earth like neon swords. The Canines screamed as their bodies were torn apart, sliced and cut, maimed and severed, gouts of dark liquid erupting from their mangled bodies.

The circle rippled again, a split second after the first, growing a hundred feet out from Grayson's epicenter. Another barrage of fire hot crystals vomited out of the earth, bringing death, the towers of glowing blue bursting from the earth's crust with violent authority.

Grayson's world went dark, the pressure and strain from overcooking blurring his vision down to nothing. He felt himself crumple over on his side, his skull threatening to split apart. The gurgles and screams of the Canine's around him bled into his ears, making its way past his hazy mind, his dimmed world.

And then there was nothing. Nothing but silence and the coo of the wind, a soft caress across Grayson's sweat stained face.

Grayson lay there for a moment, allowing his body to reset, his fingers desperately reaching for the dial in his leg. He found it and shut it down, his body releasing a shuddering gasp as it recoiled from the violence it had just dispersed.

Grayson coughed, shivered, and then threw up where he lay. The darkness gave way some and the stink of vomit filled his head. Slowly, he opened his eyes, his mouth dry, his chest creaking as if his ribs were shattered.

At first, all he saw was the dead. Dozens and dozens of them, a field of gore and carnage that fanned out before him like a graveyard.

Got the bastards, he thought weakly, his mind threatening to break beneath the pain in his skull.

But then a figure loomed over him, a shadow falling across his exhausted body. Grayson looked up at it, his blood turning cold.

"I can't wait to see what's inside of you," Golden Eyes said, the massive Canine towering over him, its eyes glowing in the night. It was grinning, as if the death of its allies meant nothing to it.

Before Grayson could react, the massive creature reached down and ripped the regulator out of his thigh in a horrible tear of flesh and blood.

Grayson screamed, the pain overwhelming, the sky shaking above him.

A moment later, a massive fist plowed into his jaw and everything went dark.

CHAPTER 9

The world was a slate of darkness that bled through Grayson's head like a slow poison. He felt it swirling around him, filling him with a sense of weightlessness. Pain pushed in from beyond the veil, a slow trickle that grew to a dull roar. It gripped his head and squeezed his skull. His body began to fill with it, a stream that grew into a surging river, coursing through his limbs and down his spine.

Grayson opened his eyes, feeling that sense of weightlessness leave him. Rock and hard packed earth scraped across his skin in pulsing waves and a thought entered his mind.

I'm being dragged.

He closed his eyes, not sure if he had even opened them, and then tried again. He coughed and squinted as dust billowed around him. A halo of pain circled his wrists, cutting into the skin like rings of fire.

He craned his head up and saw that he was indeed being dragged across the ground. A heavy cord of thick wire criss crossed his body and bound his arms and wrists tightly across his chest. His wrist reader had been taken, along with his boot knife, leaving him isolated, weaponless, and utterly alone.

The golden-eyed Canine held the end of the cord and continued to drag him, its back turned. Grayson blinked the dirt from his eyes and saw that it was still dark, though the first bruises of dawn had begun to fill the horizon across the tops of the distant mountains.

He coughed again and the Canine stopped. It turned and stared down at Grayson, its figure huge. Grayson stared up at his captor and noted its pale skin, its long blond hair, its golden eyes. The thing smiled then, flashing its razor sharp canines. When it spoke, its voice was low and calm.

"Welcome back."

Grayson flexed in his restraints, testing them. "The hell are you doing with me?"

The Canine's smile grew, its teeth white and huge.

Grayson felt his thigh burning, a gaping pit of molten agony. He looked down at his leg and saw blood still drying across his armor.

My regulator, he thought, *oh god it's really gone.*

The Canine held something up. "Looking for this?"

Grayson's eyes snapped to it, the tubes dangling from the small metal box. Dread filled him, pooling in his stomach like a frozen lake.

"You went down pretty easily once I removed this," the Canine continued, its eyes flaring. "I wonder what secrets it holds?" Its gaze swept over Grayson's bound form. "I wonder what secrets *you* hold."

Grayson struggled to sit up, but found it useless. "Where the hell are you taking me?"

"We're going to Voratarium."

"And where is that?" Grayson asked, trying to ignore the rising fear that crawled up his throat.

"Not much further."

Grayson grit his teeth. "How about you let me go and we can stroll there together?"

The Canine sniffed, its tall figure leaning down toward him. "So you can attack me?"

"You're not as stupid as you look."

"And yet we look so similar, don't we?" the Canine said, tracing a finger over Grayson's body. "Remarkable isn't it? That two races can appear so similar and yet function so differently."

"Why don't you tell me what you are?" Grayson spat. "I would like to know exactly what it is I'll be killing."

The Canine shook Grayson's regulator again. "Are you certain you could? I'm still learning about you people, but I have been watching you rather closely since your arrival. I don't know if you're much good without this contraption."

"How about you give it back and we can find out?"

The Canine gripped Grayson's chin then and tilted his head up so their eyes met. "You and your companions—you're not like the other ones on this planet. There's something special inside of you. Something similar to what courses through my own veins."

"Is that why you look different from the others?"

"Voratarium has gifted me its life source," the Canine said, its golden eyes glowing. "Of course I'm not like the others. It's why your attack didn't affect me."

Grayson shifted in the dirt. "What's this Voratarium you keep talking about? And for the last time—where the hell are you taking me?"

The Canine fingered the cord binding Grayson. "You aren't as afraid as the others were. Why is that?"

"You mean the other people you took? The people from Typhon?"

"Were they your friends?"

"No. But I was hired to get them back."

The Canine smiled. "Oh, they're far too valuable to return. Despite your people's stupidity, they possess the capability to right what they have wronged."

"How about you cut the poetry and talk straight?"

The Canine stood, all eight feet of it pulling up with a groan. "We will have much time to talk once we arrive. But we must press on. We're nearly there."

"Nearly where!? Your ship?"

"Quiet now."

"Fuck you."

The Canine turned without warning and booted Grayson across the chin, rocking his head back and bringing forth an explosion of stars across his vision. The taste of warm copper filled his mouth and he gasped, wincing.

"Do as you're told," the Canine said calmly, stooping to pick up the end of the cord. "Once we arrive, you may ask your questions."

Grayson spat out a mouthful of blood and complied, not feeling especially eager for another kick. He winced as they continued onward, his body sliding across the rough terrain. Small rocks and pebbles pounded his muscles with a dull ache as they went, a hundred pressure points that all poked and prodded, wearing his already exhausted body down.

He didn't know how long they went, only that when they stopped he was completely spent. His mouth was full of dirt and his face was caked with dust. He was thirsty, horribly thirsty, and his head throbbed. He blinked back grit as the Canine dropped the cord once more, the sky just beginning to bleed red across the purple and black.

"Would you like to see?" Golden Eyes asked, walking back to Grayson.

Grayson opened his mouth to respond, but hacked up dust instead.

"I'm going to untie you," the Canine said, its long fingers already working the cord. "I'm sure our journey has drained you of your strength. And even if you are eager for combat, keep in mind that I have bested you once already. There's no need for a second match."

I'll be the judge of that, Grayson through bitterly, though he knew the creature was right. He felt like he could barely stand, let alone take a swing at this thing.

The Canine stripped the cord away and then pulled Grayson to his feet. Grayson buckled, his legs cramping horribly, and he fell back to the ground in a heap.

Get up. Get the hell up.

The Canine reached down and pulled Grayson to his feet once more. "At least I know you won't be running away anytime soon. Now find your legs and come with me up this crest. You should know what you'll be saving."

Grayson took an unsteady step, every ounce of him screaming to rip this thing's throat out. But he didn't, the thing's words echoing in his head.

Saving?

Shoulder to shoulder, the Canine led Grayson up a small rise, the sandstone hills sloping upward to overlook a massive valley below, backed by towering white-rock mountains.

But it wasn't the mountains that took Grayson's breath away. It was what lay before them.

Lying across the belly of the valley was an enormous black mass, it's rectangular shape perfect in its symmetry. The expanse of it was over a thousand feet long, its corners sharp and orderly. The long walls of its exterior were smooth and shimmering as if they were made of glass rock. There were no holes or divots, no windows or boarding ramps—the surfaces of its exterior modeling sheets of coal black metal, as if the entirety of it was a titanic support beam that had been expertly cut away from some colossal alien structure.

"Do you see what you people have done?" Golden Eyes asked, pointing toward the far end of the strange block. "Do you see how you have hurt us?"

Grayson followed his finger and saw that the back end of the huge mass was damaged, a portion of the eerie construct caving in and smoking. The exterior walls were crumpled inward around the hole, gaping inward to reveal something entirely different underneath.

"What am I looking at?" Grayson whispered.

Beneath the wreckage lie a twisting mass of squirming biology, a wet, pulsating tangle of slithering folds and regurgitated ooze. It looked as if there were layers of wriggling muscle hugging the blast radius, hugging the outer walls in a desperate attempt to pull the smooth exterior back together.

"What have we done to deserve that?" the Canine asked darkly, its gaze transfixed on the wound in the long construct. "What did we do to counter such an attack?"

Grayson just stared at the massive block of shining mystery before him. "I wasn't here for that part. But you must have done something to spook Typhon."

"They hailed us and as we scrambled to adjust our language, we were fired upon," Golden Eyes hissed into Grayson's ear, its breath hot. "Tell me, how does that merit such defilement?"

"Defilement?" Grayson asked. "Your ship got knocked out of the sky. It wasn't personal."

Why the hell am I trying to reason with this thing?

The Canine gripped Grayson's shoulder painfully, its voice a growl. "Do you know what that is down there? What it means to us?"

"Not a clue."

The Canine sniffed, its huge form bristling with violent energy. "You're a cowardly race. Our attempts to decipher and respond to your language was enough to send you all scurrying into a frenzy. The unfamiliar terrifies you and your first reaction was to lash out—because if something is alien to your common understanding, then it must be dangerous."

"You're not exactly proving them wrong," Grayson said quietly, knowing he should just shut up.

The Canine turned on him. "You have forced us to mend the damage you doled out upon us. We didn't start this. You did. And now your people are being held accountable. They have become our tools to mend this... *disaster.*" Golden Eyes leaned down and brought his face inches from Graysons.

"You have done the worst and now you will *all* suffer for it."

As the Canine pulled away, Grayson watched as the sun began to blossom over the distant mountains, its brilliant yellow warmth spilling down across the glimmering white slopes. He felt exhaustion sweep through him in a torrent, and in that moment, all he wanted to do was to just lay down and never get back up. His eyes traveled down the mountains and then back across the massive block of darkness that sat smouldering across the sand and redstone plains.

"What are you doing to them?" Grayson asked wearily, fearing the answer.

The Canine shoved Grayson forward, beginning the final stretch toward the otherworldly construct below. When it responded, its voice was laced with hatred.

"We're draining them of their lifeforce to replace what they took from Voratarium."

Grayson's boots kicked down the slope, Golden Eyes at his back. "Is that what you're going to do to me? Drain me of my lifeforce?"

Golden Eyes smiled grimly. "Not before we find out exactly what's inside of you."

CHAPTER 10

Shinji moved away from the wall of rock he had dragged himself behind. His regulator scraped across the sandstone, showering dirt down into his hair. He scanned the scorched valley before him, his eyes sweeping across the dead.

Grayson, he thought, *where the hell did that thing take you?*

When Grayson had overcooked, Shinji had crawled away from the point of impact and hidden himself behind a flat plot of rock that jutted from the valley wall. He had seen Grayson ascend and then drop like a ball of overpressurized electricity, exploding and killing nearly everything when he fell from the sky.

Nearly everything.

He had seen the massive Canine amid the carnage, had seen the way it had swatted away Grayson's attack as if it were nothing. He knew it was going to kill or take Grayson away and he knew there was nothing he could do to stop it. Not in the state he was in. And so he had watched helplessly as the huge creature clubbed Grayson, bound him, and then dragged him away.

"Just hold on, you old bastard," Shinji muttered. Wincing, he stood, feeling a fist of pain slam into his head and bleed into his aching muscles. He was dehydrated, worn down, and exhausted. He hadn't overcooked in a couple months and he was reminded why he didn't rely on it to solve all of his conflicts.

Grayson said dusters were coming. But when? And how long has it been since he was taken?

He looked to the sky and saw the sun, a halved eye of burning orange that peered at him over the horizon. The darkness was starting to retreat, giving way to the growing heat and warming light.

Slowly, he walked toward the field of death before him, a hundred dead Canines in all manner of mutilation. Grayson's attack had been merciless and brutal, leaving the dry earth soaked in blood, body parts, and gore. Shinji walked between the dead, stared down at them, feeling his strength beginning to return. Seeing the carnage helped. It gave him something to hate, something to harden against. He had never been on a job like this one, hadn't ever faced a foe so strong or alien to him.

And he welcomed it.

He looked around the empty stretch of desert and his thoughts fell back to his companions.

Ada. Titus. Where the hell had they gone? Grayson said they had fallen into the earth, but Shinji feared the worst.

It's their own fault, he thought, kicking at a severed torso. *They should have been smarter. They knew what I was about to do. What I needed to do.*

And yet, a trickle of guilt heated his spine.

Shinji turned away from the dead and walked back toward where Grayson had found him. His regulator felt heavy across his back and he checked the tubes in his arms, making sure they were secure. He could feel the pulse of glo inside of him and he reached up to trace the new scar that had formed beneath his eye, mirroring the other.

Full blown freak now. Guess the day had to come eventually.

He walked up a small incline and crested a hill, staring back in the direction of Typhon. He hadn't been expecting to see anything and so he was surprised to see a pair of dust clouds headed his way.

I guess Reston wasted no time.

Shinji climbed another foothill and stood atop it, waving his arms. At first he thought they weren't going to see him, their path tracing west of his position. But then one of the dusters broke off and the other followed.

Ten minutes later, they came to a stop in front of him. Four Orbital Clerks emerged from the two dusters, their copper face shields reflecting the rising sun.

"Where are the others?" One of them asked.

"Just me," Shinji said, striding toward the vehicles.

"Did you find our people?" Another asked. "What the hell happened out here?"

Shinji pushed past them and climbed into one of the dusters. "We have to get back to Typhon."

The Orbital Clerks looked at each other. "Why? We've brought you supplies, weapons, and rations. Shouldn't you continue with the job? With what we're paying you to do?"

Shinji eyed them, the blue glow of his scars flaring. "I plan to. But first I need something."

As they roared back to Typhon, Shinji tightened his hands into fists, his teeth grinding together.

Hold on, Grayson.

CHAPTER 11

Grayson stood before the expansive construct, its size dwarfing him and his captor. They had traveled down into the valley in silence, each step bringing a deeper sense of dread as the colossal craft grew closer. Grayson's leg burned, the gash from his removed regulator scabbing over, the exposed flesh filled with grit and dirt. He tried to ignore the pain, tried not to think about the infection that was surely taking root.

On approach, a host of Canines and Tusks had emerged from the side of the construct, a stream of ten that began to make their way across the sandy earth, away from Grayson, toward Typhon. When they exited the construct, it was as if they were pulling themselves from a pool of water, the black surface rippling slightly to allow their bodies to pass through with ease. Now, Grayson watched as they vanished over a hill, picking up speed as they went.

Gone to get more people, no doubt.

"How many are you?" Grayson asked quietly as his eyes traveled south, down the length of the craft, its smooth walls absorbing the sun.

Golden Eyes shoved Grayson from behind, "Too many for you to fight. And more every hour, at that."

How the hell am I going to get away from this?

They stopped at the foot of the massive craft, its walls towering high overhead, its width running left to right at an impossible scope. Grayson studied the surface once more, the smooth ebony walls perfect in their glassy darkness.

Golden Eyes stepped around him and pressed his hand to the surface, as if probing for something. A moment later, he pushed Grayson ahead, straight into the side of the construct.

For a second, Grayson thought he was going to break his nose, the flat surface rushing toward his face. But instead, his skin cooled as he was enveloped, sucked inward to vanish from the outside world, accepted into whatever lay beyond.

Here we go, he thought with some panic.

Before he could adjust to his new setting, Golden Eyes was at his side, dragging him forward. Grayson stumbled as the world around him darkened, the interior hidden from the blaze of the sun.

"Keep moving," Golden Eyes growled.

Grayson kept pace, his eyes going wide as they entered the belly of the craft. It was unlike anything he had ever seen before. The walls and floor were a blend of metal and something biological, the two tangling and sliding over the other in a mix of dark purple and dull gray. It looked as if some kind of infected muscular tissue was growing over the long sheets of metal, the colors warping and shining as if wet.

They were traveling down an immense hallway, the ceiling high overhead, the passage lit by some unknown source, the length of it glowing the same purple color as the strange flesh that patched the walls. As they walked, they passed a dozen connecting hallways, each one snaking off the main corridor.

"Don't stop," Golden Eyes said, prodding Grayson in the back. They rounded a bend and entered a massive room, the expanse of it broadening out all around them, the ceiling thirty feet overhead.

As they entered it, Grayson felt his throat tighten, his eyes widen.

Hanging from the ceiling were countless Canines. They appeared dead, or perhaps asleep, their limbs hanging limp at their sides. A cord of flesh ran from the ceiling down into the back of their necks like some kind of umbilical cord. Grayson could see some kind of dark liquid pulsing through the tube into the Canine's bodies. He craned his head back and took it all in, his stomach twisting, the countless Canines gently hanging twenty feet above his head like some kind of gallows.

"Voratarium continues to breed new life, even now," Golden Eyes said almost proudly, allowing Grayson to take in the sight. "Even when it is suffering, it continues on."

Grayson continued to stare up at the haunted vista. "Is that what this ship is? Some kind of living vessel?"

"This place is merely one of its organs," Golden Eyes said, now pushing Grayson forward again. "A connection to us."

Grayson stumbled forward, his leg burning, as they headed toward another long hallway. "How many rooms are there like this?"

"Too many to count."

"Is this how you were born? Dangling from the ceiling?"

"It is how we are all born."

"But you're different from the others. Why?"

"I proved myself to Voratarium and I was gifted with its life force, chosen as one of his pilots. It is what we all aspire to. What we live for. We are grown so that we may give back. And with that comes reward."

They entered the hallway and passed a group of Tusks that slithered and crawled along the walls and ceiling, giving Golden Eyes a wide berth. Their strange metal heads chirped and buzzed with static at the sight of Grayson, their long, fleshy sacks tightening.

They entered another room a moment later, a mirror image of the one they had just come from. But below the hanging mass of Canines above, in the center of the room, was a large mound of pulsing flesh. It rose like a small mountain, its surface a bruised purple. Dark veins spider webbed across the throbbing abnormality, and the mass seemed to shiver and shift slightly, like it was alive.

Encased in the walls, as if trying to escape, were a host of Tusks. Their bodies were small and curled into themselves like they were asleep, their long arms wrapped around their flesh sacks. To Grayson, it looked like a pile of purple jelly that imprisoned the small creatures.

"Is this some kind of womb?" Grayson asked as they skirted it, his eyes drawn to the motionless figures inside.

"We all come from somewhere," Golden Eyes said. "Is this a surprise to you?"

"Against all odds."

They continued deeper into the labyrinth. They passed through seven or eight more of the grow rooms, wound their way down a maze of hallways, skirted around a steady stream of Tusks and Canines as they slithered and strode through the construct, until finally Grayson walked into a new area.

The room was even larger than the others and rounded, its walls forming a dome overhead. In the center of the room was a large pool of dark water. To Grayson, it looked more like tar, despite the gentle ripples that unfolded from the center. Circling the pool, was a host of Canines, all on their knees, watching as something took place.

A golden eyed Canine, who looked exactly like Grayson's captor, was gently lowering another one of its kind into the murky water. It was careful not to touch the surface itself, but instead it carefully guided the unmoving body beneath the surface where it sank out of sight.

"What is this?" Grayson asked as they passed along the outskirts of the encircled Canines.

"Our companion is being returned to Voratarium, guided by the Traveler's Water," Golden Eyes said. "It has ended its cycle and it goes now to hang in the Floating World."

"The Floating World—is that your home?"

"It is where Voratarium awaits our return. It is the heart of our species."

"Why does that other Canine look just like you?"

"Because it was gifted with life force."

Grayson was led out of the room and down another hallway, the odd burial now at his back. He looked at Golden Eyes, feeling lost.

"Why are you answering all of my questions?"

Golden Eyes looked at him, its face smoothing out. "Because I hope you will return the courtesy."

"What do you mean?"

"Your veins are filled with power. Power that I think could help restore this vessel and prolong the life of our home."

"I'm not going to help you."

Golden Eyes smiled slightly. "I'm sure your friends in Typhon thought the same thing before we took them away to rebuild this place. And yet here they are."

As the words fell from his mouth, they entered another area, this one darker than the others, the light dim and full of shadow. Grayson slowed as they entered, the air thickening, warming.

When his eyes adjusted to the new light, he felt the pit of his stomach fall away. He craned his head back and stared at the ceiling, a repulsed horror surging up his throat.

The captured residents of Typhon hung overhead, naked and out-stretched, suspended in the air as if frozen in a free fall. Cords of flesh curled down from the ceiling, holding them in place, the purple muscle wrapped around wrists and ankles, pulling the victims outward in a spread eagle formation. Large, living tubes had been inserted into each of their mouths and rectums, forcing the captive's mouths and legs apart to ac-cept the vibrating member. Grayson could see the pulsating tubes bulging from inside their throats, tearing into their rectums, a steady drip of blood and drool falling from above in a steady *plink-plink-plink.*

There were dozens of them, spread out overhead like the mapping of the cosmos, each one very much alive. Their eyes were closed, but the sound of low moaning echoed across the wide room.

"What the hell have you done to them?" Grayson whispered, his voice a low croak. His heart hammered in his chest and he felt a sickness clutch his stomach.

"They're feeding this place," Golden Eyes hissed.

Suddenly, pain exploded across the back of Grayson's head and he sank to his knees, letting out a grunt of shock as he did so. Before he could shake the stars from his eyes, Golden Eyes struck again, this time flattening Grayson to his stomach. The room swam in and out of focus as he struggled to keep consciousness, the back of his skull throbbing from where he had been struck. He let out a growl as he was lifted by his graying hair, his back arching. Golden Eyes leaned down and buried his teeth into Grayson's shoulder, the violent action catching him off guard. He cried out as blood squirted from the pierced flesh and as Golden Eyes compressed his jaw, Grayson felt something warm enter his bloodstream through the wound.

Without warning, Golden Eyes released him with a gasp, wiping its mouth with a disgusted grimace. Grayson fell back to the ground, his shoulder alive with searing pain. He grit his teeth, forced his vision to steady, and tried to stand, but was knocked back down and then grabbed and dragged across the room. All facades of a truce vanished from Golden Eyes' features and Grayson realized that it had all been tactfully fabricated to get him down here, to this room, with as little effort as possible.

"Get off of me," Grayson growled, but lacked the strength to resist, his arms weakly flailing, his fingers digging into the fleshy metal ground for purchase that did not hold. He tried to roll away, but Golden Eye's grip was like an iron clamp around his ankle, pulling him across the room in long, powerful strides. The canopy of naked bodies spun overhead, dancing across Grayson's vision like some kind of sick dream.

Golden Eyes came to an abrupt stop and stooped to throw open a latched door in the floor. Without pause, he pulled Grayson close and then shoved him down into a hole. Grayson went sprawling three feet down and spilled out across the low space with a thud, his hands squishing and sliding across the terrible, wet ground. He rolled onto his back and was about to spring for Golden Eyes, but the hatch slammed down overhead, banging loudly as it did so. Grayson cursed and stared up at the grated slats of metal as Golden Eyes locked it. It stared down at Grayson, its face blank.

"I'll come visit you soon. We have much to reveal, you and I."

And then he was gone, leaving Grayson in the dim light and the dark hole. Blood and drool oozed in from the grate overhead and he grimaced as it splattered onto his shoulders and dripped into his hair. He scooted away from the grate, into one of the corners of the small hole and heard something slither overhead. He glanced up and saw a Tusk had replaced Golden Eyes, its long teeth jutting from its eerie boxed head. It stared down at him with an eyeless gaze, as if guarding the room.

I'm really in the shit now, Grayson thought, wiping his face clean. He scanned the small enclosure and saw a pair of shadows huddled in the gloom across the space, on the opposite side of the grate. At first he thought they were dead bodies, but then they moved.

And then they spoke.

"Grayson?"

One of the forms crawled forward and when the faint light that filtered in through the grate lit the man's face, Grayson felt a surge of shock.

"Titus?"

The big man let out a sigh of relief, the scars beneath his eyes glowing the faintest of blue. "Aren't you a sight for sore eyes. They got you too, huh?"

"Yeah, not long after I lost you."

The second figure crawled forward next to Titus and Grayson felt relief course through him. "Ada? You too?"

Ada nodded. "We fell into some kind of cave system, but they found us."

"What the hell happened?" Titus whispered, casting a look up toward the Tusk standing guard.

Grayson shook his head. "More of them came after the earth opened up and I lost you. I overcooked and took out most of them, but that damn golden eyed bastard didn't seem to be affected. He clocked me pretty good, ripped out my regulator, and dragged me here."

Titus tapped an angry gash in his thigh. "They got mine too."

"Where's Shinji?" Ada asked. "Is he with you?"

"I found him," Grayson said quietly. "I don't know what happened to him after I overcooked, but he wasn't captured when I was taken."

"Do you think he'll come for us?"

"I don't know what he could possibly do. This place...it's huge. And there seems to be no end to the Canines and Tusks. He would have to bring firepower beyond what we have. And even then..." he trailed off, feeling frustrated and helpless. He looked at Titus. "How are you holding up? What the hell are they doing to these people here?"

Titus lowered his voice. "This place is a nightmare, man. Just listening to those poor people above us makes me want to scream."

"They said something about feeding this place...?"

Ada nodded, looking sick. "We overheard a couple of them. The ones that were speaking our language. It sounds like they're sucking the blood out of their bodies and this...place...is using it to mend itself."

Grayson felt his stomach roll. "I'm assuming that's what's going to happen to us, sooner or later."

Titus looked up at the grate. "They seem particularly interested in you and me, Gray. They know we're different, that we got something in our blood that's not like the rest. They want it. Especially those golden eyed Canines. The elite ones. The pilots."

"The one who took me said they were the ones who had received Voratarium's life force. Like they're at the final stage of their evolution or something."

Ada frowned, her face streaked with dirt and grime. "We kept hearing them talk about this Voratarium as well. I think this place is part of that—some kind of link to it."

Grayson nodded. "Yeah, they said it was one of its organs."

Titus ran his hands across the top of his stubbled head. "This is some next level psycho shit. And without my regulator, we're just stuck in it. I don't like it. Not one bit. I mean, we got to get out of here. We got to get those poor people *out* of here."

"There's too many of them," Ada said, her voice a tired exhale. "Even if we could get out of this hole there's no way we could make it to an exit."

"I may not have my regulator," Titus said. "But I can still crack a couple skulls if we need to."

"We'd be overrun," Grayson said, trying to recall his journey through the ship.

"Well there's got to be some way to even the odds," Titus said stubbornly. "I can't just sit here and wait to die. We gotta try *something*."

Grayson's eyes narrowed. "On the way here, we passed through this room that had some kind of...hole in it that was filled with black sludge. It looked like they were conducting some kind of burial there. They said it was a place where they were returned to Voratarium, to a place called the Floating World."

Ada grunted. "Yeah, we passed through that room too. What are you thinking?"

"Well, this Voratarium thing—it seems like everything revolves around it. If we can find it and destroy or kill it-"

"I like where this is going," Titus said, nodding. "These freaks seem to worship it. I think there's some kind of give and take, some kind of exchange that they rely on."

Grayson tapped his leg, thinking. "They take life from us and give it to this Voratarium and in turn, it grants the elite some kind of power. I don't know if they become immortal or just untouchable, but there's a yin and yang to it."

"And the dead who aren't given the lifeforce are returned to a place called the Floating World," Ada finished. "And yet none of this gets me any closer to finding my sister Marah or getting these people out of here."

Titus touched her shoulder. "If we kill whatever it is that's feeding off these people, maybe they'll be released and we can get them out of here. Your sister has to be here somewhere."

At the mention of family, Grayson went silent, his thoughts unexpectedly pulling him to his daughter Claire. He felt impossibly far away from her and the idea that he might never see her again sent a worm of unease slithering through his lower stomach. She didn't even know where he was.

"We have to get the fuck out of here," Grayson whispered.

CHAPTER 12

Shinji could see Typhon now, the great city rising to rest on top of the colossal towers of rock, balanced upon the fingertips of the planet. The sun splashed its blinding yellow rays across the sea of sand before them, the pair of dusters humming toward their destination. The Orbital Clerk who rode with Shinji had peppered him with questions, but the younger man had ignored him. He was thinking about Grayson and Titus, of Ada and her sister. Of all the people who had been taken by the Canines and Tusks.

He didn't really care about the captured residents of Typhon, the ones he had been hired to rescue. He would never admit it to his contractor Reston, but had no interest in their suffering. They were strangers to him. Numbers on a chart. But Grayson and Titus, even Ada...they were different; they were relying on him, they had faith in him, trusted him to stand tall.

And he refused to let them down, to become someone who abandoned his duty and passed the torch because things had gotten too hard. He had been exposed to enough of those people growing up, surrounding his wealthy parents and their disgusting, wasteful, excessive lifestyles. He wasn't like them, wouldn't allow himself to become someone who shrank away the moment something became too difficult to overcome—he wouldn't shrivel into his power because it was more convenient.

He had been challenged by the Canines, had met them in combat, and they had overwhelmed him, despite their massive losses. They had bested him by sheer numbers and taken his companions.

And that drove him absolutey red with anger.

"Go faster," Shinji ordered, his thoughts constricting in a ball of fury.

"I'm going as fast as I can," the Orbital Clerk responded from the driver's seat. "I still don't know why-"

"Shut up," Shinji snapped, returning his eyes to the rolling dunes and sun bleached hills. He replayed Grayon's descent over and over again, the carnage he had inflicted on the second wave of creatures.

How did that one survive? He thought, his mind's eye bringing forth the image of the tall, golden eyed Canine. *And what the hell did it do with Grayson?*

He curled his hands into fists, his regulator creaking in the tight space. There was something out there that could withstand the devastating power of glo. Something that could beat down a fucking *Vagabond*.

He hadn't been on this planet long, but his hatred for the strange creatures had grown fast and burned bright. Absentmindedly, his fingers found the bite marks on his leg, the memory rising like a blazing sun.

They hurt me. Almost made me kill myself.

He grit his teeth.

Nothing should be able to hurt me.

"Sir?"

Shinji was pulled from his thoughts as he looked over at the Orbital Clerk who pointed out into the desert, at a cloud of dust that trailed toward Typhon.

Shinji squinted and then his mouth formed a snarl. "It's more of them. They're headed right for the city. Looks like four or five Tusks, if I had to guess."

"Are you sure?"

"They're burrowing just beneath the sand. We saw them travel like that before. I bet they have a couple Canines with them too."

"Are they going to attack the city?"

"They're probably going to wait until dark and then slither in to take a couple more of your people."

The Orbital Clerk tightened his grip on the wheel. "What do you want to do?"

"You said you brought guns with you right?"

"In the case behind you."

"Then floor it," Shinji ordered. "And you point this thing right at them."

He reached around the seat and unsnapped the large case as the Orbital Clerk did as he was told, thumbing his wrist reader to notify the tailing duster what the plan was.

Shinji pulled an auto-rifle from the case and inspected it. It had an eighteen inch rapid cooling steel barrel with a two hundred and twelve round clip. The trigger was an electronic duel grip that sported a second release for the pressurized shrapnel grenade that was loaded into the second barrel, just below the primary.

This oughta piss them off.

For good measure, he plucked a twelve inch knife from the case as well and strapped it to his bicep. Turning back to the windshield, he watched as they roared toward the dust cloud, his blood pressure building.

He reached behind him and clicked the dial on his regulator a couple notches.

"Get right up alongside them," Shinji said darkly, feeling his body tighten and harden as the glo did its work. "And when I jump out, just stay out of my way."

The Orbital Clerk nodded, turning the wheel on an intercept course. Shinji's knuckles popped as they raced closer to the churning trail of sand, his head burning with the pulse of glo.

Fuck I hate these things.

And then they were on them, the duster jerking to course correct, the submerged Tusks slithering right outside Shinji's window.

"Don't slow down," Shinji barked, positioning himself. A moment later, he retracted the window, stuck the barrel of the auto-rifle out, and emptied half his clip into the gurgling sand, turning the dust to mud as blood exploded from the trail of creatures.

Quickly, he discarded the half empty clip and slammed another one into the receiver, watching as four more Tusks emerged from the sand in an explosion of fury. The two he had shot burst from the surface, their bodies shredded and oozing dark liquid. They let out a screech of electronic noise from their strange heads, a noise that sounded like agony. Then they fell over, dead, their flesh torn to bits.

The remaining four quickly snaked away from the dusters, only to whiplash back once they were a safe distance away. Their thick tail ends unfolded, the quadrants of flesh peeling back to spit out their Canine passengers.

Shinji gripped the door handle as he stared down the eight combatants as they began to charge the dusters. Without pause, Shinji shoved the door open, the hot wind blasting across his face, and dove out.

He landed on his stomach, sliding in the sand, and brought the auto-rifle up in one smooth motion. His attackers were twenty yards away when he pulled the secondary trigger, firing the shrapnel grenade straight at the lead Tusk's face. It made contact with a meaty thump of power, the detonation blasting apart the Tusk and the two Canines next to it, their bodies reduced to pulpy chunks that fell to the sand in a wet shower.

At ten yards away, his foes still at a full sprint, he fired the auto-rifle. He focused on the three remaining Tusks and he managed to down two of them before the rest fell upon him. The three Canines lunged for his throat as he rolled away and got to his feet, the last Tusk slamming its massive teeth down into the sand where he had just been lying.

Shinji back pedaled, firing from the hip, and blew the top half of a Canine's face away before he was tackled by the remaining two. He felt their weight take him to the ground, their snarling, biting faces snapping at his throat, their claws sparking his combat armor. One of them gripped Shinji by the hair and slammed his head into the ground, while the other swiped a handful of sand into his eyes, blinding him.

Coughing, Shinji bucked, his glo-fueled muscles contracting and then expanding. He shoved the pair of Canine's away, his eyes burning from the grit, and he fired blindly at them. One of them screamed as its chest was embedded with scorching lead, bringing forth a splash of wet darkness as it tumbled to the ground.

Shinji wiped his eyes clean a second before a Tusk slammed into him, using its boxed head like a battering ram, taking Shinji full in the chest. Even with the glo coursing through his veins, Shinji grunted and the breath was knocked from his lungs as he flew backwards, his gun flying from his grip. He landed hard on his back and his head whipped violently, bringing stars as his skull connected with a stray rock.

In a daze, he saw a shadow soar toward him. Without thought, he snatched the knife strapped to his arm and stabbed upwards as the shadow fell, the remaining Canine gasping as the blade was buried into its stomach. It collapsed mid-leap into Shinji, its guts punctured, its mouth vomiting a torrent of dark blood into Shinji's face.

Snarling, Shinji kicked up and flipped the gurgling corpse over him, yanking his knife free as he did so. He wiped blood from his face, gasping, head aching.

The last Tusk slammed into him without warning, racing at him from the side, and used its fleshy back end to smash Shinji over onto his side, his bones creaking from the impact. His regulator shuddered in protest as he was plastered to the ground once more, and Shinji knew he would have been dead if not for the glo in his system.

The Tusk rose over him, its long, bony arms reaching for Shinji's eyes, its metallic head screeching and chirping.

Knowing he had only a second, Shinji grabbed one of its clawing arms and jerked it to the side, and then sat up, jamming the blade into the Tusk's armpit. Gritting his teeth, he ripped the blade diagonally across the creature's body, opening the monster up in a torrent of gore. The Tusk howled and wavered, its organs spilling from its body in wet clumps, and then it went down, silent forever.

Shinji gasped and took a long breath. Black blood dripped from his hair and streaked down his chest. Sweat coated his neck and his armor felt like a tomb. Slowly, he reached back and reset his regulator, allowing his body a moment to readjust. His eyes scanned the bloody sand before him, traveling across the multitude of corpses.

Bastards.

The pair of dusters were suddenly at his side, their engines screeching to a halt as a dust cloud billowed around them. The doors opened and the Orbital Clerks stared at Shinji from inside, their faces hidden behind their mirrored face shields.

"You ok, sir?" One of them asked.

Shinji wiped his face clean of grime and climbed inside.

"Get me back to Typhon. I'm not done with these things yet."

CHAPTER 13

G rayson clutched his temples, his teeth practically sparking together as pain blasted through his skull. It felt as if a pillar of fire was boring through his brain, searing the pink matter to charred bits. Stars danced behind his eyelids and his body cramped so badly he thought his bones would crack.

"Easy, pal, easy, it'll pass," Titus whispered, his voice laced with concern, a large hand stroking his friend's back. Grayson could barely hear him behind the agony, his entire world fracturing beneath the strain in his head, the ache in his muscle.

"What's happening to him?" Ada's worried voice called from the other side of the enclosed hole.

"He's fringing," Titus responded, his eyebrows knit together. "Happens to our kind the older we get. Shit, breathe man, *breathe*."

Grayson buckled beneath the attack, begging the pain to leave. He knew this would come again, the attack appearing like a ghost to terrorize his glo-strained body.

Leave me alone, he begged, shuddering, feeling as if his head were being compressed. *Let me be until I can escape this damned place.*

He heard Ada scoot closer, her voice hushed. "Is he going to be ok? Is he dying?"

"His body is reacting to the glo," Titus said, distracted, his hand never leaving Grayson's back. "It's taking its seven pounds."

Grayson gasped and his eyes snapped open, tears rolling down his cheeks. Oxygen rushed his lungs and he let out a shaking gasp. He felt his body relax then, the grip lessening.

"I'm ok," he said hoarsely. "It's gone I think."

Titus eyed him. "You sure?"

"Yeah. Nearly split my head in two, though."

Titus patted Grayson on the shoulder. "We'll get you some help once we're out of here, man." It was a lie that neither of them felt needed to be acknowledged.

"We need to get our regulators back," Grayson said, still recovering. "My levels are all over the place, I can feel it."

"And you overcooked earlier."

"Yeah, that didn't help," Grayson said quietly, placing a cautious hand to his forehead. "Christ, that one was bad." He looked at Titus. "How're you doing without yours?"

"My regulator?"

"Yeah."

"Awful," Titus grimaced. "Feels like someone's punching my brain every time my heart beats."

Ada looked at the two men, their scars softly illuminating the small space in a pulse of blue light. "How long do you think we've been in here now?"

Titus shook his head. "I dunno. Couple hours at least." He looked up at the frozen Tusk that stood guard above the grate. "Looks like our friend hasn't gotten bored of his post yet either."

A strand of slime dripped down from the grated hatch and landed on Ada's shoulder. She grimaced, looking distressed, and wiped it away quickly. The moans from the people suspended from the ceiling continued to beat down on them, a relentless, miserable soundtrack to the dim prison. The longer they were down here, the more it started to affect them, press in on them, worm its way into their minds.

Grayson looked down at his shaking hands. "We have got to get them out of here."

He said it quietly. He didn't have a plan to back up his declaration, but simply acknowledging the suffering above felt better than trying to block it out. It felt more human. Hopeful.

It made the pit feel less like a grave.

"Something's coming," Titus said.

They all looked toward the grate to see four purple eyed Canines, along with two golden ones, staring down at them. Grayson's heart skipped a beat, their sudden presence seeming to materialize out of thin air.

The purples pulled the grate open and then stood back as the two golds squatted down and pointed to Ada.

"Come with us," one of them said, its face blank of expression.

Titus got between them. "I don't think so."

The second gold pointed past Titus, at Ada. "You are not like these other two."

Ada spat at them from behind Titus's shoulder. "I'm not going anywhere with you."

Grayson crawled to his feet, his pulse quickening. "What do you want with her?"

"That's none of your concern."

"I'd say it is."

The two golds stood and nodded to the four purples. "Retrieve her."

Titus balled his hands into fists, readying himself as the four purples made to come down. But before he had the chance to act, the Tusk slithered into view, its large, curved teeth clacking against the floor. It leaned its boxed head down into the hole and emitted a sharp, chirping frequency of static, holding the wavering note as it did so.

Grayson's eyes bulged the second it happened, his head igniting in a fresh torrent of pain. Titus seemed to suffer the same reaction, his mouth tearing open in a howl, his hands clutching his shoulder, the blast of noise bringing him to his knees.

Grayson felt his eyes watering and suddenly the bite he had received from the golden canine burst to life as if someone had poured acid into the wound, draining it down into his veins to inflame his entire system. He grabbed at the puncture wound, his throat pulsing in a scream, his body quivering. As the static garble continued, he began to feel the inexplicable urge to stop breathing. It came as an impulse, a desperate, primal reaction to the noise blasting overhead. His shoulder felt as if it were being branded by a white hot iron, and the desire, the need to end it all became an overwhelming roar in his head. He could feel his hands going to his face, his thumbs reaching for his eyes. He wanted to plunge them into the soft jelly, reach all the way back and crush that terrible, screaming urge in the back of his mind. He knew it made no sense, knew it was only pain, but the feeling encompassed him like blazing inferno.

He felt his thumbs meet his eyes and a second before he sank them deep into the sockets, the static frequency stopped.

Grayson gasped, falling to the ground, and banged his chin, his tongue caught between his teeth. Blood filled his mouth as the echo of the onslaught faded from the corners of his head, retreating, leaving a shocked hole where it had been a moment before. Grayson blinked, the world returning, and realized that Ada was screaming.

In a daze, he looked up to see the four purple eyed Canines hauling her out of the pit. She thrashed and spat, kicked and punched, but it was no use. Titus reached out to her, his face twisted in rage and pain, his voice an agonized groan.

"No! Leave her ALONE!"

The golden Canines just watched as the lesser creatures began to tear the clothes from Ada's body. They did it without emotion, a practiced ceremony that held no interest to them. Grayson felt horror pool in his guts as one of them slammed a fist into Ada's jaw, knocking her to the ground. The other three joined in the beating a moment later, pounding the fight out of her with brutal efficiency. Her grunts of rage turned into whimpers of panic as four pairs of fists thudded into her exposed, naked body.

"Stop it!" Grayson cried weakly, his body feeling as if it had been electrocuted. He tried to get to his feet, to stop what was happening, but his legs were jelly and he simply crumpled beneath the effort.

Slowly, a pair of fleshy tendrils extended down from the ceiling, each one hollowed and puckering, expanding, contracting, almost breathing as they reached for Ada's bloody form. The Canines hoisted her up into a standing position and spread her legs with a kick. The first tube slithered around her thigh, searching for its entry point. Ada shrieked weakly, realizing what was happening, but a blow to the stomach knocked the howl from her throat, doubling her over.

The wet tube slithered into her rectum a moment later, burying itself deep inside her, crawling up her insides, forcing her apart. Ada, still held, stood bolt upright, her mouth creaking open in a scream. But before she could, the second tube found her and crammed itself down her throat, causing her esophagus to expand, swollen around the intrusion.

"Jesus Christ let her go! STOP!" Titus shrieked, his eyes wide and brimming with terror. He tried to stand, to throw himself toward the lip of the floor above, but found that he couldn't. He slammed down next to Grayson, snarling, whimpering, foaming.

The tendrils, now fully inserted, pulled Ada up toward the ceiling, toward the rest of the trapped souls of Typhon. Four more of the flesh tubes blossomed from the web of purple muscle above and slithered around Ada's ankles and wrists, keeping her suspended so that the inserted members could function without obstruction.

Titus thrashed and pounded on the floor, lost in a horrified rage. Grayson tried to stand, to heave himself upward, but the lasting effect of the Tusk's screech still echoed in his mind, its hold over him heightened without the blast of glo through his bloodstream.

The two golden Canines pointed to the pair of thrashing men. "Bring them to the chamber. First the big one, then the other." One of them turned to the Tusk and spoke to it in another language, something lost and forgein to Grayson's ears, but he could guess what the command was.

If they struggle, blast them again.

The four purples leapt down into the pit and hauled Titus up. He managed to headbutt one, but the effort seemed to drain him of the final ebb of strength he possessed, his body slumping as he was dragged up and out of sight. The Tusk hovered over him, its metal head squawking its strange static, as if it were talking to the Canines.

Grayson came next, and despite his overwhelming urge to murder the things, he found that he was completely expended. He cursed the Canines as they came back for him a moment later, dragging him up and out of the hole.

The wail of the suspended humans seemed to fall over Grayson like a physical weight as he was pulled up and out of the room. He knew one of those voices now belonged to Ada and the thought nearly shattered his resolve. His chest heaved and his head thundered as the Canines pulled him along, his feet dragged behind him. Titus cursed their captors, his weakened voice laced with a defiance that wasn't matched by his drained strength. Together, they were taken from the room and into a hallway, then marched directly across into an adjoining chamber. As they entered it, the pit of Grayson's stomach fell away.

Nothing good happens in this place, he thought miserably as his eyes adjusted to the dim purple light.

A platform rose waist high in the center of the room, like a hospital bed if it were fabricated from muscle and mucus. Off to the side, on the other side of the room, was some kind of metallic tray that slid out of the wall. When Grayson glanced at it, his dread solidified. Sharp, deadly instruments lie in waiting, each one looking more grisly than the last.

But a glimmer of hope wavered inside of him as well when he saw his regulator, along with Titus's, mixed in with the tools.

The two golden Canines instructed Titus up onto the raised platform, their large size and seemingly infinite strength used to push the big man into place, onto his back. Straps came next, large clamps that clacked loudly over Titus's wrists, throat, and knees, holding him down.

The Tusk entered the room last, and with a nod from the golden eyes, it let out a low volume screech that brought Grayson quivering into himself, his eyes watering, muscles draining. The voice returned, a malicious whisper that urged him to cut off his own oxygen supply.

Gasping, the sensation left as soon as it came, leaving Grayson drooling and panting on his hands and knees, his vision dancing around a swarm of stars.

"You will assist us," one of the golden eyes said as the four purples stepped back against the wall to observe.

Grayson blinked back his daze and looked up at the lanky figure. "I'm not doing a damn thing for you."

The second golden Canine circled the table where Titus moaned, his eyes fluttering. "You will if you want him to survive."

Grayson sucked in an unsteady breath, wiping his mouth. "The hell are you talking about?"

"We are going to open your friend up and inspect the power he has within him. You will assist us in this task."

Grayson met Titus's eyes as he lay across the platform. He took a moment before answering.

"If you cut him open, you'll release his power and kill everyone in this place," Grayson lied.

The first golden Canine shook its head. "I don't think so. That doesn't appear to be how you function." It went over to the table of tools and plucked Titus's regulator from the pile. "Not without this to aid him. But your attempt at deception is noted and it is not appreciated."

"I'm not helping you hurt him," Grayson spat as the Tusk slithered over to his side, swaying over him.

The pair of golden Canines looked at one another and then shrugged. "We will see."

Without another word, they went to the table and began selecting tools. Grayson felt bile rise in his throat and he begged his body to wake up, his eyes snapping over to lock with Titus's.

"I can't move!" Titus whispered desperately, spittle flying from his lips. His eyes were huge. "Grayson, I can't get out!"

Grayson felt misery begin to seep down his throat, into his chest. "You have to stay strong." He hissed back, his voice cracking, knowing what was coming. "I'm here with you—no matter how bad it gets, I'm not leaving you."

Titus's eyes shot over toward the pair of golden eyes, his voice pregnant with looming fear. "I'm not ready, Gray, I can't *do this*! You have to help me! Please, oh god please!"

"You can handle this!" Grayson called, his voice rising with despair. "You're the toughest son of a bitch I know! You can handle anything! Together, you and me!"

"Oh shit," Titus moaned as the golden Canines returned to the table. "Oh shit, no, no, please, don't do this. I'll tell you anything you want!"

The Canines held long, curved blades that looked like altered scalpels. Their faces were expressionless as they began to take off Titus's chest plate and then his undershirt.

"We can tell you everything!" Grayson yelled, lunging forward from the ground. The Tusk grabbed his shoulder with a long, clawed hand and pulled him back, returning him to his knees. Its grip was overwhelming and Grayson felt tears begin to form in his eyes as his friend's rising panic began to fill the room.

"Grayson don't let them do this! PLEASE!" Titus shrieked as the Canines exposed his naked torso, positioning themselves at either side of the platform.

"Cut me open instead!" Grayson yelled, his voice cracking. "He's old and sick! You won't get what you want from him! Use me instead!" He began to thrash beneath the Tusk's relentless grip. "USE ME YOU BASTARDS!"

The two Canine's ignored him and placed their thin blades on either side of Titus, just below his ribcage.

And then, they began to cut.

Titus shrieked, his body jolting in agony as the knives parted the flesh, the thick folds curling away from the slow moving blades. Blood gurgled up from duel wounds and began to run down the sides of the platform. Grayson opened his mouth and howled, tears running down his face, as Titus's face bulged beneath the pain.

The Canine's continued to trace the blades down the length of Titus's body, to his hips where they paused. Then, they began to slice horizontally just above the pelvic line, connecting the two initial cuts.

"Hold on Titus!" Grayson cried, wrestling against the Tusk's grip. "Jesus Christ, please STOP *HURTING HIM!*"

The two Canines slid their fingers into the new horizontal incision and then pulled the flap upward, tearing the chunk of compact skin upward to reveal the bloody mess below.

Titus vomited onto himself, his mouth frothing, his eyes rolling into the back of his head. Tears ran down the corners of his eyes as his screams gave way to gurgling. He began to cough then, choking on his own puke, his chest bucking, each movement spilling blood across the table as his opened stomach rolled.

"He's drowning!" Grayson screamed, his eyes bloodshot. "HELP HIM!"

One of the Canines looked at Titus's face and then quickly turned his head to the side so that the vomit could drain out of the gasping man's throat. As quickly as it did so, it returned to the opened torso, its fingers prodding the naked, blood soaked organs before it. Coils of intestine slithered around the Canines' fingers as they poked and tested the alien biology before them, their eyes wide and focused, searching for some clue to the power Titus held.

"He's DYING!" Grayson howled, his head spinning, watching as Titus's eyes began to flutter, his gurgling fading.

The Canines looked at Grayson. One of them spoke, its voice calm. "Where is his power?"

"You're bleeding him DRY!"

"Where is his power? What is his source?"

Grayson grit his teeth, his vision blurred by tears. "You took that away, you brainless fuck!"

The Canine's looked at one another and then the second spoke, as evenly as the first. "But he must possess some kind of source? Some epicenter that is controlled by the device?"

Faint traces of blue began to flow out of Titus's guts, electric cords of liquid that mixed with the blood. The Canine's noticed and their eyes alighted. They reached down into Titus and stained their fingers with it, raising their hands so Grayson could see.

"What part of him creates this?! Tell us!"

"We don't produce glo! We inject it! That's why he and I are different from the others!" Grayson yelled, drool leaking from his chin. "We alter ourselves! It doesn't come from us!"

"Glo?" One of them asked, staring down at its bloody fingers. "Is that what you call it?"

"Fix him!" Grayson shrieked, watching as Titus's chest began to slow, his breathing becoming fainter and fainter.

The two Canines looked at one another. "Do you think somehow they've tapped into Voratarium's power? Stolen it?"

The other shook its head. "We are not like them. This is something different. This glo that runs in their blood—it is not the same lifeforce we are gifted." It rubbed its slicked fingers together. "Perhaps there is another world out there, beyond the Floating, that this race of creatures has discovered. This substance is similar to the lifeforce in us, but it is not of Voratarium."

"What should we do then?"

"We should dig beneath its organs to see if his friend is telling the truth."

"But what if the subject dies?"

The Canine paused and looked at Titus who appeared to have mercifully lost consciousness. "That would limit things. Perhaps, in its weakened state, we could attach the device back to its leg to see if we can increase the flow of this liquid glo. Identify the source, cut it out, and then repair the creature. See if it can survive."

The other Canine nodded. "Creatures like this would be an incredible offering to Voratarium. If their lifeforce is as strong as we think-"

"We would prolong the life of the Floating World by a millennium," the other finished.

Grayson knelt, half listening, his eyes frozen on Titus's sickly face. The big man had passed out, blood pooling out of his stomach at an alarming rate. Traces of vomit clung to his lips and he seemed to be at the precipice of death.

The Canines went to Grayson suddenly and hauled him up. "You will attach the device to your companion." One of them shoved Titus's regulator into his hands and Grayson stared down at it with red rimmed eyes.

"What?"

"He is beyond consciousness," the other instructed. "But he is not dead. Attach the machine back into his leg. Hurry."

Grayson was shoved forward toward the table where he stared down at the grisly mess that was his friend. His hands were shaking as he examined Titus's regulator, his eyes sweeping over his unconscious friend's face. In this state, the regulator was a gun without a bullet and all thought of annihilation left Grayson's mind as he stared down into Titus's unresponsive features.

"Hurry!" One of the Canines barked and Grayson heard the Tusk crawl closer toward him, static buzzing.

Grayson wiped his face miserably and examined the regulator. Titus used an older model, but he was familiar with it. He began to untangle the wires, stripping away the bits of flesh that still clung to it.

Misery engulfed him like a storm as he worked, his head a drum of agony, his limbs weak, his throat dry. His whole body felt as if it had been drained of water, his muscles cramping, his lips chapped. The sight of Titus before him swam in and out of focus and he fought with his stomach, begging it not to revolt.

How did we get here? Grayson thought, wiping his eyes again. Everything he knew and loved felt an eternity away, as if his past self had died somewhere far beyond himself. He thought of Ada, hanging from the ceiling, he thought of Reston and Typhon and the job they had been contracted for. He thought of Ada's sister, Marah, whom he had never met. He thought of his conversation with Ada on top of the duster, at the start of the Negative. He recalled how she had spoken of her sister, the bond they shared, the memories they held dear. She had relied on him to find her. To help her. To help the horde of prisoners that had been stolen away from Typhon and now hung from the ceiling of this awful place.

You failed, his mind buzzed as he began to insert the array of wires and tubes back into Titus. *You didn't save anyone. Ada never even got to see her sister before she was strung up. Hell, you don't even know if she's here or if she's alive. And all those people are still hanging like sacks of meat, drained of their blood—used like pieces to a broken machine. You didn't accomplish anything here and now you're going to watch your friends die. And then you'll go next. You won't even be able to say goodbye. What is Claire going to think? What will she do when she doesn't hear from you again?*

The thought of his daughter brought him shuddering from his thoughts. It had seemed like a lifetime since she had crossed his mind and the realization filled him with a miserable self hatred. The image of her face rose in his mind's eye and he clung to it, clung to a relationship he wished he had more time to nurture. He had never been a great father, never dwelled or stressed over his daughter, never thought of her much when he was working offworld. But now, at the end, he found himself yearning for her. Wishing he had just another hour to be with her, to tell her all the things he had been too distracted or preoccupied to say.

Why aren't you back on Lighton, in Malice, with your pregnant daughter? Why are you here? Why would you do this? Why? Why? WHY?

Grayson swallowed hard, his eyes misting, and finished attaching the regulator into Titus's thigh.

"Did you finish?" One of the Canines asked impatiently.

Grayson said nothing as he adjusted the dial, bringing the device to life. He felt himself draining, fading away, lost in a past he didn't have time to regret. As he was about to step away, he happened to glance at Titus's face.

His eyes were open.

Grayson felt a surge of electric energy rattle him, shake him into alertness, his mind exploding with realization.

Titus opened his mouth, knowing he had only a second.

"Crank it, Gray," Titus croaked, barely a whisper.

Grayson froze, eyes bulging, and felt the Canines surge for him, the Tusk at his back reaching, panic erupting throughout the room.

Like lightning, Grayson grabbed the dial on the regulator and jacked it up to its maximum level.

"Take care of the kids," Titus hissed.

And then his back arched as the influx of glo erupted into his bloodstream. Grayson threw himself to the floor as Titus's opened abdomen spat neon blue, his hands knotting into fists, a howl bellowing from his chest, a final cry of rage and defiance against the terrible creatures.

The Canines grabbed at Titus, shouting, scrambling, but the damage was done. A blue glow surrounded Titus, exploded out of him like the sun, pulsing from every pore and orifice, a burning, sweeping heat that blazed through the room.

Grayson covered his head, flattening himself as much as he could against the floor. Titus overcooked a moment later, a blast of raw energy that billowed out from his body like a blade of raging death. The arc of energy cut through the air like a sword, burning horizontally in all directions, slicing, destroying, and severing everything in its wake. The blade of power knocked the two golden Canines back, sliced the Tusk in half, just above its flesh sack, and eviscerated the four purple eyed Canines who had been watching the process from the far wall.

Grayson felt the curtain of death pass over him like the blade of an axe, his skin heating beneath its trajectory. He looked up to see the blast strike the walls, tear through them, and pass on deeper into the ship. Screams echoed in its wake as Canines and Tusks were swept up in its path, the interior of the construct creaking and bending, folding in slightly as the supports were destroyed.

Grayson blinked, eyes watering, and looked at the two golden Canines. They were on their backs, dazed, but not severed. They clutched their heads and looked at one another, horror in their eyes. The dark blood of their companions oozed across the floor and found them, the opened walls around them funneling the sound of death into the room.

Run, Grayson's mind screamed. *RUN! GO!*

Heaving himself up, heart crunching into his ribs, Grayson stood and allowed himself a single look at what remained of Titus. His body was a ruined mess, a pile of gore and blood, his opened stomach a soggy marsh.

And he was dead, his eyes closed, the scars beneath his eyes empty of light.

Goddamn it, Grayson sobbed, knowing he had only a second. *Goddamn it, I'm so sorry Titus.*

And then he ran out of the room with a sob, bolting forward with all the strength he could muster. His body howled in protest, but he grit his teeth and endured, his booted feet taking him quickly into the hall and back into the room he had been imprisoned in.

The trajectory of the blast had ripped open the interior of the ship, the metal and flesh parting and torn where the blades of power had been sent. Dozens of dead Canines and Tusks littered the floor, their bodies cut in half, taken in the eruption.

Grayson stepped over them, barely giving them a thought. Above the grated hole now, he looked up and saw that many of the captured humans had been knocked free in the blast, their bodies sliding to the floor in wet, soggy piles.

"ADA!" Grayson screamed, the moans of the dead and dying filling his ears, both human and alien. "Ada, where are you!?"

Men, women, even a few children lined the floor, freed from the flesh tubes that had held them for so long. They were only half conscious, most of them gagging bile onto their naked bodies, confused and dazed, sick and crying. They didn't know where they were, what had happened to them. They were just as lost as Grayson felt.

"Ada!" Grayson screamed. He spotted her then as she crawled to her knees, yanking the torn flesh tube out of her mouth and then puking a second later. She was trembling all over, her skin sickly pale.

Grayson rushed to her, his head hammering. "Ada! Ada, it's me!"

She looked at him with bewildered eyes. "Grayson?"

"We have to go right now!" He shouted in her face, bending to scoop her up into his arms.

"I can walk," she said, pushing him away. She looked around at the destruction, at the dozens of moaning, crying people around her.

"Oh my god," she whispered thickly, still looking deathly pale.

"We have to leave right now!" Grayson barked.

Ada swept her eyes across the room, life returning to them. "I recognize these people. Oh god, look at them!"

Grayson shook her, his voice a rattle. "Ada! NOW!"

"We...we have to take them with us!"

Grayson grabbed her by the shoulders and hauled her up, already hearing the scramble of Canines and Tusks flooding down the corridors all around them. "We can't! We'll come back for them I promise!"

Ada's eyes found his and he saw a fire burning in her sockets. "I'm not leaving them! Marah is here somewhere and I'm not leaving this ship without her! Without every single one of these people!"

Howls of static rage screeched down the ruined halls, a chaotic scramble to return order and decipher what had happened.

Grayson ran for one of the passageways, dragging Ada behind him, his voice a growling plea. "If we stay, we die! We don't have the resources to take them right now! Come ON!"

Ada wrestled herself free, tears now forming in her bloodshot eyes, her face a pasty white. "Stop it! Marah is here, I know she is! We have to find her!"

A flurry of alien language roared down the passage at their back as a host of Canines flooded the damaged drainage room, the sight of the freed humans sparking an outraged panic.

Grayson could feel a mental clock ticking down in his head, an alarm blaring in his brain. He reached out and grabbed Ada's naked arm once more, hauling them away from the growing horde.

"We're all dead if we don't leave RIGHT now!" he yelled over the noise, the damage from Titus's blast apparent all around him. The walls buckled where the blast had cut them, the purple-fleshed metal panels groaning and bending.

"Grayson, please!" Ada cried as she stumbled forward at a run, dragged without choice.

They came to an intersection and Grayson assessed their options quickly. To his right was another empty hallway, to his left-"

"Oh no," he hissed. A trio of purple eyed Canines ran down the length of the hall toward them, their faces igniting with hateful recognition as they spotted Grayson and Ada.

"Move!" Grayson yelled, shoving Ada forward down the opposite hall, his booted feet slapping the flesh-patched metal.

They sprinted down the throat of the hallway and were dumped into a familiar room, the exit opening up into a massive, high ceiled arena. A pool of blackened liquid sat in the center, a wide circle that stood between them and the opposite hallway, their only way out. At their backs, the Canines surged, gaining ground.

"Go! GO!" Grayson ordered, heart hammering, head pounding, his lungs feeling as if they had been punctured. Sobbing, Ada charged forward, across the room and toward their exit with Grayson panting at her back. When they were halfway around the large pool, they skid to a halt, their eyes going wide.

"No, no, no," Grayson exhaled, sucking air, feeling sick. Panic laced his insides as four Tusks slithered out of the hallway in front of them, blocking their only way out.

Ada looked over her shoulder and grabbed Grayson. "They're coming! They're right behind us!"

Grayson looked back and saw the Canines had entered the room, trapping them. His blood turned to ice and fear rose in the back of his throat. He spun around to see the Tusks advancing, their metallic box heads buzzing an unknown frequency.

"What do we do!?" Ada asked, her face alive with terror. Grayson knew she was thinking of the ceiling, knew where she would go if they were caught again.

He spun on his heel and faced the pool of dark liquid. Its surface was perfectly calm, the unblemished waters seemingly unaffected by the death blow Titus had exhumed.

You have no idea what that water even is! His mind roared.

He checked his sides and saw that the Tusks and Canines were alarmingly close now, almost close enough to lunge for them.

This is where the Canines were put to rest, returned to Voratarium they said, he countered frantically. *They called it the Traveler's Water. There's something in there, a way out, an escape, something, anything!*

He grabbed Ada by the arm and looked into her eyes.

"We have to go in!"

Ada's eyes darted toward the eerie waters. "Wha-"

Grayson didn't let her finish, the Tusks and Canines reaching for them now at a full sprint. Taking a deep breath, he threw himself and Ada toward the surface of the water, squeezing his eyes shut so hard he thought they would rupture.

A splash followed, and then he went weightless, the world vanishing.

CHAPTER 14

Shinji stepped out of the duster and headed straight for the lifts. He felt sore and dried out, his armor plating caked with grime and dirt. His eyes burned from the constant desert glare and his head thundered. After the skirmish with the Canines, he had instructed the drivers to take him straight to Typhon's auto garage, a mental clock ticking down in the back of his head. He knew Reston was going to want an explanation, a reason as to why he was back, alone. A confrontation was almost assured, but the clock told him it needed to be brief. He didn't have time to hold these people's hands, he had a job to do and not a lot of time to do it.

The auto garage was a hum of activity and he drew more than a few eyes as he strode across the concrete, his regulator swaying at his back. The Orbital Clerks called for him to wait, but he ignored them, along with the dozens of curious, fearful faces he passed.

He had the lift to himself and as he ascended toward the Orbital Dome of Typhon above, his mind examined the plan he had slapped together. It was reckless, foolish, and massively dangerous, but he didn't care. Grayson, Titus, and Ada were still out there and they were relying on him, probably praying he would come to their aid.

If they're not already dead.

In truth, beneath the bravado of his mission, he felt a burning desire, an urge, to just wipe out as many of the horrible purple-eyed creatures as he could.

When the lift came to a stop and the doors opened, he was greeted by Reston and a host of Orbital Clerks at his back. It was an inevitability he had hoped to avoid.

"You're back," Reston stated, his face laced with concern. "Alone, I'm told?"

Shinji stepped off the lift. "For now. I don't have time to explain, there are things I need to do."

Reston held up his hands, blocking Shinji. "Hold on, I need to know what's going on."

"Didn't Grayson message you earlier?"

"Some, but he didn't tell me much. Where's the rest of you? Where's Ada?"

Shinji frowned. "I don't know. Gone. Taken. I didn't see."

The Orbital Clerks shifted and Shinji could see a crowd of anxious citizens gathering behind them. Reston's face hardened.

"What the *hell* happened out there?"

Shiniji felt his patience thinning. "These creatures, the Canines? There are way more of them than we imagined. They knocked my team around pretty bad and one of us was taken. I need to gather some things and head back out there or some very nasty things are going to happen."

Reston's face went pale. "Who was taken?"

"Grayson."

"And Ada? You really don't know where she is?"

"We were attacked. I lost her in the commotion, but last I heard she was with Titus. If she is, then you shouldn't worry too much. Titus is a monster with a heart of gold. He won't let anything happen to your daughter."

Reston ran his hands over his face and turned around, clearly distraught. He noticed the gathering crowd and he set his jaw, turning back to face Shinji.

"We hired you to do a job," he stated quietly.

"And I'm fucking doing it," Shinji spat back, feeling his blood begin to boil.

Reston's voice turned to iron. "I was told the Vagabonds were the best in the business for situations like this. I was assured by your network that we would be taken care of. I have a city full of terrified people that I need to protect, that I need to make feel safe again. I have responsibilities I need to uphold and families that are demanding answers." Reston's eyes hardened. "And now I'm down another daughter, no closer to saving my people, and you *dare* tell me you're doing your job?"

Shinij didn't know if Reston was putting on a show for the crowd or if he actually felt genuine outrage. Neither option cooled the sudden fire in his throat. Gritting his teeth, Shinji stepped toward Reston, causing the Orbital Clerks to half raise their rifles in alarm.

"Listen to me," Shinji growled. "Those things out there have infected this planet. They're a way larger threat than you first let on. There are thousands of them. I don't care if you hired a dozen Vagabonds—what we're dealing with is a fucking outbreak." Shinji stood nose to nose with Reston now. "So if you want to keep polishing your halo in front of all these people then be my guest, but I don't have time to listen to it."

Shinji made to step around him, but Reston grabbed his arm. "We're not done here."

Shinji looked down at Reston's hand and then back into Reston's face. "I get it," he said dangerously, his voice low. "You're scared and your loved ones are missing. But if you don't take your hand off my arm in three seconds, then I'm going to turn this place into a *fucking sun.*"

Reston tightened his jaw, but removed his grip a moment later.

Shinji forced a breath down his throat. "I'm not here to argue with you. I know you're pissed and I get it. But we're in over our heads, all of us, and we need to adjust our expectations."

"What is that supposed to mean?" Reston said crisply.

"It means I'm going to need your help."

Reston blinked, as if not expecting the confession. "How?"

"I want you to round up every single duster you have and follow me back out into the desert. I saw Grayson get captured, I saw the direction they were headed. I know where to find their ship, their source. I know where your people are being held. I can find it. And when I do, I want transport to shuttle as many people back to Typhon as we can manage."

Reston let a beat pass before answering. "And then what?"

"Then I'm going to wipe out the Canines."

Reston cocked an eyebrow. "How?"

"Leave that part to me," Shinji said. "But we're not going to have a lot of time."

"Have you even seen where my people are being held?"

"No, but I'm sure it won't be hard to spot once we're through Begger's Valley. I can find it and when I do, I need your dusters. Can you do that?"

Reston bit his lip and then nodded. "You better know what you're doing."

The scars beneath Shinji's eyes flared. "I guess we'll find out."

Shinji finally pushed past Reston, leaving the conversation where it sat. He was furious, white hot with anger, but he forced it down. Throwing a punch Reston's way wasn't going to solve anything and he tried to remind himself what the other man must be dealing with.

He's not like you. None of them are. They're terrified of everything that's stronger and meaner than they are.

Walking quickly, Shinji rose up the flights of circular disks that made up the floors of the Orbital Dome. He headed for the docks, where Titus's ship the Afterburner sat. He kept his attention focused and ignored the trail of bulging eyes he left in his wake, his boots slapping the metal plates of the stairways.

When he reached the Afterburner, the sun blasting down from overhead, he trotted the final distance across the landing platform and hurried up the ramp of the ship. As he entered it, he realized just how easy it would be to dust off and leave this mess behind him. He wasn't bound to any of this, didn't need to risk his life for these people or his companions. He could simply fire up the engines and leave.

And you'd be no better than everyone you grew up trying to get away from, he mind spat. *You'd be just like them—abandoning those weaker than yourself.*

A memory rose then, a single image of his parents publicly screaming at him in front of all their friends. He had brought home a stray dog, a pathetic, tiny, starving thing that could barely walk. He had found it earlier

in the day while he was out picking up something for his father. He didn't
know why he had been drawn to it, but it had looked so pathetic and so
desperate that he had impulsively plucked it from the streets. When he
returned home with it, his parents had been horrified and their friends
had laughed at the state in which the dog lay in the boy's arms. Instead
of returning it to the streets, he remembered how his parents had forced
him to drown it in the pool out back, with all of their friends looking on.
He remembered how he had cried, refused, and his father had hit him,
screamed at him to put the thing out of its misery.

Shinji dismissed the haunted thoughts with an angry snarl, and then
dismissed all thoughts of flight almost as quickly as it had come. He
pounded down the empty hallways of the Afterburner and entered the
tail end of the ship where the glo drive was installed into the main engine.

You really going to do this?

"Fuck it," Shinji whispered after a moment.

He reached down and ripped the docking tube out of the glo drive,
the thin rubber hose that bridged it to the main engine. He held the
severed hose in one hand while he slid his regulator off his back with a
thud. Then, he fired up the glo drive and attached the hose to his regulator.
With a rising groan, the glo drive warmed up and began pumping copious
amounts of raw liquid glo into the massive regulator. Shinji watched it,
knowing the danger of his plan.

God this is going to be miserable.

When the regulator reached capacity, Shinji pulled the still spurting
tube out and capped off his regulator, sliding it onto his back as he did so.

Then, with the neon blue still gushing from the severed tubing, he
opened his mouth and shoved the hose down his throat, drinking deeply.

CHAPTER 15

Ada was lost in darkness. She could sense that she was moving, falling or perhaps floating, a sensation of speed enveloping her. Her eyes were closed and she couldn't hear anything, not even the rush of water.

When Grayson had thrown them into the pool, she had had only a second to fill her lungs with oxygen before the dark liquid engulfed them. Now she could feel pressure building in her chest as the air began to run out. She waited until the last possible second before opening her mouth to gasp, dizzy and sick with desperation, fully expecting her lungs to be flooded with water. Instead, she found that she could breath easily, her body gulping down air in shuddering relief.

She realized a moment later that something had changed. The sensation of flight had left and the darkness that surrounded her seemed to be leaving. Her body slumped with its own weight once more and she struggled to rise and stand, her hands grasping for purchase.

Suddenly, she felt someone grab her wrist and haul her up, a rush of sound and air coming with it. She blinked, feeling something slick slide off her skin as the world shimmered and shook, colors adjusting into focus.

"Ada? Ada, breathe!"

Ada collapsed to the ground and panted, sucking down deep pulls of air. Her naked body shivered with a sudden cold and her teeth began to chatter. Her mind reformed and she shook herself into a state of consciousness.

"Are you hurt? Are you ok?"

It was Grayson. She could tell by his voice that it was him. She pulled her eyes open with some effort and the universe realigned. Grayson's concerned face stared down at her, his scars glowing with their eerie color.

"You with me?" He asked.

Ada nodded and sat up, arms covering her exposed chest. "I'm good. I'm just winded. What the hell happened to us?"

Grayson stepped away from her, allowing her eyes to sweep across the landscape, across the dull gray sky and all the horrors it held.

Her face drained of blood. "W-what the hell is this...?"

Grayson's face was grim as he responded. "I think we're in their world."

Ada didn't know how to process the awe inducing terror of what she was seeing. Slowly, she stood, her eyes absorbing every tiny horrible detail.

They stood beside a black pool, similar to the one they had leapt into back on the ship. The ground around them appeared to be made from metal plating, with patches of purple muscle littered across it, much like the interior of the massive Canine construct. Ada's eyes traveled toward the horizon and saw that huge, geometrically perfect masses of towering darkness lined the edges of the world, like some kind of carved mountain range. Everything was perfectly squared off, the looming constructs a smoothed black color. Colossal coils of wire ran between the structures, as if they were parts to a greater machine. The space between was a long empty plain, perfectly flat in all directions. Black pools stretched out in a line and as Ada turned around, she saw that the one they had exited was just one of hundreds, all neatly stretching from horizon to horizon in a perfect row.

But all of that wasn't what stole her breath away. The alien pools and the distant, towering constructs weren't what drove a blade of fear into her heart.

In the distance, across the flattened plains of metal plating and fleshy ooze, stood an absolutely titanic creature. Its humanoid body filled the sky like a looming planet, its long legs rising from the surface to stand towering over the grayed world. Its body was naked and sexless, its skin the color of glossed coal. Its head was shaped like a metallic box, much like the Tusks, but it was the size of a small moon. There were no features on the surface of the enormous abnormality, no eyes or mouth or teeth. The entire entity stood motionless over the world like some kind of cosmic nightmare.

Lining the length of its torso and shoulders were millions of snaking black wires that fanned out and floated all around it, high up in the heavens. Ada went cold when she realized that at the end of each tube was a Canine. They simply floated in space above and around their host, like fetuses in the womb. Except their eyes were open, staring down at them in cold silence, a countless number of purple stars hovering in the gray expanse.

As Ada struggled to process what she was seeing, her mind frantically trying to make sense of it all, she noticed a sound. It was the only sound in the entire world, a low, muted thing that made the silence in between even more haunting.

Thump-thump...thump-thump...thump-thump...

Slowly, she turned to Grayson, who also seemed to hear it.

"Is that...a heartbeat?"

Grayson hadn't taken his eyes off of the colossal monster standing motionless against the horizon. Slowly, he nodded.

"I think so."

Ada swallowed hard, shivering, realizing just how cold this place was and just how naked she remained. Grayson glanced at her, seeming to notice her distress, and he quickly removed his chest plate and slid out of his undershirt. He handed it to her and then strapped his armor back on. Ada took the shirt gratefully and wordlessly. She pulled the stinking thing over her head and was grateful when it fell down to her knees. The warmth was appreciated more than the dignity.

"What is this place...?" Ada finally whispered, her eyes returning to the endless Canines in the sky.

Grayson kept his voice low. "They kept calling it the Floating World. I think this is where they were trying to get back to when your father shot them down."

Ada forced her teeth to stop chattering. "What makes you say that?"

Grayson pointed toward the massive entity's squared head. "Look."

Ada squinted toward where Grayson was pointing. When she saw what he was looking at, her eyes went wide.

Rectangular pieces of the titan's head were slowly sliding out of the construct, like pieces to a complex, interlocked puzzle. The pieces that slid out were silver and they slowly floated up and away from the body of the creature, rising high into the heavens to vanish into the clouds.

Almost instantly, a pair of smooth black pieces drifted down from the opposite horizon and hovered toward the immense being, their flight paths going directly over Ada and Grayson's head, magnifying just how huge the pieces were.

"They look just like the ship we were held captive on," Grayson said quietly as the pair of perfectly angled crafts passed them by, reaching the boxed head of the silent monster. A moment later, the pieces adjusted course and then slid perfectly into two empty spaces in the things head. From this distance, it looked like they had barely filled a gap, giving perspective to just how enormous the entity was.

"What are they doing?" Ada whispered, watching the whole process with bewildered eyes. She felt sick and alone, isolated and horrified by the strange world

"I think they're keeping it alive," Grayson said quietly, watching as another silver craft slid out, only to be replaced by a new arrival a couple minutes later, this one pure black.

Grayson waved a hand up toward the floating Canines, at the millions of purple eyes that watched them in utter silence. "I think this is all some kind of cycle, an exchange of life force that keeps both the Canines and that thing alive."

"Hell," Ada whispered, pulling the shirt tight against her chilled skin. "Is this why they took us? To bring us here?"

Grayson shook his head. "I don't think so. I think they just wanted to repair the damage you did to their ship. I think we were just tools to get them on their way again. The Canines, they kept talking about life force. I think their ship was some kind of tanker. I think they were returning back to this place to continue fueling the cycle."

Ada stared at the cosmic sized entity before them. "If they only needed us to fix their ship, then who or what did they use to fill it up on life force in the first place?"

Grayson shook his head. "I have no idea. But I think the universe is a lot bigger than we think. Hell, we don't even know where glo comes from. Not really."

Ada's mind suddenly alerted her to something and she snapped her eyes over to Grayson. "Where's Titus?"

Grayson slowly stared down at the flesh-patched ground, his face creasing in sorrow. It was a look she wasn't used to seeing on him and it made her heart race in terror.

"No…"

"They dissected him," Grayson said carefully, quietly, his voice threatening to burst. "Cut him open right in front of me."

Ada's eyes bulged, her throat tightening. "What…?"

Grayson swallowed hard and pressed his fingers to his eyes. "I think they wanted to use us. To use the glo we have in our veins. I don't think they've ever encountered people like us before, Vagabonds, and they wanted to know more. I think they wanted to use us to fill their ships, use the power of glo to fuel whatever the hell that thing out there is. They were extremely interested in our capabilities. If they use life force as an engine to keep their cycle of life alive, then glo might be the grease to keep the gears running for another millenia."

Ada covered her face with her hands and allowed herself a moment of grief. She couldn't believe Titus was gone. He had been so strong, so good. So goddamn *good*.

Thump-thump…thump-thump…thump-thump…

Ada looked up, the muted noise rolling across the world.

Grayson scanned the distant towering structures, as if searching for the source. He spun slowly, taking in the array of bizarre mysteries that surrounded them as the beat of the drum continued.

"What do you think those metal towers are out there?" Ada asked, watching him.

"I haven't the slightest idea."

Thump-thump...thump-thump...

"Ada, look over there. At that tube, the small one, over by those structures. Do you see it?"

Ada turned slightly and saw what Grayson had spotted. It was a rogue cord that flowed out of the giant creature and sloped downward, floating across the sky to disappear inside the clusters of eerie, distant buildings. She couldn't see what it was attached to, but it was clear something was different about it.

"What do you think it is?"

Thump thump...thump-thump...

Grayson paused for a moment before speaking. "I don't know, but it sounds like that drumming, that heartbeat or whatever it is...I think it's coming from over there. Maybe the two are connected?"

"Actually connected?"

"Sure, why not?"

Ada chewed her lip. "Should we head that way then?"

"Unless you want to hop back into one of these pools."

Ada shook her head. "No. Not yet. But before we go, we should mark the one we came out of."

Grayson lifted his eyebrows, as if he hadn't considered that. "Good idea." He patted himself down, searching for some kind of marker he could use. After coming up empty, he took his gloves off and laid them at the lip of the wide basin. Ada caught his eye and he shrugged.

"Better than nothing."

Ada shivered in the cold air and nodded, pointing with her chin toward the strange, isolated tube that floated lazily across the world. "You want to lead the way?"

Together, they began to march across the empty, silent world. The row of black pools seemed to lead directly toward the distant structures and so they walked down the length of them. Their feet clacked and squished against the flesh lined metal ground, the icey air chilling them to the bone as they went. Ada found it hard to keep her eyes ahead of her and not stare up into the countless hordes that drifted soundlessly above them. She could feel the Canines watching her, a million purple stars all boring into her skull. If Grayson was bothered by them, she couldn't tell. His face was a hardened plate of pale rock, his scars a muted blue. He looked older than he had just a couple days ago, the wrinkles around his eyes seeming deeper, harsher.

Titus, she thought. *I'm sure he's thinking about Titus.*

She didn't know how long they had been walking, but the structures in the distance were getting closer now, growing out of the horizon like some kind of abandoned city. Great cords of wire curled and twisted from each building, connecting them like some kind of network. She saw no sign of life as they continued down the row of black pools, her eyes searching for any flicker of movement.

Grayson stopped suddenly, raising a hand. Ada craned her head back and saw why he had halted. A long, reaching strand of tubing was slowly descending ahead of them, extending from the body of the great, silent titan.

"Just wait," Grayson whispered, watching it carefully. It dipped down, crossing the sky, and reached into one of the pools ahead of them. After a moment, it retracted, pulling with it a lifeless Canine. Dripping, the body was slowly reeled in and then raised up into the heavens, aligning with the others. A beat passed and suddenly a shudder ran through the corpse, its eyes sparking and coming alive with purple life. The limbs relaxed as awareness returned to the creature as its place in the sky cemented.

"I really don't like this place," Grayson said quietly as he picked up the pace once more.

"Let's just see what's at the end of that tube," Ada responded, her eyes trained on the thin cord that vanished into the structures before them. She shivered again, violently, and she saw Grayson watching her. He stepped close then, his body relaxing some, and embraced her. The movement caught her off guard and she bristled at his touch. A moment later, as his hands began to rub warmth into her arms, she breathed a sigh of relief.

"You're practically blue," Grayson stated quietly. "We have to get your circulation going."

There was no intimacy in the exchange of warmth, no question that hovered around Ada's head, and she gratefully accepted his help. The older man's hands were rough and his chestplate was hard against her cheek, but the warmth flowing out of him and into her frozen limbs was a mercy she desperately needed. After a couple minutes, Grayson released her and stepped back.

"Any better?"

"A little. Thanks."

"No problem."

Together, they continued on. Their path down the length of pools was a silent one now, the towering dark structures rising before them. The coils of wire that seemed to jump from one construct to the next appeared greater in size at this proximity and they reminded Ada of mechanical snakes without features or fangs.

"What do you think this place was?" She asked as they entered the outskirts of the sprawling, empty grid.

Grayson was silent for a moment before answering, his boots squishing over the fleshy metal. "I think this place was once very much alive. Maybe some kind of city or capital."

"What do you think happened? Some kind of extinction or war?"

They passed the first of the blackened buildings, a faceless rectangle that rose from the ground in perfect symmetry.

"I think everything reaches an end," Grayson answered quietly. Ada noticed him touching his head, wincing, as if he were experiencing some kind of pain. His jaw tightened and his lips became a thin white line, but he didn't slow.

"You ok?"

"I'm fine."

Thump-thump...thump-thump...

Ada looked ahead and to the left, deeper into the expansive cluster of dark structures. "It's close." She looked up and traced the wavering tube above them that marked the direction of the noise.

"Keep your eyes open," Grayson said, lowering his voice. "We have no idea what we're headed toward."

They continued deeper into the grid of structures, their placement having no apparent function or reason. Some were wide and tall, others were low and narrow, like some kind of planetary puzzle that hadn't been deciphered yet.

The thumping grew louder and Ada knew they were getting close to the source. The echo of the beat washed over them in muted waves, as if the world itself was broadcasting their path.

They rounded a massive corner and Ada reached out and grabbed Grayson, yanking him back, her heart exploding up her throat.

"Get back!" she hissed, a breath caught in her throat. Grayson fell against her and they hugged the corner together, the beating drum pressing in all around them. Ada peeked around the structure and confirmed her alarm.

Two Canines were kneeling in the center of a small natural square, their heads pressed to the ground, their forms motionless. Grayson spotted them and cursed quietly. The Canines had their backs to them and didn't seem to notice their approach. As Ada studied them, she realized and saw what held their attention and the sight of it filled her veins with ice once more.

A small, golden eyed Canine was on its hands and knees before the two purple eyed ones. It looked different than the others, younger, like a child. Rising from its naked back, pressing its form down, was a massive, beating organ, twice the child's size. It was purple and its mass was snaked with angry, pulsing veins. The walls of its quivering form seemed to shudder and expand, sending out a wall of noise with every contraction. Plunged into the top of the organ was the end of the heavenly tube, connecting it to its host.

Thump-thump...thump-thump...

"I think we've found Voratarium's heart," Ada whispered.

"No shit," Grayson said, staring at the golden-eyed child, its body seeming to struggle against the weight of the pulsing organ that grew from its back.

As they watched, the heart child slowly opened its mouth, its figure quivering violently. It was an unceremonious action that appeared more animal than human. A moment later, a pool of golden liquid dribbled out of the child's mouth and onto the cold ground. The heart child coughed and then began to crawl away from the other two Canines, almost as if it had forgotten about them. Ada watched it go, the tube connecting it to its host marking its direction.

When it had vanished from sight, the two Canines scrambled forward and began greedily lapping up the golden pool of vomit. Their fanged teeth scraped and sparked the metallic ground as they did so, their tongues coated in the liquid. When it had all been digested, the Canines stood slowly, as if intoxicated.

Then, as one, they clutched their heads and howled, their bodies violently contorting and expanding. Ada could hear the pop and grind of bone as they realigned, the flesh stretched and pulled.

"Oh hell," Grayson whispered venomously.

When the spasms passed, the Canines slowly pulled themselves up, a full two feet taller than they had been previously. Their eyes glowed gold now, their faces shadowed with a passive elation. They looked at one another, examining their new features, their large hands and long fingers reaching out to touch and prod the others.

"We must find an organ to captain," one of them stated, its voice a low rumble.

"We will," the other answered. "There are many vessels. Voratarium will instruct us. Come."

As one, they turned away from Grayson and Ada and walked in the direction of the towering titan, their new forms lost as they disappeared into the labyrinth of structures.

"What the hell did we just see?" Ada asked after a full minute had passed, the frigid air finally returning to her lungs.

"Evolution," Grayson said grimly. He looked up into the sky and traced the direction of the floating tube that marked the heart child. "Come on, we shouldn't let it get too far ahead."

"What's the plan here?"

Grayson took her hand and pulled her after him, his voice hard. "We have to kill that thing and get out of this goddamn place."

Ada followed him deeper into the sprawling weave of structures, her eyes tracing the floating tube overhead that marked the location of the heart child. A million thoughts collided in her head, tangled with a host of emotional trauma that she dare not examine. She could feel an immense weight hanging over her, waiting for her to catch her breath before dropping to crush her. So much had happened and they were still so far away from what they had set out to accomplish. Thoughts of Marah fluttered through her mind and Ada balled her hands into fists, a hopelessness filling her.

Did they string you up like they did me? Are you still there, waiting for me?

Grayson limped along ahead of her, his jaw set, and she realized just how worn down and beaten he really was. His face was ghostly pale and he seemed to be fighting against a constant pulse of pain. What had Titus said back in the pit? That he was fringing?

"Keep up," Grayson urged as they twisted their way through the labyrinth. Ada shivered, her bare feet slapping against the growth beneath her. As she ran, the alien world filling her senses, she realized that there was a good chance they'd never leave this place. For all of Grayson's grit, even he couldn't perform miracles, especially in his state. She noticed the patch of blood on his leg, where his regulator had been torn out, and she couldn't imagine the burning pain he must be feeling with every step.

"There it is," Grayson whispered, halting.

They had rounded a corner and come to a stop, everything freezing in place like some kind of holo image.

The heart child stood crouched in front of them, only a couple feet away. It was bent over and trying to stand on two legs, but the massive beating growth on its back made it nearly impossible. The child staggered back down onto its hands and knees in a pitiful expression of defeat while the drumming of the heart continued to pulse all around them.

Grayson detached himself from Ada and began circling the creature, his eyes hard and laser focused. The heart child spotted him in a sputtering jerk of surprise, its eyes going wide, a small sound escaping its crusted lips. It turned away from Grayson and saw Ada, its expression crumpling into fear.

"Careful," Grayson instructed, moving closer, his arms outspread. "We have no idea what this thing can do."

196 · ELIAS WITHEROW

But instead of launching an attack, the heart child suddenly curled up beneath the weight of itself and began to cry. It caught Ada off guard and she felt her stomach churn as its lonely wails rose into the gray sky.

Grayson inched himself closer, his face draining of blood. Ada could tell he was put off, shaken even, as the child continued to weep, an almost uncontrollable sobbing now. Great golden tears streamed down its face as the growth, almost twice the child's size, continued to beat.

"Grayson…?" Ada called, the cries infecting her, rooting her where she stood. She felt pity and disgust rise in her chest and she begged the heart child to silence itself.

Grayson said nothing as he strode closer, now standing directly over the child. It looked up at him with big, wet eyes that were horribly huge and sickeningly human in appearance. Its lower lip quivered and it said something in a language neither of them understood, a desperate plea that fell on unhearing ears.

Then, in one massive motion, Grayson raised his boot and brought the heel of it crunching down over the child's head. Ada felt her chest surge with repulsion and empathy as the child's head bounced off the ground, bringing forth a spurt of golden liquid from its mouth. It howled in pain, the most pitiful, soul crushing sound Ada had ever heard and she felt sick.

"Fuck!" Grayson cried shakily. "Fuck fuck FUCK!"

Grunting, his face creased in misery, Grayson brought his boot up again and delivered another blow. This one split the heart child's mouth open, popping its jaw off to the side. Another scream followed and Grayson's chest heaved.

But then he struck again. And again. Until he had turned the child's skull to mush, finally silencing the thing. The quickness of the violence left Ada wide eyed, the execution a lightning bolt of shock.

Panting, Grayson stood over the ruined corpse, a look of shame and repulsion creeping into the corners of his eyes. He looked up at Ada and then almost immediately turned away. The dead heart lay before them like some kind of evidence to a crime of necessity.

As Grayson caught his breath and as Ada stared on in stark disbelief, the pulsing heart that grew out of the child's back began to slow. Fade. Sputter.

And then it stopped altogether.

In an instant, a bellowing, grinding noise exploded over the world. It was as if a colossal iron building were buckling and falling beneath its own weight. Ada and Grayson spun around and started up over the tops of the black constructs that surrounded them, toward the titan that towered over existence.

Its squared head was slowly, horribly, sliding apart. Great, colossal pieces fell out of their slots like a deconstructed puzzle. The blackened masses fell down the length of the titan's body and boomed to the earth, sending shock waves up Ada's legs as each one struck. The Canines floating in the sky all began to shriek as one, a wall of noise that pierced Ada's skull like a knife. The wires and tubes that held them, suspended them in the sky, began to fall as well, dragging the screaming Canines with them.

"Run!" Grayson barked suddenly, grabbing her arm and yanking her forward. "We have to get out of here right now! Back to the pool! HURRY!"

The world shook and buckled, the grinding, shrieking cacophony of sound blasting over the world in massive, ear splitting waves. The ground trembled and rumbled as thunderclaps echoed, the pieces of the head continuing to fall.

Ada felt her lungs burning as they bolted through the maze of dark structures, sprinting back the way they had come at a full tilt. Above the world, she saw the great titan begin to sway, its long, dark limbs beginning to give out as more pieces of its head were disassembled.

They were almost out of the labyrinth when Ada spotted them. Her heart sank and fear seized her. Ahead of them, between the last building and the open plains, were the two golden Canines. They were clutching their heads in apparent agony as the world fell apart around them, but when they spotted Grayson and Ada, they righted themselves and faced the pair with a snarl.

Grayson didn't even slow. He ran full speed at the lead one and leapt for it, kicking out hard. His boot caught the lead Canine in its chest and it tumbled backward with a jolt of shock, its eyes wide. Grayson came down on its throat, his knee falling at the point of impact to deliver a bone shat-tering kill strike that ended the thing's life in an instant.

The second Canine took a step away from Grayson, its eyes huge and shocked and terrified at the brutality of the action.

"Keep going! Run!" Grayson bellowed, pulling himself off the corpse to follow Ada as she blew past them and out into the open plain.

Grayson followed, his legs churning, chancing a glance over his shoulder at the remaining Canine.

"We can kill them!" He yelled over the wind whipping through his hair. "The bastards can die!"

Ada didn't have the breath to respond, grateful for Grayson's quick execution and fast reaction time. She had no idea how he was keeping up with her, a trail of blood leaking down his leg now.

The bastards can die.

The thought was enough to spurn her on, taking her down the length of dark pools. Grayson panted and wheezed behind her, the world shak-ing and crumbling all around them. The great titan Voratarium groaned and swayed, as if a pillar of the universe were about to come crashing down. Massive blasts blew across the world as the enormous pieces of its head, the Canine's ships, continued to fall like dead stars across the sky. The Canines that had littered the heavens were falling too, plunging toward the earth at a dizzying velocity.

Grayson and Ada reached the pool marked by Grayson's gloves right as the Canine's began to splatter across the ground like biological hail.

Ada grabbed Grayson's hand, pulled him to the edge of the pool, and then threw them both into it without a second look back.

As the waters enveloped them, Voratarium fell.

CHAPTER 16

Shinji gripped the wheel and vomited onto himself. It came out in a gurgling splash that struck his legs and ran down to the floor of the duster. His stomach rolled violently and he grit his teeth, spitting.

The Oribital Clerk that rode next to him winced, but said nothing, an aura of fear emanating off of him. Shinji didn't blame the guy. They were roaring across the desert at a reckless pace, a stream of dusters at their back.

"Are you ok, sir?" the Orbital Clerk asked after a moment.

Shinji wiped tendrils of blue drool from the corner of his mouth. "Do I look ok?"

The Clerk silenced at that.

Shinji could barely see, his world a swarm of darkness and pooling color, like his eyes were filling with liquid. He knew he shouldn't be driving, but he didn't care. He had to push harder, go faster, make the distance in record time. If he didn't, Grayson, Ada, and Titus might die before he did.

Blue tears streaked down his face and Shinji suppressed a moan of misery, swallowing hard as the duster tore across the wide plains. They were almost back to Begger's Valley, hours of travel left in their wake. His regulator felt as if it weighed as much as the Afterburner, its cells filled to capacity with the ship's glo deposits.

Why did you do this? He thought with bile burning the back of his throat. *Why'd you have to drink that shit?*

His face slack, he decided it didn't matter. He wanted to wipe the Canines off the face of the planet and he was going to need all the power he could hold to do it. His head thundered beneath the level of glo in his system, his heart racing, skipping beats, his ribs aching like they were going to pop out of his skin. His gut rolled with the liquid power—consuming him.

Shinji retched, hanging onto the wheel for dear life, and felt blood and glo leak from his nose, stream out of his eyes, fill his mouth. He spat again and wiped his face, gasping, panting for air. He felt like every breath came after a punch to the stomach.

"Shinji, come in," a voice chirped over the duster's radio.

Shinji ignored the request, guiding the duster down a long dune and around a rise of redstone. It was all he could manage.

"Shinji, this is Reston, you're going too fast!"

Shinji snorted, a bubble of blue snot running down his face, and he glanced at the Clerk next to him.

"What do you think? Am I going too fast?"

The Clerk shook his head miserably. "Whatever you think is best, sir."

"Good answer."

Shinji blinked burning liquid out of his eyes, clearing some of the darkness that pressed in. He squinted and licked bloody glo off his lips, gagging, his body shuddering. He fought back another groan, swallowing it along with a second gurgling wave of vomit.

Pull yourself together, pussy.

He braked slightly and turned sharply to the left, the slopes of Begger's Valley coming into view. They were getting close now. He checked his mirrors and saw that the convoy at his back was doing a decent job of keeping up. He didn't have any kind of concrete plan, didn't have a tactical maneuver he was planning on executing—he didn't have much of anything to offer the troops he led. He just knew the general direction of the Canine's ship and he knew he held enough power in his system to blow it to hell and back again. If Reston and the Orbital Clerks could get a couple people out before that, well, that was up to them.

He felt a momentary pang of guilt as he recalled Reston's bitter words from earlier. He knew they had fucked up this job. He knew they weren't living up to their reputation, that they had gotten in over their heads. But if he could show them that he was willing to give it his all, that he wasn't a coward, that he wasn't afraid of these purple eyed freaks—it would have to be enough. For himself, if nothing else.

They dipped down into Begger's Valley and raced across the wide basin, the duster bouncing wildly.

So close now, Shinji thought through a haze of pain.

He gunned the engine.

CHAPTER 17

Grayson and Ada burst from the pool of liquid with a gasp. The world reoriented itself and Grayson hurried to get his bearings, along with a breath of air. He splashed and sputtered over to the side of the dark pool and hauled himself out of it, Ada at his side. Spitting, he quickly stood and looked around him.

They were back in the Canine's ship, the massive room empty now, but he could hear that they were not alone. From the snaking hallways, he could hear howling, screaming, pain and rage mixing as the aftermath of Voratarium's demise in the Floating World was felt throughout the ship.

"Sounds like they know what we did," Ada said, coughing, looking alert.

Grayson caught himself as the walls and ground shuddered, like something had fallen or had been caved in. A low, rolling groan of metal followed, accompanied by another rumble.

"We need to get back to that room, the one we were held prisoner in, and gather as many survivors as we can," Grayson said quickly as the howl and buzz of Canine's and Tusks continued to fill the air. "I don't know how many people we'll be able to take or how many are still alive, but we have to try or all of this will be for nothing."

"Couldn't agree more," Ada said. "Let's hope those animals didn't string them back up to the ceiling." As she said this, her hand went to her throat as if she were remembering her own brief time.

"It sounds like they're a little preoccupied," Grayson noted darkly as the wailing and screaming continued. "But remember - there's not much we can do to fight back right now. If it comes down to it, we run, no matter who's with us. You got that?"

Ada set her jaw and said nothing, but she offered Grayson a small nod. Together, they bolted away from the pool and ran for the hallway they had previously come from earlier. Grayson searched his memory as they went, trying to remember exactly where the room full of people was located.

Just get out of here, you can't save them, his mind warned as the raging and roaring of the Canine's and Tusks pressed in down the hallways.

Grayson ignored the voice as they ran, taking lefts and rights from memory. His heart nearly stopped when he spotted a cluster of howling Canines at one of the junctions, but they didn't seem to notice him or Ada. They were all clutching their heads, their eyes wide, as if something was screaming from inside their skulls.

Your overlord is dead, Grayson thought grimly as they ducked into an empty hallway, jogging in the opposite direction. *Why don't you just lie down and die too.*

They entered another room, one of the breeding rooms with half grown Canines that hung from the ceiling like sacks. But as they crossed the room, not daring to even breathe, Grayson saw that the bodies were falling from the ceiling as if prematurely released. The corpses hit the floor and he heard bones break and shatter without reaction.

Stillbirths.

"This way!" Ada yelled as the ship moaned and creaked around them, the floor shaking as something passed through it. They took another passage and crossed an intersection, the two opposite halls filled with Tusks that slithered and slammed themselves against the walls, oblivious to Grayson or Ada.

They're going to wake up, you know they are, his mind urged again. *You better be on your way out before the shock wears off.*

Finally, they reached the chamber that held the prisoners of Typhon. To Grayson's surprise, most of them were still huddled on the floor, trembling, recovering from their time above. A dazed look filled the fifty odd people, a dream-like terror clinging to their faces. Most were cowering in the corner of the vast room, shaken, clinging to one another, their naked bodies slick with sweat, ooze, and vomit. Littered across the width of the room were a dozen bodies that were ghostly pale, unmoving, and appeared to be dead.

Focus on the ones still breathing, Grayson thought as they entered the space. He stepped over the first of the dead, a young girl who couldn't have been older than eight. Grayson felt his stomach roll as he noted how paper thin and snow white her skin looked, as if her innards had been deflated. He could hear Ada trailing behind him now, whispering shocked horror as she began to recognize some of the dead.

Grayson went to the people in the corner, his hands raised, his voice calm but urgent. "I know you all have been through hell, but we're getting you out of here. All of you. But you have to come with me right now. Do you understand?"

A woman met Grayson's eyes, her own empty and hollow. When she spoke, her voice was dry and cracked. "Get...out?"

Grayson knelt, feeling the ship rumble beneath his boots. "Yes, all of you. But we don't have much time. Can all of you walk?"

A man about Grayson's age slowly stood, his face a haggard mess. "Do you...have any idea...what they did to us?"

Grayson nodded grimly and cast his eyes toward the ceiling. A few bodies were still clutched tightly to it, the fleshy tubes constricting their unmoving prey.

"I know," Grayson said hurriedly. "And I can't imagine how terrifying this all must be, but we have a very narrow window here. If we don't take it, we're all going to die right here in this room."

The wide eyed, sickly crowd looked at one another, a similar gaze of despair passing from one person to the next. They all appeared horribly thin and weak, their bodies shaking from shock, and Grayson wondered just how many of them would be able to follow him out of here.

A shriek came suddenly from behind Grayson and he spun, heart exploding up his throat. When he turned, he saw Ada on her knees, clutching one of the dead bodies on the floor. It was a woman. A woman who looked a lot like Ada.

Oh no...

Ada was weeping and shaking the dead woman, her mouth open in a plea. "Marah! Oh god Marah please wake up! Come on! Open your eyes for me! It's Ada!"

The woman who had first spoken to Grayson slowly stood and went over to Ada. "She's dead," she said quietly as she looked on. "They sucked her dry. I'm sorry."

As one, the rest of the survivors rose as well and circled Ada, a look of deep sadness and pain washing over their faces. Grayson stood behind them, watching as Ada continued to hug and plea for her dead sister to wake up.

Goddamn it.

The sight of Ada in such anguish made his heart sink into his stomach, her sobs wracking her body in heaving exhales of disbelief.

"Marah! Marah come on! We have to go home! *Please!*"

Grayson pushed through the small crowd and knelt next to Ada, feeling the clock ticking down in the back of his head. The howls of the Canines and Tusks had gone alarmingly quiet.

"Ada," Grayson said gently, reaching out to touch her shoulder. "I'm so sorry. But we have to go right now or all these people are going to die. We don't have time to mourn right now."

"I know that!" Ada snapped, her eyes brimming with tears. "Just...just..."

The ship shook again and a small ripple of fear echoed from the survivors, their eyes darting around the wide room.

"We're leaving," Grayson said, standing, hating the urgency he felt. "Please Ada..."

Ada grit her teeth, her cheeks stained with tears, and then kissed her dead sister's forehead before laying her back down.

"I'm so sorry," she whispered, choked. "I failed you so completely..."

"Ada!"

Ada stood, like a lightning bolt, her grief mixed with fury. "I know! *Fuck!*" A strangled cry came from her throat and she wiped her eyes, her face alive with misery.

A howl blasted down one of the empty hallways, the shriek of a Canine. But this time, it was filled with rage instead of pain.

They're recovering, Grayson thought frantically. *And their timing can't be worse.*

"Go, GO!" Grayson yelled, pushing the survivors forward toward a passage as more snarls and growls began to fill the ship. Grayson could hear the Canine's scurrying around, could hear the furious static of the Tusks as they began to hunt for who had destroyed their creator. It was a sound that chilled Grayson to the bone.

Ada bounded forward, ahead of the survivors, leading the charge away from the noise. It was an action that surprised Grayson and cemented his respect for her. He knew she was in turmoil, knew how badly she had wanted, needed to save her sister.

And you failed her.

Grayson brought up the rear, the fifty or so survivors following Ada's lead as they entered the hallways. Grayson had no idea where the exit was, what it would even look like, and prayed that Ada knew something he didn't. At every intersection, the howls of the Canines grew closer and closer, their rage and fury rapidly approaching.

They made it further than he had hoped before the Canines found them. They had entered some kind of massive control room, purely by accident, and nearly ran into five purple eyed Canines along with a golden one who stood atop some kind of pedestal at the center of the room that was surrounded by a holo globe-map. When the Canines saw them, the golden one immediately dispersed the holo field around him and leapt from the pedestal, its teeth bared in a snarl of rage.

"This way!" Ada yelled, her voice a thin screech, taking the survivors away from their attackers, down another purple fleshed hallway.

At the rear, and closest to the Canines, Grayson had to dive out of the way as the golden Canine lunged, with the five others at its back. The Canine's claws missed him by a hair as he rolled upright and sprinted after the Ada and the others, his heart in his throat.

What he didn't see was that one of the survivors had tripped and fallen during the coarse adjustment, rendering him helpless.

By the time Grayson realized what happened, it was too late. The Canines fell on him with all the anger of hell in their eyes. Gritting his teeth, knowing there wasn't anything he could do, Grayson fled, following the others out of the room. At his back, the man was torn to shreds and the golden Canine arched its head back and howled, as if signaling for more to come.

This isn't working, Grayson thought frantically, panting. *We're going to get caught. They're going to catch up.*

His head was thundering beneath an avalanche of pain, his skull threatening to split apart. He tried to focus on the survivors ahead of him, on placing one foot in front of the other as the screams and howls echoed throughout the passages all around him. His thigh burned like fire from where his regulator had been ripped out and he knew his glo levels were in an agonizing flux. He felt like he was going to throw up, but he forced himself to keep running. He could hear the Canines at his back regrouping, gathering, readying a kill party to come after them. Static chirped and blasted at them from every direction and he could hear the slithering of Tusks drawing nearer as the ship bellowed another croaking shudder.

"There! THERE!" Ada's voice cried out from the front. Grayson had no way of knowing what she had discovered and no way of asking and so he pressed himself into the pack of survivors, a panicked tangle of limbs and stinking bodies.

As they pressed forward as one, Grayson had a fleeting glimpse of a purple glyph on a wall directly in front of him. It rose up out of nowhere, a dead end, and he raised his hands to stop himself from slamming directly into it. But instead, he passed through the wall, as if slipping through a sheet of cool water, and went tumbling out into the blinding dusk of Pratus.

CHAPTER 18

Grayson's boots churned through the thick sand, the roar of Canines and screech of Tusks echoing across the orange tinted sky. The colossal ship lay a couple hundreds yards behind him now as the sun dipped and fell over the world, splashing warm, brilliant color across the open plains. The strange, milky disk in the sky moved with it, marking the inevitable Negative that approached.

Grayson felt as if his throat was filled with shards of glass. His breath blew hot and dry across his chapped lips as he urged the survivors ahead of him to keep moving. His skull felt as if it were splintering apart, one fragment at a time. The loss of his regulator could be felt with each awful step, a thunder between his ears.

Ada bellowed her encouragement at the head of the group, her voice shrill and filled with exhaustion and pain. The naked survivors were crying and gasping as they ran, the roar of the Canines blasting across the sand at their backs. Grayson knew they were coming and once they did, there would be nothing to stop what followed.

As they crest a dune, almost to the lip of Begger's Valley, Grayson chanced a glance over his shoulder at the massive, world stretching ship at his back. From its walls streamed hundreds of Canines and Tusks, flowing out of the construct like a burst pipe. They merged into one column of rage and anger, their path directed right at Grayson and the others.

We can't outrun them, Grayson thought frantically, pushing the man in front of him, urging him to move faster.

We're going to die out here.

The finality of the thought cut through his mind like a blade. He continued to run, his legs burning, his mind fevered. He could feel a weary acceptance enter his chest and spread through his body, a tired, worn out realization that sat and waited for him.

"Faster, down into the valley!" Ada yelled from ahead. Grayson and the survivors quickly began to scramble down the steep bank before them, the redstone slopes full of loose rubble and windswept sand. Grayson steadied the people ahead of him, placing a balancing hand on their arms when needed.

The Canine construct dipped out of view as they made their descent, but the howl of their pursuers could still be heard, washing over their heads like a death cry. Grayson could feel fear somewhere beneath all the exhaustion and the thundering of his head, but he was too worn out, sore, and pained to find it. He kept his eyes on the bodies ahead of him, listened to their weeping sobs as they fled for their lives, and silently he wished he could do more to help them.

"We're going to die!"

"I can't do this! I'm not ready!"

"Please, someone!

"Run, just run!"

"They'll be on us soon!"

"Make them stop!"

The cries of fear that echoed from the group wafted up into the deepening purple sky, the reds and oranges melting into something more spectacular. Grayson tripped on a rock and almost went sprawling, but he caught himself and ran the rest of the way down the slope. Once they were all on level ground, the open stretch to the other side of the valley looked impossibly far away. At the speed at which they were going, Grayson knew they'd be cut down before even going half the distance. He glanced up at the magnificent sky and he felt a rare breeze brush his face.

This is the last good thing I'll ever feel.

The eerie disk overhead was nearly across the skyline and Grayson knew that even if they did manage to get across the valley, once the Negative came, all was lost. The loss of clear sight would slow them to a crawl and the Canines would find them, the Tusks would come for them, and they would all die in a colorless world.

Gasping, head pounding like a gunsmith's anvil, throat parched and ragged from running, Grayson longed more than anything to see Claire one last time and tell her he was sorry for not being there more. That he could wish her the best in life and tell her he cared for her.

The Canines reached the upper slopes, roaring behind the desperate pack of survivors, their prey sighted once more. As one, hundreds of the creatures began to charge down the long decline, teeth bared.

We have maybe eight or nine minutes before we're all dead.

Just as the thought filled his mind, his ears picked up the sound of engines. A lot of them. He quickly looked up, wiping his dust caked face to squint across the valley, a sick, hopeful current running through him.

Engines. Vehicles. A lot of them, he thought as the sound rumbled more into the forefront of his senses.

A moment later, he spotted at least twenty dusters roaring over the far lip of Begger's Valley, their wheels bouncing and skidding down the steep slopes. The growl of their engines filled the air now as they charged the survivors and it was the most beautiful thing Grayson had ever heard.

They came for us, Grayson thought. *I can't believe it. Goddamn, Reston. Thank you.*

Cries of hope and tepid relief rose from the group of naked, exhausted survivors and Grayson couldn't blame them as he watched the cluster of dusters roar ever closer. He shot a look over his shoulder to see if the arrival of vehicular force would give the Canines pause.

It didn't. The creatures continued to stream down the slope at Grayson's back like water off rock, a tangled, enraged mass that pulsed with violent intent.

Grayson turned back to the dusters and saw that they had already almost reached him. They blazed across the wide plain, a trail of thick dust in their wake.

When they reached the survivors, brakes engaged, and a host of Orbital Clerks exited the vehicles and began to yell for the survivors to hurry, get in, move, move, *move!* It all happened so fast that Grayson simply stood at the back of the small crowd and watched, thankful for a moment to catch his breath.

The horde of Canines and Tusks drew nearer and Grayson swept his eyes between them and the survivors boarding the dusters. There were only twenty or so Orbital Clerks and even though they were armed, they stood no chance against the hundreds that came from across the valley.

Suddenly, a hand gripped Grayson's wrist and spun him around. With a jolt, Grayson stepped away from the man who had touched him, his bloodshot eyes going wide, his voice a hissing whisper.

"Shinji...?"

The young man looked nothing like Grayson remembered, save for the darkness in his eyes.

"Where's Titus?" Shinji asked, bent over, gasping.

Grayson examined the young man, shock rippling through him. His skin was ghostly pale, his veins a blackened spiderweb beneath the paper thin white. Blue liquid streamed out of his ears, nose, and mouth, dribbling down across the front of his armor. It streaked from the corners of his eyes, mixing with faint traces of blood, giving him a haunted, deathly look.

"What did you do?" Grayson asked, horrified,

Shinji sucked in a wet, shaking breath, his regulator like an anchor to his back. "Where the fuck is Titus? Where's Ada?"

Ada suddenly appeared at Grayson's side, a terrified look cast at the still charging Canines, but when she saw Shinji, she nearly froze.

"What have you done?" Grayson asked again as the last of the survivors boarded the dusters.

Shinji winced, his face wrinkled and worn, the scars beneath his eyes blazing, appearing bigger now. "Going to end this," he coughed, spitting neon. "All of it." He wiped his lips. "You have to get out of here. Right now. You just have to tell me where Titus is. Did he make it out?"

Grayson shook his head, feeling his stomach roll. "No."

The roar of the Canines shook the sky, a hundred yards away now. Shinji tightened his lips and then grabbed Grayson and Ada and shoved them toward the last duster as the others began to speed away, back to Typhon.

"Run. Go. I'll take care of this."

Grayson stumbled forward. "Jesus Shinji, come with us! You don't have-"

"GO!" Shinji screamed, his entire body trembling, blue drool dripping from his chin.

Ada gave Shinji a pained look and then ran for the duster. Grayson took a half step toward it.

"You're going to die out here."

Shinji offered Grayson a small, sad smile, his scars flaring. "Yeah."

Grayson turned and jumped into the duster, slamming the door behind him. The others were already racing across the valley, taking the survivors as far away from their pursuers as they could. The Canines were horribly close to Shinji now as Ada gunned the engine, the duster leaping forward in a spit of dirt and dust. Grayson turned back in his seat and stared at Shinji who stepped confidently toward the wall of Canines before him, his regulator looming over his back.

Shinji reached for it, cranked the dial, and then he vanished.

"Go faster," Grayson urged Ada.

His eyes caught something in the sky, a flickering light.

"As fast as you can," Grayson pressed.

"On it," Ada said, flooring it.

The Canines slowed once they realized Shinji had disappeared, their charge disintegrating into a trot, their eyes roaming their ranks for any sign of where the lone man had gone. They stood in the valley, pooling, as more continued to stream over the walls of the valley and join them, hungry for violence.

Grayson turned his eyes to the heavens and felt his breath drain away.

The entire corner of the sky was slowly turning blue, a pulsing, building mass that pulled clouds and lightning toward it like a black hole. Flashes lit the valley, blinding, silent snapshots that flickered across the extending volume of cloud cover. The Canines stared up at it, a ripple of unease starting to spread among their ranks.

"Oh my god, Shinji…" Grayson breathed as he continued to watch.

He felt as if he were observing the formation of a world ending catastrophe. The flashing clouds and blazing blue sky continued to grow and blow across the valley, the wind picking up speed, gusting great gouts of dust across the world. A boom of thunder shook the heavens, followed by another that rumbled and growled like the snarl of a wild beast.

And then, at the epicenter of the massive cloud formation, the sky began to split open. It was as if the claws of a cosmic god reached down and tore open the very fabric of creation to allow its nightmares access to all beneath it.

The dark ocean of space filled the center of the sky, bordered by flashing, sparking, boiling blue clouds, rolling across the ceiling of the world as the wind howled and screamed and threw sand and rock against one another.

From the center of the cosmic gash, the wound that split the length of the horizons, an enormous, swirling vortex of electric coiled light and power came roaring through. It was as if all the power of the universe had met at a singular location only to be cast down into the world.

When the Canines saw what was happening, as the wind and grit beat against them, they turned as one and fled back the way they had come, screaming in terror.

From his seat in the duster, Grayson watched all this with a horrible terror. His eyes traced the colossal trail of blue and white power that arched out of the sky, spitting cobalt chemtrails in its wake as it burned toward the surface. Thunder blasted and crashed all around them in massive, hammerblow waves and the duster rocked and shook beneath the hurricane of wind and sand.

The city-sized mass of power nearly blinded Grayson as it dipped across the sky, headed directly for the location of the Canine ship.

There was no mistaking the moment of impact. It felt and sounded as if a thermonuclear moon had been thrown from the sky and onto the world. The flash of light blotted out all existence as it exploded out of the epicenter, followed by a blast of super heater chemical fire that shot out and across the valley like flash burned death. It took the horde of Canines and Tusks into its blazing jaws, searing, scorching, and charring everything it absorbed.

As soon as the fire came, it went, and in the chaos, Grayson knew that if he hadn't been in the duster, he would have been turned to ash. He blinked blindly and begged the white spots in his eyes to fade as Ada cursed and yelled, struggling to maintain control over the vehicle as the waves of infernal power pulsed around them.

Scrubbing his pained eyes, Grayson looked out his window and felt his heart stop.

"Ada, go left! NOW!"

Without thought, Ada gunned the engine and jerked the wheel left as hard as she could. A moment later, a massive, hundred foot piece of the Canine ship came blazing out of the sky to explode like a bomb across the valley as it struck earth.

"Hold on!" Ada screamed as debris blew into the duster, slamming it, denting it, threatening to rip it in half. As she struggled to maintain control, more pieces came raining down around them, as if some celestial city had been knocked from the heavens.

Grayson gripped his seat, gritting his teeth, watching and praying helplessly as thunderous chunks of the obliterated ship continued to fall and smash around them, as if made of glass.

Then, without warning, Grayson felt something huge crunch across the front of the duster, the world lost in sound, sand, and fire. His body went weightless for a moment and he could hear Ada screaming as they flipped.

A second after, his head smashed into something miserably hard and the world went black.

CHAPTER 19

Grayson knew that quite a bit of time had passed when he finally opened his eyes again. It had been the darkness, the calm ocean of nothing that he had floated in that assured him of this. He had grown used to it, comfortable with it. It was a place just beyond awareness, that strange, sleep drunk state of unconsciousness. The void had enveloped him, welcomed him, and he had sunk deep into its waters, lost to time and consequence.

Now though, as he felt the weight of the world sharpen, his eyes fluttered and sound, light, and smell returned. When he realized what was happening, that he was waking up, a dull sense of shock coiled through him.

How am I not dead? He thought as bright white light filled the space all around him. He could hear people talking, conversing along with the steady beep and trill of medical monitors.

He shut his eyes again, not ready for the world again.

The duster...we were crushed.

He cautiously did a mental inspection of his pain levels. His head still felt like it would tear open at any moment, but found that the rest of his nerves were mercifully out of touch.

You're heavily medicated. Probably suffered massive internal injuries with multiple broken bones. When you open your eyes again, you're going to be strung up with medical tape and plexi-mold.

He sunk further into his thoughts, content to let the machines and staff chirp and buzz around him. His mind returned to the events at Begger's Valley. The Canines. The survivors. Titus....

He felt his chest swell and he allowed himself a moment of grief. He ushered it in carefully and let it fill him, the weight and extent of his friend's death coursing through him like fire before being gently put out and shut away again.

He examined their escape from the ship. Ada. She had led them out of there. Kept them all together and pushed them forward until there was nothing left to push. And it had been enough. He knew he'd be dead if it hadn't been for her last minute leadership.

Is she alive? He thought suddenly.

And what happened to everyone else? Did Shinji ever make it out?

He dreaded the answers to his questions, but he knew there was only one way to find out. Slowly, head drumming, he peeled his eyes open. For a moment he was blinded by the stinging white light, but he adjusted to them after a moment. When he looked around he saw that he was in some kind of medical ward. A host of portable medical machines sat on a cart around his bed, with a host of multi-colored tubes flowing into the crook of his right elbow. Upon further inspection, and to his absolute shock, he found that he wasn't locked in a plexi-mold cast. Instead, a single casing had been fitted to his right forearm and hand, just below the elbow. He studied it, wondering what the damage was underneath, relieved that it appeared to be the only damage.

"How's your head?"

Grayson turned to see a woman walking toward him holding a holo-board. She looked to be about forty with short blond hair and a tall, thin frame. She wore a white coat and black pants. But the most shocking part of her appearance were the blue scars beneath her eyes, two tiny slits that cracked through the smooth skin.

"W-where am I?" Grayson croaked after finding his vocal cords.

The woman placed herself at the foot of the bed and examined the holo-board, her fingers drifting across the screen.

"You're in Typhon. You've been unconscious for three days now. I'm glad to see you're awake, I wasn't sure there for a while."

Grayson tried to sit up, the details of the room sharpening some. "Three days? Shit." He looked around and saw that four more beds lined the long room across from him. Three of them were filled with men who looked like they had suffered some kind of physical trauma. In the fourth, unmistakable, lay Ada. Her eyes were closed and her head and arms were wrapped in white, fiber-gel cloth. She appeared to be breathing, her chest rising and falling in shallow pulls.

"Ada, is she ok?" Grayson asked sharply, pointing with his cast.

The blond woman looked over her shoulder and then nodded. "Yeah. Tough little cookie, that one is. She was awake yesterday for most of the day, insisted she was alright and then tried to disconnect herself from the med-monitors."

"What happened?"

The woman smiled slightly. "She's been given a sleep aid. I slipped a little cocktail into her IV. It was for the best. She's still a long way from well."

"What's the damage? Is she ok?"

The woman eyed Grayson over the holo-board before putting it down. "Why don't we focus on you right now."

Grayson stared up at her, at her scars. "Ok. Sure. But first I want to know where you came from. There's no mistaking your face. You're a-"

"- a Vagabond, yes," the woman interrupted. "Very astute of you. I'm Dr. Tarson. But since you're part of the network, you can call me Maddy. Short for Madeline."

Grayson studied her. "Okay Maddy, what are you doing here?"

Maddy smiled and tapped the sheet that covered Grayson's leg. "We got an urgent call from Typhon that there was a Vagabond without his regulator that needed immediate medical attention." She pointed with her chin. "Go ahead. Have a look."

Shocked, Grayson flipped the sheet off himself and saw that a brand new regulator had been installed into his thigh. It was smaller than his previous one, with less wires, he noted. His fingers brushed it, touched the tiny dial along the side, and then he looked up into Maddy's eyes.

"Thank you. I had no idea the network had doctors in its ranks."

"We're not all brutes," she said lightly. "Some of us want to understand the science behind the substance." She lowered the holo-board. "And you're welcome. But I'm afraid you went a long time without your regulator. Too long. The damage the unchecked glo in your system did couldn't be reversed."

"I figured as much," Grayson said quietly.

"How's your head by the way?"

"Hurts like all hell. And I mean all *hell*."

Maddy bit her lip. "I'm afraid that's just something you're going to have to live with. No offense, but you're old for a Vagabond. You've been doing this for a long time. The glo in your system has sucked you dry for years now. I don't even have to ask if you've started to fringe."

Grayson nodded silently.

"It's not going to get any better. I'm sorry."

Grayson raised his eyes. "How long do you think I have?"

Maddy looked down at her shoes and Grayson saw her shoulders droop slightly. When she spoke she kept her voice low.

"Six months. Maybe a year if you really take it easy."

Grayson hissed sharply, his face going numb.

"I'm sorry," Maddy said softly.

Grayson slowly wet his lips. "I know it's been coming...I've been feeling it for months now. But when you put a number to it..."

"I know. That's why I came. When I got your file, I saw how old you were." She paused before continuing. "We live hard lives. The least I can do is to make the end as comfortable as possible for you."

"I appreciate that," Grayson said numbly, feeling the edges of his vision darken. Six months...maybe a year...

"Did any other Vagabonds make it back?" He asked quietly.

Maddy shook her head. "I'm afraid not."

"What about the survivors, the ones we brought back? How are they doing?"

"Forty-seven made it back. Three died within twenty-four hours and five are critical."

"Jesus..."

"Considering what they went through, and if Ada's account yesterday was accurate, then it's a miracle you got any of them out of there. You should be proud."

Grayson shook his head, staring down at his legs. "Proud...sure."

Maddy reached out and touched his leg, her voice gentle. "Why don't you get some rest. When I leave here in a couple days, I can take you with me."

Grayson looked up. "Why would I go with you?"

"I spoke to Reston earlier and he said your ship, the Afterburner, isn't functional in its current state. So unless you want to stay here for a while..."

"I'll go," Grayson said. "I have to get home."

"Ok. Until then, I'll be checking in on you. Get some rest."

Grayson turned away from her and let his mind fade into the pillow, his eyes staring at nothing.

A FEW DAYS LATER, Grayson found himself standing on the docks, staring at the small ship he was bound to board. He had a small bag slung over his shoulder, the remnants of his journey, along with a few things he had taken from the Afterburner until it could get towed. He wanted to bring Jace, Titus's son, a couple of his father's personal belongings, something to remember him by. He hated the thought of delivering the terrible news, dreaded it, but knew he was duty bound to it. It had to be him.

Doesn't feel right leaving here without you, Grayson thought as flight crews prepped Maddy's ship, a buzz of activity along the wide port. He gripped the shoulder strap of his bag and sighed heavily, the weight of his excursion nearly crippling him. His head still thundered like artillery fire, a constant barrage of merciless pain, but the rest of his body had healed quickly once his new regulator had been installed by the Vagabond doctor.

What the hell am I going to tell Claire? He thought, the ache in his skull a foreboding signal of what was coming. *Should I tell her? Should I just...*

He stopped thinking about it. He squeezed his eyes shut, trying to filter through the trauma he had suffered over the past few days. It occupied a part of his mind now like a shadow that couldn't be issued away.

Titus...Shinji...all those people...

222 • ELIAS WITHEROW

"You trying to sneak away without saying goodbye?"

Grayson turned, opening his eyes, and saw Ada striding across the deck toward him. Her head and left arm were still wrapped in bandages, but she seemed confident on her feet. She came to a halt beside him and smiled sadly.

"After all we've been through, you were just going to ghost me?"

Grayson returned the smile, but it was without humor or cheer. "Didn't think it was appropriate, considering. Thought it might be best if I just left."

"What do you mean?"

"I failed this colony, Ada…"

Ada's lips came together tightly. "You did the best you could. No one questions that."

"Then why hasn't Reston allowed me to debrief him?"

Ada sighed quietly. "He lost a daughter. That's all he sees right now."

"And you lost your sister."

Ada nodded carefully. "Yes. Yes I did."

"Right. So I figured it was best if I just left."

Ada looked up at him sadly. "You lost two of your friends as well."

Grayson said nothing, his eyes staring straight ahead. He felt his chest stir.

"Did you get your payment?" Ada asked after a minute.

"Yeah, it came through this morning on my wrist reader."

"Good."

Grayson watched as the crews of dock workers finished fueling the small ship before them. "Did the Orbital Clerks find any Canines this morning on their sweep?"

Ada shook her head. "No. Nothing. Not a peep."

"And their ship?"

"Still blown to hell. No Tusks either. Shinji massacred them and I mean *all* of them. I still can't believe we got away."

"How are the survivors doing? Have any more passed?"

"No. And they're doing well. As well as they can. They'll get there."

Grayson raised his eyes to meet Ada's. "And how are you?"

Ada looked away from him. "I'm ok," she said softly after a moment. "It's just going to take some time."

"And you be sure to take it."

"I am. I will."

Grayson let out a long, shuddering breath, his head creaking. "I guess this is it, huh?"

Ada nodded.

Grayson glanced at her. "You should know that I was damn impressed by you. We wouldn't have made it out of that ship without you leading the charge. You kept those people going. You kept me going. You should be proud of that."

Ada said nothing, her eyes misty.

"Alright then," Grayson said, hoisting his bag up. "I think it's about time I got on that ship and got out of here. Maddy is waiting for me."

But before he could go, Ada stepped forward and embraced him in a hug, her cheek pressed against his chest.

"You take care of yourself, Gray," Ada said into his shirt, her voice quiet and muffled. "And if you're ever orbiting Pratus, you better come down and say hi."

Grayson smiled a little at that. "Sure. I can do that."

He pulled away. "Goodbye Ada."

"Goodbye Grayson."

CHAPTER 20

Grayson lifted his grandson over his head and smiled while the little boy gurgled and cooed down at him, a big goofy grin plastered to the infant's face.

"Aw, he's smiling at you Dad!"

Grayson glanced at Claire on the couch next to him and then back at Lan, the baby waving his small chubby arms in delight.

"We'll get him on a spaceship one of these days," Grayson said, swooping Lan back into his lap. He rubbed his finger across the baby's cheek, his rough skin sliding across the unblemished flush of his grandson's face.

"He's gotten so big already," Grayson said quietly, never taking his eyes off Lan.

"He'll be three months next week," Jace said from the recliner across the room. He was finishing his drink, a contented smile on his lips, his eyes traveling to meet his wife Claire's, then Lan's, then Graysons. He smiled.

"I'm glad you've been able to spend so much time with him lately," Jace continued. "Means alot to have his grandfather around."

Grayson cradled Lan to his chest. "Not sure what good I'll do him." He paused. "But I am glad I got to meet the little guy."

Claire scooted closer to her father across the couch. "That's a weird thing to say, Dad. You planning on taking another offworld job without telling me?"

Grayson shook his head, a tremor running through his skull. "No. I told you months ago that I was done with that. My place is here, in Lighton, with you three." His voice faded some. "There's no place I'd rather be."

Claire smiled and reached out to scoop up her son. "Good. Lan gets cranky when he doesn't see his Pop-pop. Don't you sweetie? Yes you do, my little butterball." She planted a kiss on the delighted child's face and then stood up and passed him to Jace across the room.

"Little Lan the Man dropped a bomb in his diaper for you."

Jace grimaced and set his glass down. "Couldn't even let me finish my drink, could you?"

Lan gurgled a response and played with his fingers. Jace gave his son a small smile. "Ok, let's get your ass sorted out, shall we?"

Grayson hauled himself off the couch, trying hard not to show how horribly the room spun around him. He took in a steadying breath.

"I think that's my cue to go."

Claire turned to him. "Aw, really?"

"Yeah. It's getting late and this old man needs his eight hours."

Grayson walked across the room and planted a kiss on Lan's cheek. "See you later pal. Don't give your old man too much trouble in there."

Jace snorted and offered his hand to Grayson. "Knowing him, he'll shit on me mid-change."

Grayson pumped Jace's outstretched hand. "You're going to have to keep an eye on this one, I think."

Jace smiled. "It was good to see you, sir."

Grayson waved a hand. "How many times do I have to tell y-"

"Grayson," Jace corrected himself. "It still feels weird. Sorry."

"Until next time," Grayson lied.

He went to the door and felt Claire shadow him to it. He pulled his coat on and faced her after forcing the pain from his face.

"Same time next week?" He offered lightly.

Claire embraced her father in a hug, her voice muffled against his collar. "Please. It's been so good to have you around lately. I've missed you."

Grayson nodded. "I've missed you too. You're doing a great job with the kid, by the way. He's so happy." He paused. "How's Jace been? I didn't want to ask, but I've been thinking about him a lot lately."

Claire pulled aware. "He's been ok. It's almost been a year since you came back and told him what happened." She wrapped her arms around herself. "I can tell he misses Titus. I do too. But we're getting by. It gets easier to live with that hole."

Grayson put a hand on the door handle, feeling his body start to shake. "Yeah. I miss him too." He turned back to her, his eyes brimming. "I love you, sweetie. I'll see you later, ok?"

But before he could leave, Claire reached out and touched his arm, her voice soft and knowing. "Are you ok, Dad?"

A moment of panic flared in Grayson's chest and he fought with a sudden surge of misery that overwhelmed him. He felt a dampness in his eyes and he cursed it.

"I'm great, hon," he rattled, his voice an unsteady croak. He forced a smile. "I'm just so glad I got to see you tonight."

He opened the door and left before she could say or see anymore. As soon as he heard the lock click at his back, Grayson gripped the railing along the stairs in front of him and nearly collapsed. Pain roared through his head like a burning train. He felt as if his skull was slowly being compressed, an immense, agonizing vice that nearly blinded him. He coughed into his sleeve, his body finally releasing the tension he had been holding. His eyes watered as the cough drew blood, his sleeve splattered with red and neon blue.

"Goddamn it," Grayson rasped, reaching into his coat pocket.

His hands were shaking so badly he could hardly extend the portable cane, the poly-plastic prosthetic clicking and then locking into place. He leaned heavily on it, his body slumping as the thunder between his ears continued its endless war.

Carefully, Grayson made his way down the stairs to ground level where he exited the building onto the busy streets of Malice. Rain lashed the streets, beating at the hordes of people that patrolled the sidewalks, the cold water splashing against the push of traffic, indifferent to the honk and hum of autos that filled the roads.

Grayson began to walk down the street, his legs like anchors, his muscles flaring with every step. The cane creaked beneath his weight as he walked, the neon pinks and blues from the buildings above filtering across his face, dancing over the black tape beneath his eyes.

He made it the four blocks to the bar, a place called North Road, and he pushed his way inside and out of the rain with a grateful groan. Since his return to Lighton, he had made it a point to come here after visiting Claire to reflect on his visit. It was one of the few things left in the world that he enjoyed, the slow, ponderous examination of an evening spent with loved ones, each fresh memory and joyous moment sealed into an amber capsule and stored away.

He hobbled over to the bar, the establishment littered with the low conversation of scattered patrons, and slid onto a stool. He hissed through his teeth as he did so, a shock of pain shooting up his spine to erupt across his skull. His vision swam for a moment and he hacked a wet cough into the crook of his elbow. Wiping moisture from his lips, grimacing, he retracted his cane and stashed it in his jacket.

"How you doing tonight, Mr. Grayson?"

Grayson looked up and greeted the barman with a nod. "A little achy, truth be told. How's the family these days?"

"As soon as I get one, I'll be sure to let you know," the barman responded without missing a beat. "You want a drink?"

"Please."

Grayson rubbed his eyes as he waited, black spots swimming in and out of focus. Every breath felt like inhaling glass, his limbs like blocks of aching concrete. He reached down and touched his regulator through his pants, silently cursing it.

"Here you are, sir."

Grayson picked up the drink and took a slow pull, sucking the foam off the top. He nodded his thanks and allowed his mind to slowly unfurl, drifting away from the pain to focus on his visit with Claire and Jace.

"You really shouldn't drink alone," a voice said from behind him. "It's a pretty bad look."

Grayson turned to see a man slide into the stool next to him, his heavy jacket dripping rain off the black leather. His dark hair was soaked through and hung in long strands over his eyes. Stubble lined the man's jaw and he scratched at it as he leaned heavily against the bar.

When Grayson saw his face, he felt the blood drain out of him.

"Shinji?" He whispered, his eyes going wide.

The man's lips curled in a smile. "Took me a long time to find you, Gray. Heard this was a usual spot for you."

Grayson felt ripples of shock coarse through him as he stared into the man's face. Shinji looked at least ten years older than the last time they had met. His eyes were dull and dark, with wrinkles creasing the corners. The scars below them had grown, cutting deep beneath his sockets to curve down his sharp cheekbones.

"I thought you died," Grayson whispered.

Shinji grunted. "So did I."

Grayson's voice was a hushed exhale. "What the hell happened to you? Where have you been all this time?"

Shinji said nothing for a long while. When he finally spoke, his voice was a soft rumble. "I don't really know. I remember falling from the sky. I remember killing the Canines - destroying their ship. After that..." he raised a hand. "There was nothing for a long time. Then I started to wake up inside my regulator, just like I always did."

Grayson shifted his eyes and noticed that Shinji wasn't wearing his regulator, the massive contraption absent.

"I stayed in that metal box for a while," Shinji continued. "Don't know how long. Hours, days maybe. I couldn't move. I felt like I had been ripped apart and thrown back together. When I was finally able to pull myself out of there, I realized where I was. What had happened. My memory returned. All of it."

"If I had known you were still out there-" Grayson started, but Shinji waved him away.

"Don't. I'm not here for that. To the best of your knowledge, I was dead."

Grayson gripped his glass. "I wouldn't be sitting here if you hadn't done what you did."

"I know. Again, not why I'm here."

Grayson nodded slowly and took another sip of his drink, his mind a sparking mess of memory and shock.

"Where's your regulator?" he finally asked.

Shinji patted his thigh. "Got myself one like yours. I needed to downgrade. I can't do what I used to."

Grayson touched the tape beneath his eyes. "Your face…"

"Different, isn't it?" Shinji said, cocking an eyebrow. "That much power really rips it out of you. I've been a little more careful since then. Don't want to get any uglier, you know?"

"How long has it been?" Grayson asked. "A year?"

"Just about."

"Shit."

Shinji studied him. "And what about you? Still holding on? I honestly wasn't sure what to expect when I started looking for you."

Grayson grimaced. "I've…been better."

"You ever get back to see your kid?"

"Yeah. Just came from there actually. Been spending as much time as I can with them."

A spear of fiery pain spiked suddenly through Grayson's skull and he gripped his head, wincing, inhaling sharply. His eyes watered as the fit coursed through him, traveling down the length of his body.

"Jesus, Gray," Shinji whispered once Grayson relaxed some, blowing out a long, shaking breath.

"I'm fine."

"Of course you are."

Grayson stared at the counter. "I knew what I was doing when I shot glo into my veins that first time. I don't need your pity."

"I don't pity you," Shinji said. "I just want to know what's waiting for me when my time comes."

Grayson said nothing for a while and then he turned to the younger man. "What are you doing here, Shinji?"

Shinji smiled slightly, as if waiting for the question. "I got a job for you, if you're interested."

Grayson blinked. "What?"

Shinji spread his hands. "I know you're at the end of your rope, but I figured I'd give you a chance to go out in a blaze of glory, so to speak."

Grayson shook his head slowly, grunting. "Kid, there is nothing in this universe that could get me back on the Vagabond network searching for work. I'm done. Hell, just look at me."

Shinji shrugged. "With enough glo in your system, you'd be ok."

"And how long would that last?"

"Is it any worse than what's happening to you now?"

"My family is here," Grayson said pointedly. "When I pass, I'd like to do it close to them, not out on some meaningless battlefield."

Shinji looked at him for a hard moment and then sighed. "Ah, you're probably right. Honestly, I didn't think you'd be this bad off. I knew you were starting to fringe, but…"

"I'd be more of a burden than a help," Grayson said. "But I guess I appreciate you asking."

"Sure. How's Titus's kid doing these days?"

"He's good. He takes good care of my daughter and grandson."

"Titus would have liked that."

"Yeah."

Shinji looked down. "I think about that guy a lot, you know."

Grayson pressed his lips together. "Yeah. So do I, kid."

A beat passed and then Shinji took a long breath. "Well, I don't want to sit here and waste your time."

Grayson looked at him. "What's the job?"

"Huh?"

"What's the job you're doing?"

Shinji spread his hands. "Ah, that. Yeah. It's another offworld gig. There's this Vagabond doctor that thinks she's discovered the source of glo. Or rather, *a* source. I'm going along as extra muscle. The place we're going…it's out there. I mean it's *way* out there, man. No telling what we'll find."

Grayson took a long drink from his glass before answering, his mind spinning. "No kidding…" he paused. "This doctor…what's their name?"

"Madison, but everyone in the network calls her Maddy."

Grayson grunted.

"What?" Shinji asked.

"I met her once. Right after the shit on Pratus with the Canines. She installed my new regulator."

Shinji's brow furrowed. "No kidding. Small world."

"She seemed sharp. I'm sure your expedition will be informative, if nothing else." Grayson took another drink. "The source of glo, huh? I honestly don't know if I want to know where this shit comes from." He tapped his regulator. "I doubt it's anyplace safe."

"Which is why I'm going," Shinji agreed.

Grayson sighed and felt a feverous shiver run through him, followed by a thundering rattle inside his skull. He squeezed his head.

"You be careful out there, Shinji," he said quietly. "I'm glad I got to see you again."

Shinji pulled himself from the stool. "Yeah. You too, Gray. We've been through a lot, you and I." He placed a hand on Grayson's shoulder. "You were always straight with me and I appreciate that. However you choose to end your days, I hope you find some peace."

Grayson smiled through the current of pain. "Thanks. Take care of yourself, kid. I hope I run into you again."

"Me too."

Shinji patted Grayson's shoulder one more time and then he turned and left, vanishing into the rain soaked streets as the door closed at his back.

Slowly, Grayson returned to his drink, his eyes misting behind an avalanche or agony. It rose with every beat of his heart and his vision blurred and darkened around its crushing grip. He focused his breathing and felt the room grow dim.

After a few minutes, the seizures subsided a little, allowing Grayson a moment to breathe. The noise in the bar returned and his senses calmed, returning him to the present.

"Was he a friend of yours?"

Grayson looked up at the barman and then over his shoulder toward the door.

"Yeah. Something like that."

"Are you ok, Mr. Grayson?"

Grayson stared down at his drink, memory flowing through him like a tide.

The barman nodded toward Grayson's glass. "You want another one?"

Grayson felt his eyes watering as another attack readied itself on the fringes of his consciousness, a coiling of agony that he could feel tingling across his body. Faces rose and fell like mountains in his mind, past and present colliding like tectonic plates. He could feel a hole opening up, waiting for him to fall into, a darkness that promised an end.

"Sir? Another drink?"

Grayson wiped his eyes with the back of his hand, his voice a hoarse whisper.

"No. I think this is it for me."

THE END

ELIAS WITHEROW is a New England based author with a passion for writing that can only be matched by his love of the mountains. He hopes to create stories that stir the darker side of imagination while bringing a fresh perspective into the horror genre. Elias can usually be found muttering over his keyboard or inspecting his lawn. If you ever run into him, he'd love to talk horror.

TWITTER @ELIASWITHEROW
FACEBOOK.COM/FEEDTHEPIG

MORE FROM
THOUGHT CATALOG BOOKS
+ ELIAS WITHEROW

Outlast Your Gods

Final Sky

Return To The Black Farm

The Worst In Us

The Third Parent

The Black Farm

The Worst Kind of Monsters

THOUGHT
CATALOG
Books

THOUGHTCATALOG.COM
NEW YORK·LOS ANGELES

Made in United States
Orlando, FL
01 May 2024

46389388R00143